Turning the Tide

A Novel by Elizabeth Harvey

Prologue

Sadie held onto her tightly, pulling her close whilst rhythmically stroking her hair to calm her. Her blouse was now stained with tears. She sat curled up on Sadie's knee, her long limbs balanced precariously on the chair. She was much too big to do this now and hadn't done it since she was a girl. Her head was buried into Sadie's neck, the sobs barely above a whisper but every one shook her to her core. Sadie was angry. Very angry. She bubbled and fizzed but nothing could be done about that now. She had to put her own feelings to one side and focus on her granddaughter.

"Shhh." Sadie whispered, rocking back and forth as she clung to her. "It's alright now. Grandma is here. You're alright." She knew this wasn't true but willed herself to believe it. She hoped that by saying it she would convince herself. "We are going to pack it into a tiny box and you are going to give it to me. It is not yours to worry about anymore." The once guttural sobs over time became laboured breathing and then light sighs. Her breath tickled Sadie's long grey hair, causing it to sway. Sadie kissed her forehead. "You're alright." She repeated softly.

Her granddaughter looked up, wide-eyed with pure terror. She had been on the cusp of the sleep. She began shivering again.

"You should go to bed, my love. You're exhausted."

"Please." She whispered, a tremor in her voice.

"Okay, okay. It's alright. Just sit here with me."

She burrowed in closer. "I'm scared."

"I know, petal. I know. It's ok."

"What about Mum?"

"I'll deal with your mother. There's nothing for you to worry about anymore."

"Don't tell her. You can't tell her. Please."

Sadie shushed her granddaughter and stroked her head once again. "I won't tell another soul for as long as I live."

"Promise?"

"Promise." Sadie's anger began to bubble again but she pushed it down, her emotions threatening to boil over. As much as she wanted to scream, she remained quiet and still, the picture of calm. Her feelings didn't matter anymore.

"I just want to forget, Grandma."

"You will, my love. One day it will just feel like a bad dream."

"I love you, Grandma."

Sadie held back her own tears. "I love you too, petal. With all my heart."

Chapter One

I don't know why I applied for the job. I don't know why I did the Skype interview, accepted the position and agreed to move to the very North-West corner of Scotland. Looking back, a part of me believed my entire life had led to this. A part of me believed that my life was about to irreversibly change and that I was letting it. Picking the path of most resistance had always been my speciality. I let these thoughts wash over me as I drove towards Inverness with a car-full of worldly possessions, an old road map and my drowsy fiancé Steven.

***

Steven and I had been sweethearts in High School. He was everything a girl could have wanted: athletic, popular and charismatic. Many of the girls in my year swooned over him but, ironically, I was not one of them. I had been sitting alone in the library studying for my prelims when he sauntered over to my table.

"What're you reading?" he had asked, pulling a chair over to sit next to me. I looked at him quizzically for a few seconds before returning to my book. Steven sat with me for a while before taking the hint and leaving the library. The whole thing was rather odd. I was quiet and studious, nothing that the likes of Steven could ever be interested in. At the time, I had thought some of his friends had dared him to do it. Why else would he want to talk to me? I continually rejected his advances, thinking he would soon get bored. What I hadn't anticipated was that Steven was rather persistent. He told me years later that he'd walk past the library every day in some vain hope of seeing me again.

Our first date had been nothing short of perfect. I had snuck out of my house after dark (something I had never done before) and hopped into Steven's battered Ford fiesta. It was a miracle he hadn't woken my Mum up when he arrived- the thing was an accident waiting to happen with a precarious hole in the bottom at the passenger's side. Getting into his car was like an Olympic-standard long jump. After abandoning his car on a seedy side street, he took me on a beautiful tour of the city: Glasgow University; Ashton Lane; Kelvingrove Park… we walked for hours and hours and the time just slipped past. He completely surprised me. I'd assumed he'd be a charismatic flirt and I'd be dropped at the first sign of an upgrade. I couldn't be more wrong. Steven was sensitive and sincere. He waited until half way through our first date before taking my hand because he didn't want to scare me off.

One evening, many years later, we sat in our Glasgow flat eating an Indian from our local restaurant. Having never been known for my cooking ability, we were on first name terms with the owner. I was concentrating on my garlic naan bread when Steven asked me a surprising question.

"What are your thoughts on marriage, Mhairi?"

I looked up in surprise. "We've had this conversation before, Steven. You know how I feel about marriage."

"I know, I know. I just wanted to hear about it again."

I shrugged and continued eating my naan bread. "Marriage is just a piece of paper, Steven. It's the relationship that makes a marriage and not the other way around."

Steven nodded, pushing a piece of paper to me across the table.

I looked at Steven quizzically before unfolding it. It read: *This is our piece of paper and I couldn't be happier. Will you marry me?*

***

Steven had been adverse to the move initially but I talked him round. It would be the perfect opportunity for us to start afresh. It would be easy to sell our two-bedroom flat in the West End of Glasgow. It would be easy for Steven to find work in the village. It was too good an opportunity to miss.

We cruised along the A9 as the sun barely breached the horizon. The view was spectacular- an array of mountains burst with colour as the light gently wakened behind them. Steven was searching for a radio station, releasing an array of white noise as he turned the tuning dial. The change of frequency was getting on my nerves.

"I highly doubt you're going to find any radio station signal up here." I said, keeping a close eye on the traffic ahead.

Steven grunted in response and continued to turn the dial. I sighed. Hoping to miss the rush hour traffic, I shepherded Steven into the car at 4.30am. His reaction had not been a happy one. He had dozed for the first of hours but was now fully awake and getting restless.

"Why don't you leave that dial and just put in a CD?"

"It might be better if you remember that I don't need micro-managing." He said smirking, all while not taking his eye off the radio.

I eased off the gas as a tractor pulled onto the road, my grip tightening on the steering wheel. "I just thought it might save you some time."

In a huff, Steven turned the radio off and gazed out of the window.

"I'm not a fan of this lack of signal either, you know."

Steven turned to face me. "Oh really? Is someone regretting their decision?"

"No." I responded, a little too quickly.

Steven raised an eyebrow before eventually returning his attention to the window.

I hadn't been in Allaban for a very long time. My Grandparents lived there so I spent the summer holidays with them while Mum worked. My days were consumed looking for my next adventure amid the hills and glens. Time was different in those days. Summers seemed to last forever, an endless indulgence. Grandma always said that, in Allaban, time stood still. In those days, Grandma was always right.

When they passed away, everything changed. My Grandpa had aggressive lung cancer when I was nineteen years old. It took hold quickly and he died within a year. My Grandma followed soon after. They say she died of a broken heart. I'm convinced my heart also broke the day she died. The untainted memories of Allaban and my Grandparents remained intact and quietly boxed up in my mind. Until now.

I had been aimlessly scrolling through the job adverts when I saw it: Head Teacher of Allaban High School. I was immediately intrigued. Some research soon revealed that the previous headteacher hastily departed, leaving scandal and mystery in her wake. The high school was left to the depute head teacher. Once I unearthed their most recent inspection report, it was clear the school had fallen into severe disarray. I put in an application on a whim and promptly forgot about it. I had graduated from my teaching degree ten years previous. Gaining a headship a decade into your career was unheard of for a teaching professional. When I found out I had been successful, I was gobsmacked. I was so excited until I remembered I had neglected to inform Steven.

"We have just started building a life here and suddenly you are all ready to move again. What's so bad about living in the same place for more than five minutes?"

"This is a fantastic opportunity Steven. I can't just say no."

"And why not? It seems a lot simpler than upping and moving to the middle of nowhere."

"It's not like we've never moved before."

"We have moved plenty of times before! Why should we do it again? Why can't you just be happy with where we are now?"

I sighed. I couldn't help it. I couldn't settle. We had moved a lot in the last few years and I could see it slowly wearing away at Steven's patience. He had always joked that I ear-marked jobs like others would a holiday catalogue. He wasn't far wrong.

"Why can't you just include me in these conversations, Mhairi? You always have your mind made up before you've ever given me a seat at the table."

I shrugged. "I didn't see the point if it came to nothing."

"You've got to include me in the narrative. I'm not a mind-reader, Mhairi. I can't guess your next big escapade. This is *our* life. I want us to make these decisions together."

"This job will be life-changing for the two of us… in the best way."

Steven scoffed as he stormed past me, plucked a beer from the fridge and lay on the couch. This was the signal that our argument was over. He would come round eventually- it would just take a little time and persuasion.

Mum, however, had been a different kettle of fish. My Dad died when I was still very young so she had pinned all hope of success and happiness on me, her only child. In many ways I was a success- I had a job, a home, a fiancé - but I did not have the family my mother so craved. I knew Mum secretly hoped I'd have children and settle down. The problem was that predictable had never been my style. When I shared the exciting news over the phone, she sighed, deflating my enthusiasm.

"Well it's your life, Mhairi." She stated. "You are entitled to live it how you choose, I suppose.." This was Mum's way of disapproving in her own cryptic manner.

***

After a long drive, we finally turned onto the last stretch of road towards Allaban. Suddenly, a bang erupted from the car and we rolled to a stop in the middle of the single-track dirt road. Steven was jostled awake and looked at me with a baffled expression. I cursed under my breath. Our journey had been going too smoothly.

"Why couldn't this have happened in Inverness when we at least had a phone signal?" exclaimed Steven, bounding out of the car to assess the damage. He studied the wheels intently, hands on his hips. "The left tyre has a puncture. Where is the puncture repair kit?"

"It's in the boot somewhere but you might need to root around for it."

Steven sighed. "Why didn't you move it into the car?"

I ignored him and instead sat back in my seat, attempting to stretch my legs after the long drive.

Just as Steven set to work, a truck came into view, gliding along before coming to a graceful stop. The driver hopped out of the truck and made his way towards our car, wading through the weeds that lined either side of the road. He was dressed in a shabby checked shirt, worn blue jeans and black boots. He wore an old cap, successfully covering a mess of chestnut hair. He took a moment to survey the spectacle in-front of him, his face filled with concern.

"I have an electric pump in my truck if you'd prefer? Might save you some time."

Steven lifted his head from underneath the car. "We're fine, thank you." He said curtly and resumed his labour. "I'm almost finished and we will be on our way."

I studied the stranger's face, a strange sensation filling my chest. He looked inquisitively at the car before catching my eye. I smiled apologetically.

The man shrugged and made his way back to his truck. He backed into a passing place and waited patiently for Steven to finish the job.

Ten minutes later, Steven was finally happy with his handiwork and hopped back into the car. The engine roared into life. As we drove past the black pickup, it's owner gave me a curious glance. His eyes were somewhat familiar but I just couldn't place them. Steven gave him a token wave as we flew past.

"Did you know that guy or something?" Steven asked, whilst once again trying to find a radio station.

I shrugged. I had known him as a child, that much I was sure of. His warm brown eyes drew my mind to a past I'd spent fourteen years trying to forget. Time had long since eroded those memories of a happier and simpler time- a time before the event that disturbed my happy childhood. Although time had passed, those brown eyes were still a vivid beacon in my rearmost memory.

***

Just short of fifty minutes later, we reached the brow of a hill and Allaban opened up before our very eyes. The view was nothing short of magnificent. The light caught the trees in a dance of colour as the sun sat sleepily in the sky. The village was dusted with small crofts and mismatched houses staking claim to the many hills and glens stretched before us. These houses stemmed from the winding road, much like a long established oak tree with a variety of curious branches. The school was tucked in behind the right-hand side of the hill as we made our decent. It was a modest, red sandstone building with large Victorian windows on every side. It stood abreast a beautiful loch, quietly content with its picturesque location. This sight brought the reality of my decision home- I was to be the new Headteacher of this school.

Steven studied the building curiously. "It's not a very modern building, is it?"

"I guess it's been around for a very long time."

"Well they might have done a better job of maintaining it. It looks like it's about to crumble into the water."

I chuckled. "Just as well you're here to fix it all."

14

Steven paused. "I thought that was your job, love?"

I guess he was right.

Chapter Two

After an eventful journey, we finally arrived at what was to be our new home. As Steven began to unpack the car boot, I walked up the cottage. It was an odd feeling. Steven and I were to be the new inhabitants of this cute little cottage, a stone's throw away from a majestic loch in the middle of nowhere. On the other side of the loch resided the school, where I would spend the better half of most of my days. I felt strangely detached from this reality. It was hard to accept that a split-second decision I had made a few months ago had brought about this bizarre string of events.

It was clear that the cottage had been a resident of the village for a long time. It's walls were crafted from white stone proudly supporting a sturdy thatched roof. A beautiful wheel hung by the front door, its prongs intricately entwined with iron heather. I reached out to touch it, waiting for the dream to disintegrate before my eyes.

"It's called Heather Cottage."

Startled, I whirled around. I turned to face a woman, her blonde hair swept back into a messy bun, adorned with kirby grips. Her eyes were bright blue, reminiscent of the first crisp day of Spring. She wore a deep purple maxi dress which ebbed in the wind as she spoke. "My name is Emily Harris. Welcome to Allaban." She smiled.

After accepting the position of Head Teacher of Allaban High School, I immediately began drafting list of tasks I needed to complete prior to the big move. I contacted the local estate agents in search of a new home and they then put me in touch with Emily. Emily owned Heather Cottage and a few other properties scattered around the village. The woman in-front of me did not match the image I had in my mind. To me, she was a stern businesswoman, not the bright and bubbly figure that stood before me.

Steven abandoned the car and approached us, extending his hand to Emily. "Lovely to meet you. I'm Steven, Mhairi's fiancé. This place looks amazing."

"Thank you. Heather Cottage has been in the family for a few generations. We recently refurbished the inside but the stone walls you see are the original architecture."

"I can believe it. It looks like a hurricane couldn't topple it."

Emily laughed. "With the winter winds we get up here, sturdiness is a necessity! I'll let you inside."

It was a modern space with two floors separated by a winding spiral staircase. Downstairs was a small kitchen and living room separated only by a couch, whilst upstairs was a bedroom and en-suite. The cottage was very cosy- mostly thanks to the log burner which sat on the far wall of the living room. The plush purple walls and splashes of tartan on the furnishings had a homely feel with a modern twist. It was clear that Emily had a flair for interior design. The décor was the perfect fusion of highland heritage and modern design.

"My grandfather built this cottage. It's always had a special place in our family."

I smiled. "It really is beautiful Emily."

"I've always enjoyed decorating. I like to update the place every so often- far more often that my husband George is aware of. Ignorance is bliss." She chuckled. "I'll leave you two to settle in. If you need me I live in the house just along the road. It's the one with the yellow door." With that, Emily was gone. She was clearly passionate about her family's legacy. This fire burned far brighter than the log burner could ever compete with.

Steven put down the bags he was carrying and let out a huge sigh. "Well. This is home." He looked around. "I've seen worse places."

"High praise from you!" I teased, going to collect the rest of our belongings from the car.

The car was precariously packed with all of our prized possessions, a jenga of junk. It always baffled me that, no matter how much I cleared and tidied, I still owned far more that I could fathom. Steven always said I was a hoarder but I refused to believe him. Better to keep something just in case than to regret it later. After a few relentless hours of moving in, we sat cross-legged on the couch cradling a pizza, the contents of the car scattered around the room.

"What kind of pizza is this?" asked Steven, studying his slice. "what are the green bits?"

"Green peppers."

Steven frowned. "Nothing green belongs on a pizza."

I rolled my eyes. "It's good for you."

"It's a pizza, Mhairi. It's not supposed to have anything good for you on it."

"It won't kill you."

"If it does, I'm blaming you."

"I'll be sure to mention it in the obituary."

After concluding that the pizza was up to his standards, Steven jammed a full slice in his mouth. "I didn't except the village to be so spread out." He said as he chewed. "We must have driven past at least 100 houses."

I nodded in agreement. "The population of Allaban was 300… and that was at least fourteen years ago."

Steven let out a long whistle. "300?! Wow. It's bigger than I thought it would be, that's for sure."

"Doesn't stop them all from knowing if you sneeze before breakfast. Grandma always warned me to be on my best behaviour."

Steven cocked his head to one side. "Is it weird being here without them? Your grandparents, I mean?"

"We are on the other side of the village. If we were in their house… maybe."

"Still. It's the first time you've been here in… how many years?"

"The last time I was here I was an eighteen year old. That wasn't yesterday."

"Well you don't look a day over forty."

I elbowed him in the ribs. "You were two years above me in school, old man."

"Seriously though… does it feel strange?"

"A little… I guess."

Just then, the doorbell rang. Steven gave me a puzzled look. I shrugged my shoulders. No one from the village knew we were here aside from Emily. Who could possibly have found out? My brain began churning through all the worst case scenarios as my pulse sky-rocketed. I eased myself off the couch, crossing my arms to hide the slight tremble which had begun to course through my body.

As I opened the door, I was greeted by a figure looming in the doorway, the entrance far too small for his lanky frame. He wore a bottle green jacket to shelter from the rain, his hair poking out precariously at the front. Although his hair was brown, it was starting to go grey in random patches. He wore rounded spectacles, framing his weather-beaten face.

"I'm very sorry to be calling so late." He said, his face sparkling in the evening darkness. My eyes squinted as they adjusted to the gloom. My mind was clouded. I recognised this face. My memory was obscured from the many years we had been apart. The past tug at my coattails. Then the penny finally dropped. "Rab Campbell?"

He smiled broadly. "Mhairi Sinclair. I'd recognise that face anywhere. You haven't aged a day."

I had spent most of my childhood in the company of Rab Campbell. We were often spotted wading through bogs, rolling down steep hills and playing games of "Chicken" with the cows in the neighbouring fields. The neighbours would often complain about us but they secretly loved having something to gossip about. As children, we were blissfully unaware of the rumblings we were causing around Allaban. All of these memories hit me in an instant, the past almost tangable.

"Still causing havoc around here, Rab?"

He laughed. "I actually go by Robert these days, Mhairi. Far more professional."

I rolled my eyes. "Oh yeah? I'll believe it when I see it! How long has it been? Twenty years?"

"Ever the drama queen, V. Fancy inviting me in already? I'm gasping for a cup of tea and it's bloody freezing."

I stood aside and he rushed in, pulling off his coat and throwing it on the sofa. My brain struggled to marry the past and the present. Whilst looking at Rab, I could see the boy I knew so well but also the man who was a stranger to me. His hair was greying and his eyes crinkled with age and yet his booming voice still dominated any room.

"Steven Smith. Mhairi's fiancé." Steven was on his feet in an instant, the pizza all but forgotten and hand outstretched.

Rab shook it confidently. "Robert Campbell."

Steven ushered him towards the squat dining table while I made tea, my mind still precariously joining the dots of past and present.

"So Rab," I called over my shoulder. "what brings you here? What have you been up to all these years?"

Rab twiddled his thumbs nervously. "Well, V, you may not believe me but… I'm the Depute Head Teacher of Allaban High School."

I whirled round in surprise.

Rab laughed. "It's the truth! I know I was a bit of a wild card growing up but I did eventually go to university- mostly to keep mum happy but I did learn a few things. I tired of living permanently in the grey. She always said I needed to put my mind to work and I was no use on the farm. After I graduated, a teaching job came up at the High School. Then, a few years down the line, someone thought it was a good idea to promote me… and here we are."

I looked at him, aghast. "I'm surprised, Rab."

Rab laughed. "I wish. These turns of events seem far more fateful than born of actual talent, V. I have always been a victim of being in the right place at the right time."

"I always thought you'd be somewhere in Australia busking on street corners."

"That job never materialised, sadly. Tom went to Spain for a while back in the day... but he came back to help look after the Croft when dad got ill."

I hesitated for a moment before continuing with the tea, my mind suddenly dwarfed by my emotions. "I didn't realise Tom went to Spain. How is Alan now? Is he ok?"

"Yeah he's fine. He had a bad stroke a couple of years back. He has been making a slow recovery ever since. Tom runs the farm now."

Steven interrupted. "I'm quite a handy man myself. I trained as a Joiner. If you need any work done I'm happy to be of service."

Rab nodded briefly. "I'll bear that in mind. Thanks, Steven."

Tom Campbell. That was a name that had proved hard to forget. It was Tom Campbell on the dirt road earlier that day. It baffled me that I hadn't recognised him. I needed a little time to unravel the bind of my thoughts and feelings. I carried the three piping hot mugs over to the dining table, careful not to spill any of the contents. I took a deep breath. "How is Tom doing?"

"He's fine. Still a man of few words. Mum always said you were the only one that managed to get a full sentence out of him."

I quietly sipped my tea as I took my seat, careful to be mid gulp and avoid answering Rab's statement.

Rab crossed his arms and sat back in his chair. "So Mhairi. Head Teacher of Allaban High School. I hadn't put two and two together when they said a Miss Sinclair would be joining the faculty."

I smiled, feeling the colour rush to my cheeks. "Much like you, I stumbled upon the advert and decided it was too good an opportunity to miss… we decided, I mean." I glanced at Steven. "I didn't expect to get it. That was a surprise."

"If you're anything like I remember Mhairi, I am not surprised in the slightest. You are, as you always were, irritatingly talented." He turned to Steven, chuckling. "One day, Mhairi decided she was determined to climb the old oak tree that sits on our croft. She made it eventually, after she sprained her ankle and used me to break her fall."

"Not intentionally!" I laughed, before catching a glance of Steven who looked anything but entertained. I cleared my throat, attempting to dissolve the tension. "So is there anything I should know about the school before Monday?"

Rab laughed. "You've caused quite a stir already and you've not even set foot in the building yet, V."

My face flushed involuntarily.

Rab chuckled. "I'm having a little get together at the Croft on Saturday night. I came here to issue my personal invitation. It'll give you a chance to meet some of the staff. "

"Sounds great."

"Fantastic news."

***

After a couple of hours, Rab made his excuses and left. Steven walked him to the door, playing the welcoming host. As soon as the door was shut, Steven turned to face me, looking anything but amused.

"What was that? V? Last time I checked that was a letter of the alphabet."

I rolled my eyes. "We were kids! Rab could barely say my name, never mind spell it."

"I've known you for the best part of twenty years and this guy was spouting stories about you, my fiancée, that I'd never heard before."

"The stories he was telling were very much my early childhood. I could barely remember any of them myself."

"Well his memory seemed crystal clear." He said, raising an eyebrow.

I sighed putting a hand on his arm. "The past is in the past for a reason. It's supposed to stay there."

"I know nothing about your life up here. You came here for eighteen summers of your life. No matter how much I probed, you'd never share any of it. I want to know everything about you, Mhairi. I want to know every part of you. Every part of your life is important to me."

"I know. It's just that this part of my history is one I'd rather forget." I made a move to clean up the chaos left by out unexpected visitor, hoping he would drop the subject.

"We have moved here, Mhairi. We have literally moved into your past. You can't just dismiss everything that happened."

Something inside me snapped. "Yes I bloody well can!" I screamed, dropping one of the mugs in the process. The stone floor broke its fall.

After a few moments, Steven eased his way over to me and took me in his arms. I sank into him, silent tears rolling down my cheeks. Coming back to Allaban had already proven to be a whirlwind. I couldn't let myself be swept away.

After a prolonged period of time, Steven broke the silence. "I'm sorry, Mhairi. I didn't mean to hurt your feelings."

I shook my head, still cradled in his arms. "I know. It's ok. The past just reminds me of them. Grandma and Grandpa. I had such happy times here. I took it for granted as a kid. I remember I'd come home, after I'd been on one of my many adventures, coated in mud. Grandma would ask: "was today your best day so far?" I would usually say yes. She would always reply: "there are many more best days to come, darling."" I paused for a moment. "I was eighteen when I last came here. That is one of the biggest regrets of my life."

"You weren't to know what would happen."

"I was too wrapped up in my own life, Steven. I thought I'd outgrown this place. I didn't think for one second that would be the last time I'd see Grandma and Grandpa."

Steven gave me a squeeze. "You loved them. They knew that."

I nodded, removing myself from him and started to tidy the kitchen. Suddenly my walls were raised like unwanted security checkpoints, shutting him out and keeping me in.

Steven sighed. "I'm going to bed. Don't stay up too late, love."

I acknowledged his statement with a nod and continued with my work. Steven would never understand what it was like to come back here. The clarity of my decision rained down on my like a shower of stupid. I had applied for the job on a whim, thinking that returning to the village would bring happy memories of a life I had forgotten. Sometimes the past should just stay forgotten.

Chapter Three

The Campbell brothers were known for causing havoc around the village. Rab, the older of the two, loved nothing more than an adventure. His idea of an adventure usually ended in tears, snotters and broken bones. If none of these were his, the mission was a success.

I was initiated into their gang when I was six years old. A then thirteen year old Rab thought it was a good idea to steal chewing gum from the local Spar. I caught him in the act but decided against telling on him. Rab thought I was pretty cool and, although seven years his junior, I took great delight in bossing Rab around.

Tom was his much more reserved younger brother. He found our antics rather amusing so hung about to see what would happen next. He was a boy of few words but wasn't shy. I remember thinking that he was a bit strange but that was just his way. One summer afternoon, I beat Rab in a hill race near his parents' croft. I was very pleased with myself but Rab was convinced I had somehow cheated. Tom only said "She won. Get over it." This statement cemented our friendship.

Grandma had warned me time and time again to stay away from the Campbell brothers. She would often refer to them as "a pair of scallywags" after Rab stole a pair of her underwear from the washing line. Grandma thought Rab lead me astray but quite often it was the other way around. We were referred to as "V and the Campbell brothers" around the village. Aside from sounding like a B-list pop group, we were indeed thick as thieves. That was until one particular incident when I turned eighteen.

Rab, then twenty-five years old, was still a loose cannon. Growing out of our immature shenanigans of years gone by, the three of us had taken to hanging out in an old abandoned barn at the back of the Campbell property. Tom would collect logs from the outhouse and we would make a small bonfire to keep ourselves warm in the long summer nights. One particular evening, Rab had managed to acquire some weed from a fisherman passing through the village. He took great delight in boasting about this but I wasn't interested.

"Go on, V. Have a try. It really mellows you out." Rab took a long drag and sank into a bale of hay.

I raised an eyebrow. "There is no need for you getting more mellow than you already are, Rab."

Rab laughed in a lazy sort of way. "You're too uptight, V. The old V would have tried it."

"Old V?" I questioned. "Since when have I changed that much?"

"You're just no fun anymore, V. Just give this a try. You won't regret it."

"I have no intention of becoming a stoner, Rab."

"Stoner? It's one wee spliff, V. You're just frightened you might actually enjoy yourself."

Tom interjected. "She said she didn't want any, Rab. Just drop it." Although quiet, his voice was full of fire. He glared at Rab.

Rab snorted. "Ooh Tom. Being the big protector now, are we?"

I turned to Tom. "I can fight my own battles, Tom. I don't need your help."

Tom ignored me. His eyes were firmly fixed on his older brother. "I said, drop it. She doesn't need to stoop to your level."

"You wish you were on my level, Tommy. Then maybe V would pay a little bit more attention."

"Stop trying to act like a cool guy when in reality you're just a waster."

I shrank back into the hay, unsure what to do. Tom was positively incandescent with rage. The brothers looked at each other with quiet intensity.

Rab leaned forward. "At least if I like a girl I have the courage to actually say more than three words to her." He sneered.

After that, the scene became a blur. Tom lost it. He flew at Rab, fists at the ready and landed a punch square in Rab's jaw. There was a loud crack and blood poured from Rab's face. Tom didn't so much as blink. Rab grabbed Tom by the shoulders and began violently shaking him, bloody spattering from his mouth.

I could only sit and watch as the Campbell brothers laid into each other, punch after punch. Eventually I found the courage to run to the house, not daring to look at the chaos unfurling behind me. I told Mary what happened but it was their father Alan who rose from his chair. I could smell the whisky on his breath as he stormed towards the barn, his hands already screwed tightly into fists. I crept behind him, hardly daring to breathe. On arrival, he grabbed both boys by the scruff of their necks and yanked them apart.

"Men use words, not fists. Now clean up this damn mess."

Alan spoke very quietly but the menace in his tone was clear. Rab and Tom were both panting and covered in blood. It wasn't clear who was worse off. Rab shrugged his father off and stormed off into the field. Tom just stood and watched his brother disappear into the dark night.

After what felt like an eternity of gut wrenching silence, Alan put a hand on my shoulder. "I think it'd be wise if you head back to Sadie's, Mhairi." He said.

I nodded, collected my belongings and hastily left. That was the last I saw of the Campbell brothers.

The young, rebellious Rab was merely a hazy memory. He was suddenly so different. I had always wondered what Rab meant that night. Tom and I had always just been friends, nothing more. He was always the first one I shared my troubles with. He was a close friend at the time and I had just cut all ties with him. I had started half a dozen letters to him after that year but never really figured out what I wanted to say.

***

Although the Campbell croft was on the other side of the village, it didn't take us long to get there. We could have walked but I thought it would be a better idea to drive. If things went sour it'd be easy enough to make our excuses and leave, complete with getaway vehicle.

The Campbell Croft could only be described as charmingly erratic. The house itself was an old building with an array of mismatched extensions which had been added over the generations. The surrounding farmland was littered with scrap metal, farming equipment and overgrown fields. On any other property this would have looked ridiculous, but on the Campbell's croft it fitted perfectly. The barn where I spent many summers with Rab and Tom was not visible from the front of the farmhouse but tucked away behind an assortment of trees, wildflowers and bracken.

As we pulled up at the croft, it was clear we were the only ones to bring a car. There were a lot of questioning glances from guests who had congregated outside.

I turned to Steven. "Any time you want to leave, we will leave."

"Don't be silly, Mhairi. It'll give you a chance to meet some of the teachers and I can start schmoosing some potential clients. I'm sure it will be a lovely evening."

"Just in case it isn't, Steven."

"What are you so worried about?"

I dismissed his question and quickly exited the car.

"You made it!" a voice shouted from the darkness. Rab sauntered up to us, cradling a bottle of gin. "Driving, V? I would have expected more from you! You can always leave the car if you decide to join the party." He winked. "Steven, good to see you again!"

"Unlike Mhairi, I fully intend to join the party." Steven said.

"Good man, good man! Just as well our V has a good influence."

Rab ushered Steven inside, weaving past all of the people congregated by the doorway. I remained, standing awkwardly beside the car.

A part of me wanted to leave. I dreaded the thought of entering into a room filled with foggy faces from my past. I hadn't seen the majority of the village in fourteen years. A handful I had seen at the funeral but I had, as much as possible, avoided them. This wasn't through lack of caring but rather caring too much. I didn't need to be an emotional mess around people I had known for most of my childhood. With this in mind, I was preparing for a frosty welcome at best. After seriously contemplating making a run for it, I walked as casually as I could towards the front door. None of those crowded round the entrance gave me a second glance.

I dodged my way through the hallway and into the Campbell's large living room. The room looked exactly the same as I remembered it- full to bursting with collective memorabilia from Rab and Tom's childhood. I even spotted a picture of the three of us, covered head to toe in mud, sitting proudly on the mantlepiece. I couldn't be any more than eight in the photograph.

Emily appeared seemingly out of nowhere and folded me into a massive bear hug, catching me off-guard. "Mhairi! How lovely to see you. Glad you were able to come. Are you by yourself?"

"Steven is here somewhere," I replied, glancing around the room. "Rab whisked him off just as we arrived."

Emily laughed. "A few of the men are in the kitchen taking part in a drinking game, I believe. George is somewhere in there too. Best leave them to it!"

I chuckled nervously in response.

"How is the cottage? Is it comfortable enough for you?"

"Oh yes, it's great. Perfect for the two of us. We've just about unpacked all of our stuff so it'll be nice once we have a chance to relax in it."

"Have you met anyone from the village yet?"

"Rab stopped by but other than that… no."

With that, Emily took hold of my arm, whisked me through a labyrinth of people and deeper into the house. She ushered me towards a group of three women, deep in a pool of gossip.

"Girls! This is Mhairi Sinclair. She's the new Head Teacher at the High School."

The three women turn to face me, each with a cocktail glass in hand.

"Mhairi, meet Donna, Iris and Sophie. They all work at the High School."

"Lovely to meet you all. I'm Mhairi Sinclair." I said, awkwardly extending my hand to each of them in turn. This felt a little too much like an interview panel.

"We know who you are." slurred Donna.

The other two women gave her a sideways glance which she ignored.

"You're Sadie's granddaughter. The one who left one summer and never came back." I blinked nervously.

"I went to University, actually. It didn't leave much time for visiting. What is it you do in the High School?"

Sophie jumped in before Donna had the chance. "Donna works in the office. I teach Music. This is my third year at the High School. I did my qualifying year here and decided to stay. I'm from Ayrshire originally." She was a pretty girl, face brimming with enthusiasm that only a teacher not long out of their degree possessed.

I smiled encouragingly. "A few of my friends teach in Ayrshire. It's a beautiful part of the world."

Sophie beamed. "Where are you from, Mhairi?"

"Glasgow originally, but I've moved around a bit with different jobs. Keeps things interesting."

I clocked Donna rolling her eyes, clutching her glass tightly.

"Nice way to see different parts of the country." Said Iris. Her piercing blue eyes were bright with excitement, her energy infectious.

"Absolutely." I replied.

"I teach English. In with the brick work I'm afraid- I won't admit how many years I've been at the High School! You know you're old when you start teaching people's grandchildren- especially your own grandson! I have a boat in the harbour which keeps me out of trouble when I'm not at work. You'll need to come a cruise on the Loch sometime!"

I nodded. "That would be lovely!"

Iris smiled. "Best way to see the village, in my opinion."

Donna cut in. "Am I the only one to see this woman for what she is?" she slurred, a little too loudly.

"Donna, be civil." said Iris, grabbing her arm before she toppled over. A few people turned to see what the commotion was about.

"I will not be civil!" Donna bellowed, spilling some of her drink on Iris's arm and attracting unwanted attention. "She ran around with those Campbell boys like she owned the place for years. Then, at the first sign of trouble, she

36

abandons the place. Your Grandma was broken hearted when you left, did you know that?"

My mouth went dry. "I… well…"

"Aye well indeed. You have no right to show your face here never mind take over the High School. Sadie will be turning in her grave."

Iris gasped. "Donna! You're making a scene!"

It took all of my willpower to not burst into tears or punch her in the face. Instead, I made a break for the door.

Emily called after me. "Mhairi! Wait! Please!" I ignored her. I was gone.

I fled as quickly as I could, escaping the house into the cool August air. I needed to escape the swampland of negative thoughts floating in my head. My feet took me to the one place I still felt at home- the barn.

It was just as I remembered- falling apart. The was a gaping hole in the roof and, although there was only one door, there were several entrances into the central cavity. There were weeds spouting out of every nook in the brickwork, as though trying to elude the casual passer-by that it was indeed part of the foliage. A solitary lamp hung from the roof, attached by Rab all those years ago.

I removed my heels and made myself comfortable on a pile of hay, gazing at the stars through the hole in the roof. They were scattered across the night sky like mistaken splashes from the end of a paintbrush. It was a beautiful mess. I exhaled.

Someone cleared their throat. "I guess we both had the same idea." Said a familiar voice. I sat up quickly whilst proceeding to fall further into the pile of hay.

"Sorry." I muttered, hastily throwing myself to my feet and attempting to fix my dishevelled appearance. When I looked up, a pair of warm brown eyes were staring back at me. He had traded his plaid shirt and big black boots for a shirt and cream jumper, paired with blue jeans and brown dress shoes. Although he'd clearly dressed up for the occasion, his dishevelled mess of chestnut brown hair still remained.

"Thomas. I'm so sorry. I shouldn't be here."

He laughed. "Only Mum calls me Thomas, V."

"And I didn't recognise you on the road... You just looked so different."

"I don't remember you being so apologetic."

I sighed. "Sorry."

He laughed. "Mind if I join you?" Tom said, pointing to the hay. "I'll try and be a wee bit more graceful at sitting than you were."

We both sat and gazed up at the sky.

After some time, Tom broke the silence. "I came out here to avoid the drinking game currently happening in the kitchen. What's your excuse?"

"I think I may have rubbed someone up the wrong way."

"Now that's the V I remember."

I smiled. "Not on purpose. She was angry that I left the village and Grandma and…"

"Who was this exactly?"

"Donna. She works at the High School."

Tom snorted. "Her opinions aren't worth your time."

"She has a right to be angry."

"No she doesn't, Mhairi." Tom turned to face me, taking his eyes away from the symphony of stars above our heads. "It's just what Donna's like. She pokes her nose in where it doesn't belong."

"But what if it isn't just her, Tom? She's right. I left the village. I left my grandparents."

"Trust me. Her opinion is not the opinion of the whole village."

He touched my hand.

Just then a drunken voice echoed through the darkness.

"MHAIRI! WHERE ARE YOU?" called Steven.

I sighed and stood up. "I should go. That's my fiancé."

I left the barn in search of Steven. It didn't take long to pick the drunken figure out from the crowd of people gathered in front of the house.

"BABY! THERE YOU ARE!" He bellowed.

I made my way towards him through the foliage. "Steven. You are causing a scene."

Just then, another drunken figure threw his arm around Steven's neck and gave him a kiss on the cheek. "Where have you been hiding this one, V?" crooned Rab.

I grabbed Steven forcefully by the arm. "Thank you very much for the party, Rab." I said bluntly. With that, I bundled Steven into the car.

"What a night! What a night!" yelled Steven as we drove home.

"Are you trying to wake up the whole village?" I hissed.

"I met so many people. They were all just lovely."

"I'm sure they were."

"Where did you go?"

"I was just outside getting some fresh air."

"You were gone for ages. I thought you'd left without me."

"I would never abandon you, Steven. Even in this drunken stupor."

Steven scoffed. "I'm not drunk."

I rolled my eyes. "Of course not."

"So where did you go?"

"I was just with Tom, Rab's brother."

"Tom? Who is Tom?"

"He was the guy we met on the road."

"Him?" Steven's buoyant mood noticeably darkened. "Why were you with him?"

"I just bumped into him, Steven. Can we maybe talk about this in the morning? When you're a little more... yourself?"

"I am just fine." He slurred. "I'm just asking why my fiancée bumped into a guy and proceeded to spend the whole night with him and not me."

I gave him an icy glare. "Steven."

"I mean Rab, Tom...they seem to know you pretty well."

"...And?"

"Did you sleep with them or something?"

I slammed on the breaks, coming to an abrupt stop. Steven flew forward in his seat, being caught only by his seatbelt.

I turned to him, slowly and deliberately, speaking barely above a whisper. "So help me Steven. Another word from you about Rab, Tom or anything else and you will be walking the rest of the way home."

Steven slumped back into his chair in stony silence.

We didn't say a word until we arrived at the cottage. Steven stumbled inside, trying to have as much composure as possible.

"I think you should sleep on the couch tonight." I stated, walking straight past Steven and up to bed.

Chapter Four

The next morning, I woke at the crack of dawn after seeing every hour on my bedside alarm clock. My fight with Steven still weighed heavily on my mind. Although I knew he had been drinking, I could not get over his hurtful slurs. I did not want to be spending the next day arguing so instead decided to take a walk to clear my head. I packed a small rucksack and crept past the snoring Steven, leaving my worries behind as I quietly closed the door.

It was a bright morning, a cold breeze shivering through the air. My bright blue jacket offered little protection from the onslaught of Scottish seasons. I pulled it tightly around me. A steady stream of happy memories accompanied the occasional gust of wind as my feet instinctively weaved through the maze of streets. I set off at a brisk pace it search of Feic beach.

Grandma always visited Feic beach on a Sunday morning. No matter the weather, she set out at the crack of dawn dragging me every step of the way. She called it her "weekly pilgrimage".

"We could be the only people on the planet, Mhairi darling. Just you and me." She would whisper. She always held me just a little tighter then, as though afraid I would blow away in the breeze.

As I arrived at the top of a particularly gruelling hill, the beach opened up in front of my eyes. The taste of freedom was intoxicating. It overwhelmed me like a bright light after an age of darkness. The sun shone through the clouds like pillars of light and danced on the beach below. The wind receded to a faint whisper. I felt comforted by the rhythmical sloshing of the waves. I stood motionless for a while, reaping the rewards of my long journey. It was as though Grandma had never left but instead chose to live the rest of her life at the beach she so cared for.

I hastily removed my shoes and stumbled towards the sea. The waves caressed my sore feet as I walked along the shore. The memories spilled into my consciousness. I used to spend hours running up and down the beach whilst Grandma sat and watched. The beach was always littered with hidden treasure just waiting for me to discover. As I was transported to those happier times, the sands of time stood still, moved only by the rippling tide. Grief caught me unawares but the calm constant of the water flushed out my negative energy.

As I wandered along the beach, my eyes caught sight of an old wooden bench sitting at the far side of the beach, overlooking the sandy dunes. Overcome with a wave of curiousity, I walked towards it. The bench was weathered from its time beside the beach, black paint peeling away from all sides. A gold plaque glittered from in its centre. It read:
"In Loving Memory of Sadie Munro. May sadness always be washed away by the tide."

My fingers traced the outline of the plaque, curious and quietly stunned by its beauty.

***

After my wearying journey, I entered the cottage. Steven sat on the sofa, his eyes searing my skin. I walked past him, avoiding his gaze.

"I wake up and you're gone. No phone-call, no text, no note."

"I went for a walk. There was no signal."

"I'm aware of that. I did call you at least twenty times. What about a note?"

"Steven- I'm tired, my feet are sore and I'm covered in sand. Can we do this later?"

"We always have to do things at your convenience, Mhairi. Never when they suit me."

I stopped and stared directly at Steven. "After your display last night, count yourself lucky you weren't sleeping in the car." With that, I escaped to our bathroom, locked the door and drew myself a bath.

After an hour or so, there was a pathetic knock at the door. "Mhairi? I'm sorry, ok? I was worried."

I did not answer. Instead, I sank into the bubbles.

Steven eventually got the hint and left.

My phone buzzed and lit up at the side of the bath. I glanced at the screen. Under the Twenty-seven missed calls from Steven from earlier in the day was a text from Emily:

"We should talk. Drinks at mine?"

After my bath, I didn't feel much better. My stiff and strained muscles still ached and my head was still clouded with confusion. I decided not to let this show. I made my way down the stairs. Steven was lying on the couch, still nursing his hangover.

"Going out." I stated. I picked up my jacket and promptly left.

Emily's house was just a short walk from the cottage. The bright yellow door shone like a beacon in the August sunshine. The house itself was exceptionally well-kept which wasn't a surprise. It was clear that, although Emily had an easy breezy manner, she prided a sense of order and organisation. I made my way along the front path, admiring the flowers as I went.

Emily led me into the kitchen and living space, evenly divided with a breakfast bar and an array of coloured bar stools.

"Have a seat anywhere you like." Emily said, as she began concocting our drinks.

"Thanks Emily. Your house is stunning." Emily certainly had an eye for interior design. My eyes struggled to take in the colourful palette.

She waved dismissively. "It's a bit of a mess at the moment. Waiting to get some work done in the living room."

"Your house is not a mess, Emily. As for work needing done, I'm sure Steven could take a look at it if you needed anyone." A new wave of resentment hit me as I said Steven's name.

Emily passed me a drink. "I'll definitely keep that in mind. How is he today? George has been lying in bed all day groaning."

I rolled my eyes. "Very similar but Steven is on the couch."

Emily laughed. "Men!"

"You've got that right." I took a large gulp of my gin and tonic, the warm liquid spilling into my stomach.

Emily paused for a moment, suddenly awkward. She smiled sympathetically. "I wanted to apologise for Donna's behaviour last night. She had already had a few cocktails before you arrived…"

I interrupted. "There's no need to apologise."

"Yes there is." Emily ran her finger round the rim of her glass. "I have very fond memories of your Grandparents. I've never met couple that were so devoted to each other."

I blinked in surprise. "I didn't realise you knew my grandparents, Emily."

"When your Grandpa got ill, I kept meaning to drop in. When he passed, I…" Emily's eyes began to fill with tears which she promptly wiped away. "It's all water under the bridge, Mhairi. We must live in the present. We cannot live in the past or it'll swallow us whole."

"I'm not very good at living in the present." I said, taking another drink. "Especially when Allaban is such a large part of my past."

"All the more reason to make new memories here, Mhairi." Emily smiled. "It took a lot of courage for you to come back here. I admire you for that."

I snorted. "I don't feel very brave at the moment."

***

I emerged from Emily's house into the cold night air. I looked up at the sky as I made my journey back to the cottage. I had forgotten how dark Allaban could be at night. The absolute darkness revealed a sky full of glistening stars. It reminded me of Grandma's favourite saying: "Even darkness has a way of letting the light in."

Lost in my thoughts, my phone vibrated in my pocket. I looked at the screen. It was Mum. I was meant to check in once we had arrived and that was already a few days ago.

"Hello, Mum." I said, trying not to sound too tipsy.

"She lives!" she exclaimed. "You might have phoned me, Mhairi. Just as well Steven sent me a text when you arrived."

Mum never made any attempt to hide that Steven was her favourite. "Sorry Mum it just completely slipped my mind."

"Well? How is it?"

"Yeah Mum, everything is fine."

"I need more than just fine, Mhairi Anne Sinclair. I need details!"

"There isn't really much to tell, Mum. I don't start the new job until Monday."

"Have you met any of your neighbours?"

"I have, actually. Emily owns the cottage and just lives down the road from us. I was just round at hers, actually... and Rab Campbell stopped by the cottage a couple of days ago too."

"That seems like plenty of news to me. How is Rab? Still a waste of space?"

I clenched my fist automatically. "He's quite different actually. He's grown up a lot."

"A leopard cannot change its spots, Mhairi. Once a troublemaker, always a troublemaker."

"He's actually the Depute Head Teacher of the High School. He has changed."

"Depute Head Teacher? Of the High School? Wow. Not a career path I thought he'd take. I thought Mary would have just let him work on the farm."

"Times change and people change, Mum. A lot can happen in fourteen years."

"Well. My opinion remains unchanged. I never liked that boy."

"He didn't like you much either." I muttered.

"What was that darling? The quality of this line is atrocious, Well just be careful, Mhairi. Have your wits about you."

"I'm sure I can manage the likes of Rab Campbell, Mum." I paused, remembering what I had seen earlier than day. "Mum, did you know of anyone putting a bench at Feic beach for Grandma?"

"Not to my knowledge, dear. A few people sent flowers but that was all as far as I remember. Why?"

"I took a walk there today and there was a bench with a plaque with Grandma's name on it."

"Feic beach?" She paused. "She would have liked that very much."

"Yes, I think so too."

Mum cleared her throat. "Right. Well, I best be off. This washing won't hang up itself. Take care, Mhairi. Remember to phone me."

"Yes, Mum. Love you, Mum." I said robotically and hung up the phone. Any time we got close to a meaningful conversation she was very quick to end it. How odd that she knew nothing about the old wooden bench. It was so generous and thoughtful… for the person who did it not to tell Mum was bizarre to say the least.

As I passed the front window of the cottage, I could see Steven pacing in the living room. I entered the cottage and put my blue jacket on the hook beside the door, all while

Steven watched me eagerly. I proceeded to make a cup of tea without acknowledging his presence.

"How are you?" he asked, delicately.

"Fine."

"Where did you go?"

"Emily's."

"And how was she?"

"Fine."

There was a pause. "Can we talk Mhairi? Please?"

I sighed and turned to face Steven, leaning against the kitchen worktop.

"I'm sorry about what I did last night Mhairi. It was really stupid."

"Okay."

"I shouldn't have left you on your own at the party. I know you were nervous about it. Rab was just so persuasive. I didn't think it would have upset you so much."

"Yes. Well. It was clear not much thinking was involved."

"Aww c'mon Mhairi. I was drunk."

"That was your own mistake, not mine."

"I never said it was."

I sighed. "While you spent quality time with the boys, I got interrogated."

"What? Who? What happened?"

"One of the women that works at the High School shouted at me. That was why I left the house."

Steven blinked in surprise. "I had no idea."

"Well. You were otherwise pre-occupied, weren't you?"

"I just wanted to make a good first impression, Mhairi."

"So drinking yourself stupid is a good first impression?"

"I didn't mean to get that drunk. It was Rab who suggested the drinking game."

"And if Rab suggested you take turns diving in front of oncoming vehicles would you do that too?"

"No! I…" Steven sighed, clearly exasperated. "I couldn't back out, Mhairi. I would have looked like a wimp. Something good came from it, though. George Harris wants me to do some work in their house."

I let out a dry laugh. "Oh good for you."

"Stop being so dismissive, Mhairi. I have to work too."

"You can work without having a drinking game with a group of overgrown boys."

"I'm sorry, Mhairi. How many times do I need to say it before you listen?"

"You were supposed to have my back in there. You completely abandoned me. Do you know how that made me feel? How it made me look?"

Steven shrugged. "I just thought you could manage on your own."

"And what about what you said in the car?"

Steven suddenly looked puzzled. "What do you mean? What did I say in the car?"

I stared at Steven. "You really don't remember what you said?"

"I only remember you dragging me to the car and then waking up on the couch. What happened? What did I say?"

I paused. "Never mind, Steven. You were clearly drunk. It doesn't matter."

Steven stared at me long and hard, trying to translate my gaze. He was eventually satisfied.

"Well. For what it's worth, and for the hundredth time today, I'm sorry." He collapsed on the sofa, clearly exhausted by our conversation. "So what happened with this woman then?"

I gave him a brief summary of what happened with Donna.

"Now that's just not right. It was years ago! You were just a kid!"

"I know that Steven but I suspect she's not the only person in the village to see it that way."

"Well they are all wrong then. You're allowed to live your own life. It's none of their bloody business."

I laughed. "I think a lot of these people believe that whatever happens in this village is their business."

Steven came over to the kitchen countertop and took both of his hands in mine. I looked down, unable to meet his eye.

"All I know is that my fiancée is the most talented and hardworking woman I know and she is going to be the best Head Teacher Allaban has ever seen." He brushed my hair behind my ear. "Ignore them. Ignore them all, Mhairi."

Chapter Five

As I awoke from a fitful sleep, I realised today would be my first day as Head Teacher of Allaban High School. My stomach churned. I had been awake for most of the night tossing and turning. I just couldn't help but speculate what the day would bring. I went through every possible scenario in my head, none of them filling me with much hope. The fear of the unknown overwhelmed me and robbed me of sleep. The responsibility weighed heavily on my tired mind. I was lucky that Steven was a heavy sleeper.

I made my way downstairs to the kitchen. Steven was already there preparing breakfast. I sat down at the kitchen table and he placed a steaming mug of black coffee in front of me.

I accepted it gratefully, wrapping my fingers around the mug. "You're up early this morning." I whispered.

"Need to make a good first impression. Heading to George and Emily's house today to take a look at their living room."

"That's brilliant, Steven. I'm sure they won't be disappointed."

Steven beamed. "I always like starting a new project. It's really exciting."

I nodded, still not fully awake.

"Did you sleep ok, Mhairi? You seem a little quiet."

"Not really." I smiled weakly.

Steven looked at me with concern. "You will be brilliant. The staff will love you, the kids will love you…"

"I don't think I'll be doing my job right if everyone loves me."

"Well… I love you. Will that do?"

I smiled, rolling my eyes light-heartedly. "I suppose that will have to do."

Steven kissed me on the forehead as he headed for the door. "Have a great day. I look forward to hearing all about it." With that, he shoved a piece of toast in his mouth and left.

I hastily finished my cup of coffee, hoping it would flush out my nervous energy. I grabbed my work satchel and headed for the door. Although it wouldn't be far for me to walk to the school, it was a particularly blustery day and I did not want to show up for my first day of work looking dishevelled. I could not give anyone an excuse to pick me apart. I need to look perfect and be perfect. My task today was simply to observe. I knew the school was in dire straits after their recent Inspection so it was my job to find out why. Going in too heavy-handed at the beginning would be a mistake. I would not gain any allies and I needed all the help I could get. All I wanted was to make a difference but a lot of the faculty would see me as an outsider hell-bent on changing everything the school had worked so hard to nurture. My mission for today was clear: tread lightly. I just hoped that a handful of the staff did not share the same opinion of me as Donna. Being an incomer came with all sorts of negative connotations in Allaban. I could only imagine the lies that people had concocted about me. Grandma had always said that actions spoke louder than words. With that, and a little patience, I hoped I could create a different impression. Donna might even grow to like me. The thought of it.

After a brief but beautiful commute, I drove over the cattle grid which lead into the school's car park. The red sandstone building loomed over me. My car was the first one in the car park and there was no sign of children or teaching staff anywhere. This at least would give me a little time to get my bearings before having to deal with the busyness of school life.

I went to open the front door but it was locked. I cursed under my breath. I hadn't even considered how I would get into the school building. Great start.

"Need a hand?" said a voice from behind me. I jumped, caught off-guard. "Sorry, I always lock the front door when I'm checking the grounds. Let me get that." I turned to see an older gentleman standing behind me. He smiled, fixing his glasses. His once brown hair was peppered with grey. He was dressed in a checked shirt, black trousers and black shoes, which shone from their recent polish.

He extended a hand towards me. "Bill Rodgers. Groundskeeper."

"Mhairi Sinclair. Lovely to meet you, Bill."

"Ah so you are the new Head Teacher! You're not what I was expecting."

I gave him a puzzled look. "I hope that's a good thing."

Bill laughed, heartily. He pulled a large set of keys from his pocket and began methodically making his way through them. Finally, he came across the key he was looking for and swept past me to open the door. He stood against it and folded his arms.

"Ladies first."

I breezed past him into the entrance hall. The interior of the building looked just as old as the exterior. The walls were jaded, not helped by the tired grey colour scheme. The entrance to the school felt cold.

"How long have you been here, Bill?" I asked.

"Six years past in July. Moved up here with the wife. I'm originally from Sheffield but it's far too busy there for an old fella like me. Used to be a lorry driver down there. Always driving but never getting anywhere." He laughed at his own joke. "Much nicer up here."

I nodded in agreement. "It certainly is."

"Not easy being a new face, though. I understand."

There was a pause.

I cleared my throat. "Do you maintain the grounds and the school, Bill?"

"I do indeed. I can turn my hand to most things that need doing. Keeps me out of trouble." He winked. "I best be off. Wouldn't want to get behind. Your office is just behind the front desk. Nice to meet you, Miss Sinclair." He smiled and walked along the corridor, his keys jangling rhythmically as he went.

Following Bill's directions, I found my new office. It was a cramped room filled to the brim with boxes and piles of paper. There were two desks, one at either side of the room. One desk was strewn with scrap bits of paper and coffee cups. There was a bookshelf in the corner stuffed full of old books and ring-binders covered in an attractive layer of dust. It was already clear that a lot of work was to be done.

A set of heavy footsteps thundered into the building, getting louder until they stopped at the office. "You're here early!" said Rab, erupting into the room. "Getting to know the lay of the land?"

"Trying to navigate through all of these stacks of papers, more like." I said, raising an eyebrow.

"Organised chaos, V. That's the key." Rab touched his temple with one finger, giving a look of assured charm. He winked, sat at his desk and put his feet up on a nearby stack of papers. "I'm assuming Bill let you in?"

I nodded. "Seems like a nice guy."

"One of the best, V. Nothing is too much trouble for that man. Oh, I almost forgot." Rab scrambled to his feet, diving a hand into his pockets. "It's in here somewhere... ah!" He produced a brown envelope, dog eared and crumpled. "In here is a set of keys for the building and the alarm codes. Just in case you want to do some overtime."

"Thank you." I said, putting the envelope safely into my satchel. I looked once again at the discarded coffee cups on Rab's desk. I let out a huge sigh. It seemed I had underestimated the amount of work that was needing done. If this was the level of organisation in the school it was no wonder they were struggling.

I decided to hold a Morning Assembly to formally introduce myself to the staff and pupils. This would put any rumours circulating the school to bed. I asked all staff to bring their classes to the hall for 9am sharp.

"Rab, any chance you could say a few words at the beginning of the Assembly? You are a familiar face to the staff and pupils so it may ease the tension a little."

Rab turned from his computer screen and put down his fresh cup of coffee. "No problem, *boss*. Anything in particular you'd like me to say?"

"Whatever you'd like. Just nothing informal, ok?"

"So I can't mention the time we stole all of your Grandma's underwear from the washing line then?"

I shot Rab a look.

He raised his arms defensively. "Ok, ok, noted. No silly stuff. Fine."

It was well past 9am by the time the pupils ambled in, some showcasing dishevelled uniforms while others just wearing jeans and t-shirts. The staff looked equally casual aside from Sophie Turner, the Music teacher I met at the

Croft, who was dressed in a suit and heels. While the pupils were being herded like an unwilling flock of sheep, Rab and I sat in squat plastic chairs on a raised platform at the front of the hall.

Rab leaned into me. "Nervous?" he whispered.

"Just a little."

"That's not the V I remember. She wasn't afraid of anything... or anyone."

"The stakes are a little higher this time, Rab."

"It's not about the stakes- it's how we perceive them. This is your first challenge. You'll be fine, V. Just imagine the staff are in their underwear."

I snorted.

Rab short me a final beaming smile before standing and making his way to the front of the stage. "Good morning, everyone." he began, trying and failing to grasp the attention of the restless crowd. "I'd appreciate it if we could take our seats quickly, folks. We've not got all day here." Finally the last of the pupils took their seats. The assembly hadn't even begun and it was already clear that the majority of the pupils were disinterested and inattentive.

"Thank you." Said Rab, before clearing his throat. "Good morning, everyone. It's fantastic to see you all this morning. I hope you all managed to relax over the summer holidays and you are now back and ready to learn." Rab paused, waiting for any reaction from the pupils. Sophie Turner began clapping very loudly. Much of the audience turned to stare at her which she didn't seem to notice. The rest of the faculty and pupils reluctantly joined in. Rab smiled painfully. "This assembly is a particularly important one for a few reasons. Firstly, it is the first one of our new term. Secondly, it is the first High School assembly that our new first years have experienced. Finally, and most importantly, I have the great pleasure of introducing Allaban's new Head Teacher."

I shifted nervously in my chair, clutching the sides with my hands until I could no longer feel them.

"Our New Head Teacher is no stranger to the village. She is a kind-hearted woman that wants nothing more than to see you all succeed. I know that you will all make her feel very welcome. Please give a warm Allaban High School welcome to Miss Sinclair."

Scattered applause rippled through the sea of faces. I stood from my chair, shook hands with Rab and took my place at the front of the platform. "Thank you, Mr Campbell, for your kind words. It is a pleasure to be standing here as Head Teacher of Allaban High School." A handful of girls in the front row looked unimpressed and began whispering to each other. I carried on and attempted to ignore them. "As Mr Campbell said, it is indeed the beginning of a new term. This means a fresh start for you and also for me. I look forward to getting to know you over the coming weeks and months. I have heard very good things about Allaban High School and I know I will not be disappointed. Mr Campbell also mentioned something very important- our school community. Everything we do in this school can either add or take away from this community. Wearing the correct uniform adds to our sense of community. Being supportive of our peers adds to our sense of community. Trying our hardest in class adds to our sense of community. Supporting our new first year pupils adds to our sense of community. Over the next few weeks, building a sense of community will be our goal. By respecting our school community, we can aspire to greater things in the future. As Head Teacher, I am here to support you as staff members and pupils. That is my job. I will do whatever I can to support you in achieving your potential. I will be observing classes, speaking to members of our faculty and also to you all about what you feel our community is. Also, I intend to speak to those who are not working to their fullest potential to find out why."

My opening address seemed to be going well. The pupils seemed to be listening instead of passively watching. Member of staff were also paying attention and seemed somewhat impressed. I allowed myself to feel optimistic. Perhaps I could make a difference in this school after all. Just as my nerves began to fade, my eye was drawn to a girl in the back row of the hall. Her face had gone an acute shade of green- a stark contrast to her flowing blonde hair. She hastily rose to her feet and ran out of the hall, as an array of heads whirled round in curiousity. I stopped mid-sentence and gave a worried glance at Rab, who proceeded to leap from his chair and run after her. As all of this went on, the pupils and staff turned to one another, bubbling with gossip. I raised my hand.

"That…That will be quite enough, thank you." I stuttered. The hall once again fell silent but with an undercurrent of curiousity. I had lost the attention of the pupils and staff but persevered. "As I was saying, I will spend time getting to know you all which I look forward to. I hope the rest of your day is productive and enjoyable."

With this, the entire school stood up at once and began making their way out of the hall. The teachers did little to stop this, aside from Sophie Turner who tried and failed to get pupils to sit back down again. I decided to ignore this and instead focus my mind on the girl who had bolted. Seeing her flee from the back of the hall had once again rattled my nerves. I promptly made my way back to the office. Rab was already there, his feet on top of his favourite pile of papers and sipping his coffee.

"Rab!" I hissed, careful not to speak too loudly as to catch the ear of anyone passing. "What on earth are you doing? Where is that girl?"

"Relax, V. She's fine."

I was livid but trying my best not to explode. "Where is she?"

"Still in the toilet, I think. I didn't feel it was appropriate to go in after her." he said, his voice laced with sarcasm.

"If that is ever the case, Rab, you get me. End of."

"You were otherwise occupied with the Assembly, V. Relax."

"I will not relax. That was a disaster!"

Rab blinked, surprised by my response.

I stormed out of the office, passing Donna on my way to the toilets. I approached the swing door and tentatively knocked. I could hear muffled crying from inside the toilet.

"Hello? Are you ok in there? You're not in trouble. I'm just worried about you, that's all."

Once again, there was no response except laboured sobbing. I leaned against the wall for a while, hoping the girl would immerge. After what felt like an eternity, I gave up. I returned to the office, unsure of my next move.

"Who was that girl, Rab?"

Rab turned to face me, his ego still sore from his scolding a few minutes earlier. "Beth Anderson. Parents own The Cape."

"What is The Cape?"

"Restaurant in the village."

I sighed. "You can't just go in a huff, Rab. This is serious."

"I'm not in a huff, Mhairi. I just didn't appreciate your tone."

"Well I didn't appreciate your handling of the situation." I stared at him but softened my gaze. "I need to you tell me about this girl, Rab. I need to know if there's anything I should be worried about."

Rab turned to face his computer screen. "She's not a troublemaker, if that's what you mean. She gets good grades, she has a nice family, she's fine. The incident at assembly was just a one off thing. Nothing to worry about."

I sighed. "Ok." Despite Rab's relaxed response, my gut told me to keep an eye on this girl. Something was just not sitting right.

Aside from the blip at Morning Assembly, the rest of the day ran pretty much smoothly. Rab remained in a sour mood and spent the majority of his day staring at his computer and ignoring me. At lunchtime, I stayed in the office and let the rest of the faculty congregate in the staff room to gossip about the morning's events. I relished the fifty minutes I had without Rab hanging over me like a storm cloud.

After a lot of thought, I decided it would be a good idea to call a staff meeting after school. The short notice would ruffle a few feathers but it was more important to formally introduce myself to the faculty. I picked up my phone and dialled the internal number for the school office. After an eternity, Donna picked up the phone.

"I'm on my lunch." she said bitterly.

I tried to make my voice as light as possible despite being irritated. "Sorry to bother you, Donna. Could you send an email to all staff asking them to attending a meeting after school?"

Donna scoffed. "A bit short notice, don't you think?"

"If all staff could meet in the staff room at 4pm that'd be great. The meeting should be no longer than thirty minutes. Thank you Donna." I hung up the phone. I probably shouldn't have been so hasty to end the call but Donna's attitude irritated me. Why did she think it was appropriate to comment on my decisions? What business was it of hers?

Ten minutes after the lunch break had finished, Rab swanned into the office carrying a half-eaten sandwich.

"Staff meeting today at 4pm, Rab." I said. "You should get an email from Donna about it shortly."

"The first day back?" he said, his mouth full. "I don't think the staff will be very pleased about that."

"Frankly, I think some members of staff will be unhappy no matter what I do, Rab. At least this way they can complain about it to my face."

Rab did not reply. He merely shrugged and returned to his computer.

***

At 3.50pm, I made my way to the staff room. A few of the faculty were already gathered and chatting furiously. When I entered, a hush fell over the room. I made my way to the table and began organising my papers, trying to ignore the many eyes trained on me. A familiar face approached me, a warm smile on her face.

"Mhairi, good to see you. I hope your first day hasn't been too wild!" Iris chuckled, her blue eyes sparkling. The rest of the staff stared at her but she remained unphased.

I laughed nervously. "Thank you, Iris. That is kind of you."

"Not at all. I thought your speech at Morning Assembly was great. Very well received."

"I don't think a lot of the children were listening after that girl ran out."

"These things happen, Mhairi. Nothing we can control. Beth Anderson is a lovely girl- she won't have done it with any malicious intent."

"Yes. I suppose you're right."

"Try to forget about it. Onwards and upwards."

The rest of the staff eventually ambled into the room. There were thirteen in total to cover the entirety of the curriculum for the forty five students who attended the high school. It was clear, unsurprisingly, they were not happy to be called to a meeting on the first day back. The only person who seemed cheerful was Sophie, clutching a notepad, pen and an eager grin. I busied myself with my notes, waiting for Rab to appear.

At 4.10pm, Rab stumbled into the room. "Sorry folks, got a little held up."

I gave him a curt nod, attempting to hide my irritation. Once Rab took his seat, I vacated mine and waited for silence to satiate the air. "Thank you all for being here on such short notice. It was important to me to formally introduce myself and get to know all of you as we will be working very closely together in the next academic session. There are a few things

I'd like to address this term with regards to curriculum, conduct and uniform. It's something I'd like to hear your opinions on."

A deafening quietness filled the room.

An older gentleman let out a snort, drawing my attention and that of the other staff. He was a gruff man, sporting a straggly grey beard and overalls. I assumed by his attire that this was the Technical teacher, Oliver Stevenson. He sat with his arms folded, a scowl painted on his face. "We are a village school." He said gruffly. "We are not like any of your fancy city schools. We do things a little differently around here..."

"I appreciate that, Mr Stevenson," I interjected, before he could get further into his speech. "and I am not pretending to know everything about Allaban High School. It's important to have an action plan going forward and a shared vision no matter the school."

Oliver made no attempt to hide his chortle. "The majority of our kids want to be crofters and tradesmen. They don't care about your fancy curricular strategy."

Iris interrupted. "I think what Mhairi is trying to say, Oliver, is that we need to keep our kids engaged and challenged. Regardless of the end result we want to support them. Is that right, Mhairi?"

I nodded, taken aback.

Iris' warm face adopted a sharpness. "Kindly keep your out of date opinions to yourself, Olly. We all know that you don't care about school improvement but at least have the decency to sit down and shut up when someone else is talking."

Oliver snorted but did not say another word.

Iris turned to me. "Sorry, Mhairi. Please continue."

"It would be great if we could form working groups and discuss these areas for improvement."

I talked through my ideas. Iris and Sophie were fully engaged, taking in my every word. Another handful of staff seemed mildly interested. The rest of the staff, Oliver and Rab included, shifted in their seats, clearly keen for the meeting to be over.

As soon as the meeting was over, the majority of staff bustled out of the room. This was the most energetic I had seen many of them all day.

Iris hung back until the majority of staff had left. "Good job, love." She said, squeezing my arm encouragingly. "A lot of the staff here don't like change. Have faith- they'll come around eventually." With that, she was gone. Only Rab remained by my side, picking his fingernails.

"Rab?"

Rab looked up from his nails.

"We can't go on like this, Rab."

"Go on like what? I don't know what you mean."

"You know fine well what I mean."

Rab returned his attention to his nails.

"I'm not going to censor my opinions as not to hurt your feelings, Rab. We are running a school not a Christmas party."

"No need to be rude on any occasion."

"I've always been direct, Rab. Flowery language isn't my style. It isn't me."

"Well it would be nice to be treated like a professional rather than a small boy to boss around."

I shrugged. "Old habits die hard I guess." My attempt at a joke fell like a lead balloon. "I need your help, Rab. The staff really look up to you. They follow your example. Without you, there is no hope of us making a difference."

Rab sighed. Although he looked irritated his hard exterior was visibly melting.

"I need you. You know the kids, the staff, the way everything works… We won't always have the same opinion, but we need to show a face of unity to the staff. That's the only way this is going to work."

Rab looked at me, one eyebrow raised. "So you're saying we are like the Queen and Prince Phillip?" he quipped.

"Not quite the analogy I had in mind but… yes. I guess so."

Rab smirked. "I suppose I can live with being Prince Phillip."

"I'm not asking you to blindly follow where I lead, Rab. I want you to question my decisions. We are a Management *Team* after all."

"Don't worry, V. I will always make my opinions known."

"I wouldn't have it any other way."

Chapter Six

After spending hours attempting to clear the jungle of papers, folders and books from the office, I gave up and headed home. Only Bill remained to bid me farewell. I escaped into the evening air and the sun was barely visible above the sleeping skyline.

It was an odd feeling. I had just completed my first day as Head Teacher of Allaban High School and yet it felt like I'd never left the village. I had come to a cross road in my life- my past and present were intersecting and slowly revealing the future. I had an odd sensation in my stomach which I couldn't quite put my finger on. I then realised that I hadn't had anything to eat all day so it was probably hunger. It seemed that old habits really did die hard.

I arrived back at the cottage just as the sun set, plunging the whole village into immediate darkness. The day was extinguished and only the lights from the houses illuminated the road as I drove home. There were no lights on in the cottage when I pulled up outside so I assumed Steven was still working at George and Emily's. I meandered over to their house, exhausted from the day's events.

Emily saw me from the kitchen window and waved. "That's Mhairi!" I heard her shout as I made my way up the path. She met me at the door.

"Steven's still working away in the living room, Mhairi. Can I get you something? Tea? Coffee?"

"Gin?" I asked wearily.

Emily laughed and nodded.

I sat in the kitchen absentmindedly spinning on one of the bar stools. Emily appeared clutching glasses and a bottle of gin.

"Rough day?" she said, placing a glass in-front of me.

I sipped it gratefully, the liquid slipping easily down my throat. "You could say that."

"No wonder. Starting any new job is tiring, never mind being in charge of a school."

"It's going to take a little bit of getting used to. Allaban High School is very different to other schools I've worked in."

"This village certainly has its own way of doing things."

"You can say that again."

Steven entered the kitchen, dressed in his tatty overalls. "Hi honey." He whispered as he kissed me on the forehead. "How was your day?"

"Yeah it was fine." I said, being deliberately vague. "How are you getting on?"

"Good. Done a few odd jobs in the living room but George wants me to take a look at other parts of the house. Looks like I'll be working here for a while!"

Emily smiled. "It's a pleasure to have you, Steven. I've not seen George this animated in a long time. I'll get you some tea."

Steven leaned against the counter while Emily prepared his brew. "You're late tonight Mhairi. Thought you would have been back at the cottage hours ago."

I smiled weakly. "I just lost track of time trying to wrap my head around things."

"Well don't work too hard, Mhairi."

"I'll be fine, I'm used to the long hours."

Emily turned to Steven, a steaming mug of tea in hand. "There you are. Be careful, it's hot."

Steven gratefully accepted the mug, gave me a sympathetic smile and headed towards the living room.

Emily picked up her glass and sat on a stool. "So what's up?" she said, looking concerned.

"Oh nothing."

"Something is bothering you, Mhairi. I can see it in your eyes."

"It's nothing, really. Just a niggle."

"Are you sure?"

I sighed. "Yes. It's nothing in particular, Emily. Just going to take some time for me to get used to the school and the school to get used to me."

"Just make sure you don't burn yourself out, Mhairi."

"I've always burned the candle at both ends. I'm used to it."

"Just make sure you have a bit of candle left at the end of it."

"I'll be fine. The kids always come first, Emily." Beth Anderson's face suddenly popped into my head. "Is there anywhere nice to eat around here, Emily? I was thinking of treating Steven to something other than beans on toast at the weekend."

"There's a couple of places. You can get dinner at the Allaban Hotel most nights but I wouldn't recommend going there unless you're desperate. A lot of the locals go there and things can get quite boisterous. The Cape is probably your best bet. It's at the other end of the village. Used to be a hotel back in the day."

"Was that the old Red Lion Hotel?" I asked, taking another sip of my gin.

"The very one. The Macdonald's owned it back in your day. They neglected it really- it ran into such disarray in the later days. They eventually left the village and put it up for sale. The Anderson family bought it a few years ago. It's fair bonnie inside now. It's open for dinner Thursday through Sunday, I believe."

"That sounds perfect. Would I know the Andersons?" I asked, trying to sound casual.

"Their girl goes to the High School. She must be in sixth year now. Her name is Beth. Very pretty girl but quiet. I've seen her running around with Nathan Black. I believe they're an item."

"Nathan Black? As in Iris Black the English teacher?"

"The same. His Mum and Dad died when he was very young- such a shame. Not sure what happened to them and I don't like to ask. Nice wee boy, though. Iris took him in many moons ago and raised him as her own."

"I hadn't realised that Iris's grandson attended the High School. I'll need to keep an eye out for them."

"You'll probably see Beth at The Cape. She works there at the weekends. That's the only thing about living in such a wee village- you can't go anywhere without meeting folk!"

Emily and I chatted until Steven was finished his work for the day. Going to The Cape at the weekend would be a good excuse to find out a little more about Beth Anderson and treat Steven at the same time. I hoped this would quench my curiousity once and for all.

***

"We really cannot get into the habit of working this late!" said Steven, collapsing on the couch as we arrived back at the cottage.

"We're a pair of workaholics, Steven. The perfect match."

"How was your day then? I didn't want to ask too much with Emily there."

"It was fine, really." I said, trying to reassure him. "A little rocky at times but that is to be expected."

"You'll win them round. You always do."

I smiled weakly. I wasn't sure if I'd ever manage to win the staff round. However, my chat with Rab had been progress. At least I knew he would back me up in future. Hopefully this would encourage other members of staff to do the same.

"What's for dinner? I'm starving!"

"I have some microwave meals… would you prefer Spaghetti Bolognese or Lasagne?"

"Ooooh very Italian." Said Steven in his best Italian accent. "I don't mind. Whatever is ready first."

I threw them both into the microwave. "Emily said there's a nice restaurant in the village. Fancy going there this weekend?"

"Are you taking me on a date, Mhairi Sinclair?"

"If it means not having to cook then yes."

Steven let out a long whistle. "I'm expecting no expenses to be spared, Mhairi. You will need to woo me."

I laughed. "I'll pay. How does that sound?"

***

The next few days at school passed in a similarly busy fashion. Although I'd only been there a week it felt like I'd been there forever- in with the bricks. Rab was much more supportive which helped me find my feet. I observed classes to get to know the pupils a little better. Donna was as unpleasant as ever, which made our daily dealings a highlight. I settled into somewhat of a routine but I vowed that I would eventually stop working 12 hour days…

eventually. I found myself falling into my usual routine-working long hours, forgetting to eat and inhaling coffee like it was going out of fashion. Not the healthiest of routines but it allowed me to focus on the priority- the kids.

One day after school, I was riffling through old paperwork when there was a tentative knock at my door. It was well after 5 o'clock so I was surprised anyone but myself and Bill were in the school. Usually the staff made their bid for freedom as soon as the bell rang at the end of the day.

"Come in." I said.

Sophie Turner hovered in the doorway, looking a little sheepish.

"Sophie, lovely to see you. Please, take a seat." I offered her Rab's abandoned chair.

"I'm sorry to bother you, Miss Sinclair." She began. It was clear from her inflections that this speech had been thoroughly rehearsed.

"Call me Mhairi. No need to be formal when there are no pupils present."

"Right. Yes. Mhairi." She paused for a moment. "I'm sorry to bother you Mhairi, it's just… there was an incident in one of my classes today. I deliberated whether to tell you about it because it seemed so trivial but it's been weighing on my mind all day."

"Of course, Sophie." I said delicately.

"Right… well… you know Beth Anderson?"

I nodded, immediately intrigued but trying not to let it show on my face..

"She is in my Higher Music class. I've noticed this week that Beth has been very disengaged. I had her for Music last year and she was always very hardworking and focused. Her attitude has completely changed. I know the term has only just started but I feel like she's not as attentive as she was this time last year. She is a lovely young girl but her mind always seems to be elsewhere. She doesn't answer out in class anymore. She always goes to the toilet during class even though it's only a fifty minute period."

I nodded thoughtfully. "Thank you for letting me know, Sophie. It's always better to share these concerns. You know her far better than I do."

"Thank you, Mhairi. After what happened at Assembly I thought it was important I tell you. She is a bright student. I just hope everything is ok."

"Of course, Sophie. You did the right thing."

"Thank you Mhairi. I just… I wasn't expecting you to be so nice to me. Everyone says you're a bit of a dragon." Sophie, realising what she had just said, clamped her hands over her mouth. "I'm so sorry. That was rude. I should never…"

"Sophie." I interrupted. "It's fine."

Sophie looked uncomfortable, still with her hands clamped over her mouth.

"Thank you again for coming to see me."

Sophie stood up quickly, almost knocking her chair over in the process. "Thank you again, Miss… Mhairi." She said, her hands still plastered to her face as she fled from the room.

I hoped my visit to The Cape with Steven would shed some light on the mystery that was Beth Anderson.

***

When we arrived at The Cape on Saturday Night it was clear it was the hub of the village. It was bustling with couples and families packed in like sardines. The Cape was once an old schoolhouse for the children of the village before it became the Red Lion pub. Demand became too great so they moved the school to its current location, leaving the old building derelict. The building had been the Red Lion pub when I was growing up, a hotspot for the locals most nights of the week. Upon careful inspection, The Andersons had restored a lot of the original architecture from the days of the school including an old chalk board which now displayed the evening's specials. The restaurant was a beautiful blend of old and new.

A jolly woman swept towards us donning a well-used apron.

"Good evening." She said with a genuine smile. "Welcome to The Cape. I'm Steph Anderson. My husband and I own the restaurant." She extended her hand first towards me and then to Steven.

"Mhairi Sinclair. This is my fiancé Steven."

"Oh Miss Sinclair!" exclaimed Steph. "Lovely to finally put a face to a name. I've heard a lot about you."

I smiled nervously. "Good things I hope. How is Beth doing?"

"She's fine. Settling into sixth year. I can't believe it!"

"Time flies! Is she working tonight?"

"She should be but she has an upset stomach. Poor thing."

"That's a shame. I hope she feels better soon."

"Thanks. I'll be sure to let her know you were asking after her. Let me just show you to your table." Steph ushered us to one of the tables by the window boasting a beautiful view of the loch. "When you're ready to order just give me a wee wave."

Steven smiled. "Thank you."

Steph slipped away as quickly as she had appeared.

Steven gazed at the ceiling. "They've certainly made a nice job of the place."

While we were busy contemplating what to eat, Iris and Nathan Black entered the restaurant. Iris locked eyes with me and gave me a cheery wave. Nathan followed his grandma's gaze and quickly adverted his eyes to the specials board. He was a tall, thin boy clearly in the middle of a growth spurt. He wore black rimmed glasses and a sheepish grin. His black hair was a mane on top of his head and it seemed as though he was trying to hide beneath it.

Steven leaned over his menu. "I do not miss being that age one bit." he whispered, eyeing Nathan Black.

"You were popular in school, Steven. I don't think your experience can be compared to Nathan Black's."

"Being a teenage boy was awkward, Mhairi. Even for charming and attractive men like me."

I rolled my eyes.

Steph approached Iris and Nathan, ready to show them to a table. Nathan said something inaudible and she indicated to the kitchen. He quickly disappeared through the swinging doors.

Steven and I had both ordered venison burgers for our main meals, mine with a side of salad and his with chunky chips. They were beautifully cooked, sizzling as they arrived at our table. My microwave meals could never compete. It was so nice to finally spend some alone time with Steven. It had felt like we were passing ships in the night these days-both working long and anti-social hours. Any alone time we spent together was fleeting and we were usually exhausted. It was about time we had a date night together.

Just as we began our main meal, Rab and Tom entered the restaurant. Rab clocked me immediately and made a beeline for our table, Tom at his tail.

"Evening Steven. Boss." He said with a wink. "Sorry for interrupting your romantic meal for two."

"You both in for dinner, Rab?" I asked.

"Nah. Just collecting a takeaway. Don't worry, I'll be out of your hair soon enough."

"Just as well. I don't get paid overtime."

Rab smirked and then turned to Steven. "Recovered from the party last week Steven?"

Steven grimaced. "Barely."

"It's all about stamina, my man. Got to drink a little every day to keep it topped up. I will teach you my ways, young grasshopper."

Steven clocked Tom standing sheepishly behind Rab. "Have we met?"

Tom looked startled. With Rab around, he was used to just melting into the background.

I interjected. "This is Tom, Steven. Tom helped us when our car broke down."

Steven's face darkened.

I forced a smile, trying to ignore Steven. "How are you Tom? Croft keeping well?"

Tom nodded. "Everything's ticking over."

Rab elbowed Tom in the ribs. "Too modest as always, Tom. He runs the farm single-handedly. He's started converting that old barn in his spare time. The man is a machine. Don't know where he gets the energy."

Tom blushed, looking askance.

"Well we'd love to see it when it's all finished." I said.

Rab put a hand on my shoulder. "Nonsense! You should come over for dinner and Tom here can give you the grand tour of the work in progress. I'm sure Mam would be pleased to see you, V."

I smiled. "That'd be lovely."

"Rab, here's your order love." Steph emerged with four large takeaway containers and passed them to Rab. The Campbell brothers made their exit, Rab waving as they left. I returned my attention to Steven but he was no longer making eye contact. Steven returned to his meal, suddenly very interested in the remains of his venison burger. The rest of the evening's meal was consumed in stony silence.

***

After a frosty drive home, Steven stormed into the cottage. I followed, my own anger bubbling.

"What is your problem?" I shouted.

"We cannot get a moment's peace anywhere, Mhairi."

I sighed, exasperated. "That's what living in a small village is like, Steven. Everyone will know if we sneeze before breakfast."

Steven snorted. "It's those guys. They appear everywhere we go."

"What? Rab and Tom?"

"They just pop up everywhere! You never told me you knew the other one. You acted like you didn't know him when we broke down."

""The Other One" has a name, Steven. His name is Tom. I didn't recognise him on the road. I haven't seen him for fourteen years so forgive me if my memory is a little slow."

"He was certainly paying you a lot of attention."

"We had broken down!" I exclaimed. "We were sitting right in the middle of a single track road. I don't think he had much of a choice!"

Steven's face darkened. "I didn't mean on the road, Mhairi."

My face grew hot. I had noticed that Tom hadn't taken his eyes off me throughout the entire conversation. "I don't know what you're talking about, Steven. You're talking nonsense."

Steven shook his head slowly and deliberately. "No, Mhairi. You can't do that. He stood and stared at you the entire time you were speaking to Rab. Admit it."

I shrugged my shoulders. "I don't know what you want me to say, Steven. There is nothing going on. The fact you keep bringing this up makes me question if you trust me."

Steven sighed. "I do trust you, Mhairi."

"You have a funny way of showing it. You've never been the accusing type."

"I've never felt reason to be."

"… until now? What's changed?"

Steven didn't answer. Instead he sat on the couch and turned on the TV.

There was an attraction between Tom and I and I couldn't deny it. All I could do was deflect his accusations. Nothing had happened that night in the barn but it was better to keep Steven in the dark about the whole affair.

After a few moments, it was clear that Steven was going to ignore me for the rest of the evening. Sick and tired of arguing, I grabbed my faithful blue jacket. "I'm going out."

Steven offered no response, apparently engrossed in a re-run of an old TV soap. I shut the door, leaving him behind.

It was long after dark. The darkness clung to the sky, extinguishing all signs of life. I trekked towards Feic Beach, still fuming as I replayed my argument with Steven in my head. The chilling autumn breeze alerted my senses and carried my bubbling anger into the dusk. As my anger slowly subsided, it dawned on me that the village streets were unrecognisable in the gloom. I looked around but my eyes could not adjust. I suddenly realised… I was lost. A wave of panic hit me with ferocity. I had left my phone on the kitchen counter and hadn't bothered to take a flashlight. I cursed. How could I be so careless? I resolved to keep walking until I could recognise where I was, the dread sitting in my gut like a stone. I felt like a caged animal, pacing to keep my mind occupied from my argument with Steven, hoping to escape the unfamiliarity of my surroundings.

Suddenly, a pair of headlights sliced through the darkness. Startled, I dove out of the way and into a nearby bog, immersing myself in the dirty swamp water. The water was grimy and freezing cold. I gasped in shock, trying to catch my breath. I stumbled to my feet, the icy bog water up to my knees bringing an immediate chill to the rest of my body.

The truck stopped and a familiar figure approached me. "Not my first choice of bath, V." said Tom, chuckling.

I was shivering uncontrollably, unable to breathe.

Tom's jokey manner shifted when he saw how cold I was. "You must be bloody freezing. Let's get you warm." He gathered me in his arms and bundled me onto the back of his truck. After a few moments, he re-emerged with blankets. "Here." He said, offering one to me. I took it and wrapped it around my sodden body. Tom sat next to me, waiting patiently. After a while, I stopped shaking and my breathing stopped being so laboured. The warmth was beginning to return to my extremities.

Tom's eyes were full of concern. "Better?"

I nodded, embarrassed.

Tom smiled. "It's usually sheep I have to rescue from the bogs round here."

"I was on my way to Feic. I got a little lost."

"A native like you? Lost? I'm surprised."

"The village is a lot easier to navigate in the sunlight."

"Yes, well. Most humans stick to the daylight hours when they decide to go swimming." Tom smirked.

I averted my gaze. "I get it, Tom. I'm an idiot. No need to rub it in."

"This is the most eventful drive I've had in a while. I need to milk it for all its worth."

I sighed and pulled the blanket tighter round me. I was beginning to shiver again.

"Here." Said Tom, offering me his blanket. "You were going to Feic, yeah? Do you want a lift?"

I smiled. "I'd like that."

"Not a chance of you getting into the truck, V. I just cleaned it."

Tom drove us to the beach as I lay in the back of the truck, gazing at the stars overhead. The night sky was so peaceful- uninterrupted by the chaos below. The beach sat undisturbed in the gloom as though awaiting our arrival. Tom reversed the pick-up to the top of a sandy mound, giving us a clear view of the ebbing waves. He assumed his place next to me in the back of the pick-up.

"Are you not cold?" I asked, studying his thin plaid shirt.

Tom looked at me intently. "Not as cold as you."

I shifted my focus to the waves. "This beach never fails to take my breath away."

"Aye, it is pretty spectacular, isn't it?"

I nodded. "Reminds me so much of our childhood."

"Those were the days, eh? Back before everything became so complicated."

"I was so desperate to grown up back then. I was sick and tired of being seen as young and stupid."

"After tonight's antics it's clear you're now old and stupid, V."

I punched him in the side. Tom retaliated by poking my arm. This turned into a play fight of punching and kicking. After I landed a punch in Tom's gut, he raised his arms in surrender.

"Ok, ok. You win. Some things never change."

I giggled. "I was never one to give up during a fight."

"Don't I know it! You were never one to give up on anything, V."

"The only thing I remember giving up was this place."

Tom sighed. "You didn't give it up, V. You just took a long sabbatical."

"I guess."

There was a silence.

"I am sorry, you know. For leaving." I whispered, sullenly.

"I know." Said Tom. "I'm just glad you found your way back. Even if it was through a bog."

I laughed. I had forgotten how much I laughed when I was with Tom. "I missed this. We used to spend hours just talking, remember? Rab would always fall asleep from a drunken stupor and we would spend the rest of the night just talking. It was so easy back then."

"It's still so easy now."

I took my eyes away from the waves to see him gazing at me, his eyes brimming with wonder. I suddenly felt winded but not from the cold. He took my hand in his. Despite the years that had passed I could still spend an eternity in his warm brown eyes. I struggled against my feelings, too sensitive of my sensitivity to ignore them. He edged his face closer to mine, studying my expression. I breathed him in slowly as not to paralyse myself with desire. He smelled of aftershave mixed with sand. My heart was pounding as his breath tickled my cheek. After that, instinct took over, and I was powerless to stop it. His lips met mine, kissing me deeply and passionately. I inhaled, my heart fluttering as he wrapped me in his embrace. We sat for what could have been hours or just minutes. In just a short space of time, he had managed to derail my sense quickly and passionately. Time seemed to stand still. Although I had known Tom my whole life, I felt like I was only just seeing him for the first time.

Chapter Seven

We kissed until my mind uprooted an ugly memory from the past. Tom's lips were suddenly sour and I pulled away, gasping for breath. I was thrown into the present and the realisation of what I had done hit me with full force. I was once again up to my knees but in a swamp of a different kind and of my own making.

"Shit!" I exclaimed, covering my face.

Tom was just as taken aback as I was. "Mhairi, I...I shouldn't have..."

"Damn right you shouldn't have." I shouted. "I have a *fiancé,* Tom. Another man that I've made a promise to. Another man that I'm supposed to *marry.*"

"I'm sorry Mhairi I just..." Tom began, spluttering.

I threw the blankets from my shoulders and leapt from the back of the pick-up.

Tom looked at me, pleadingly. "At least let me give you a lift back, V."

"In what universe do you think that's a good idea, Tom? What happened tonight was a mistake. It should never have happened. I think it's better if we just stay far away from each other from now on." I stormed off in the direction of the road.

"You can't keep running, Mhairi."

I stopped dead in my tracks. "What is that supposed to mean?"

"You know what I mean. You know there is something between us. It's been there for a very long time and I'm tired of not acknowledging it. We click. We always clicked. A click is rare and I've never felt it... not to this degree. I know you feel the same. You ran away from it back then and you're running away from it now."

I scoffed. "I am not running, Tom. I'm *walking* back home to my *fiancé*."

"The day you left here for the last time... you never told me why. What happened that made you stop coming back? What kept you away?"

"I changed, Tom." I bellowed. "I grew up."

"I still remember the last morning I saw you, Mhairi. We hadn't seen each other in weeks. I knew something was wrong so I went to your grandparents. Sadie met me at the end of the path, shooing me away, said I had no business being there. She said you weren't home. I could see you in your room, V. You were just sitting there, staring out of the window. You looked like a shadow."

My mouth was suddenly dry. This was not a conversation I was willing to have with anyone, especially not Tom. I had left Allaban to go to University. That was my story and I was sticking to it. I could deal with their scorn for abandoning the village. No one could ever know about what really happened. Grandma was the only one who knew my secret and she took that to the grave. That is where I intended it to stay- dead and buried. I refused to be dragged back into that quagmire. I did the only thing I knew how to do in that moment- I turned and ran.

"Mhairi, wait." Shouted Tom, but his voice was carried away by the roaring tide.

I barely recognised myself. The Mhairi of years gone by would never have done anything so callous and stupid. She would never dream of hurting Steven. *Steven.* He had done nothing but love me unconditionally and I had done this to him. My stomach churned with guilt. I ran all the way home, my sodden clothes clinging to my skin. I barely noticed- my face burned with shame. How could I do something so reckless? How could I hurt Steven? My mind was jumbled with arguments I couldn't face having with myself. Even after all the pain and the hurt, I just couldn't retire my thoughts of Tom.

By the time I reached the cottage, it was well after 1am and there was no sign of life from inside. I entered to see Steven on the couch, snoring softly. I tiptoed past him and up the stairs trying desperately not to make any noise. Steven stirred and I froze, my eyes wide. At this moment, I was so conscious of every fibre of my body- my heart thumping, my head pounding and my deep, loud breaths. He muttered something then turned over in his sleep. I exhaled. Hopefully Steven had gone to bed early and not worried too much about my disappearance. I would face a full interrogation first thing in the morning. I stripped off my wet clothes and climbed into bed, falling into a fitful sleep.

I awoke the next morning to Steven sitting at the edge of my bed.

"Good morning. How are you doing?"

I squinted, adjusting to the light streaming through the window. The evening's events hit me full force and I attempted to keep my composure. Tom's lips on mine flashed before my eyes. "Yeah, I'm fine."

"You were out late last night. I went to bed around 11pm and you still weren't back."

"I wasn't long after that." I said, maybe a little too quickly. "I just needed to clear my head."

He nodded thoughtfully. "I've been thinking a lot about what you said, Mhairi. About me trusting you."

I held my breath. My stomach dropped. My heart stopped.

"I do trust you, Mhairi. I've always trusted you. I was so stupid to question that."

I exhaled.

"I guess… I just don't want to lose you, Mhairi. The day Mum walked out, Dad was a broken man. I saw the light leave his eyes that day. I guess it's just made me sensitive to all that stuff. You're too good for me, Mhairi. I'm worried that one morning you're gonna wake up and realise that for yourself."

I shuffled forward on the bed and took Steven into my arms. "You are the best man I know." I whispered. "Don't

94

ever forget that." I clung to him a little tighter, my stomach clenched in agonising guilt.

Steven's parents had broken up when we were still in school. It was a subject he refused to talk about no matter how much I probed. The divorce had really affected him, not that he showed it. Whenever I tried to bring it up in conversation, he swiftly changed the subject or just pretended he didn't hear me. What had I done to deserve him? I had prepared myself for a confrontation, thinking the events of last night were written plainly on my face. My guilt was swallowing me whole. How could I tell him what I had done? The only thing Steven was guilty of was loving me too much. Since we moved to Allaban, Steven had always come second to my work. Honestly, Steven had always come in second to my work. He dutifully supported me through every new job and every new home. He always put my needs before his own and sought comfort in knowing that I was pursuing my dream. In spite of all of this, one question kept creeping into my mind- did I really love Steven?

To keep my mind from my guilt, I did what I always did- I immersed myself in work. My already long work days became longer. My routine became more cemented. Staff and pupils alike were becoming more used to my presence in the school. The pupils were beginning to slowly come around and a few even acknowledged me in the corridor. The staff as a whole had remained unchanged but I was lucky to have allies in Sophie, Iris and Rab. The rest of the staff would come around eventually. Oliver grunted when I passed his class and Donna was not always frosty on the phone. I had noticed a shift. It was a small shift but a shift nonetheless.

Weeks passed and I still heard nothing from Tom. Rab had mentioned him in conversation occasionally but never hinted at knowing anything. I knew I would have to tell Steven eventually but resolved to let the dust settle before having that conversation. Our relationship had been better of late and I did not want to rock the boat.

One morning I was sitting at my desk and the phone rang. It was Donna.

"Mhairi, I've just had a phone call from Steph Anderson. She said that Beth is really unwell and we shouldn't expect her in school this side of Christmas."

I was shocked. Things had seemed to improve with Beth Anderson and I'd almost forgotten about the events at the beginning of term. Sophie had said she'd been engaging more with her schoolwork. "Did Steph give any more details Donna?"

"Nope. That's pretty much word for word what she said to me."

I sighed. "Donna, can you get me Beth Anderson's home address?"

"Yes… why?"

"I'm going to visit her."

"I highly doubt Steph will be wanting visitors."

"With all due respect, I don't care."

Donna scoffed. "Suit yourself." She hung up the phone.

Donna's negative attitude only strengthened my resolve. I grabbed my work satchel and faithful blue jacket.

"Where are you off to?" said Rab, his eyes still glued to his computer screen. "The hotel bar doesn't open till midday."

I gave Rab an amused look. "You're funny. I'm off to visit the Andersons."

"What's this in aid of? Trying to get a friends and family discount at The Cape?"

"Steph Anderson phoned. Beth isn't going to be back in school until after Christmas at the earliest."

Rab turned to me, his work abandoned. The joviality had vanished from his expression. "Is she alright?" he asked, genuinely concerned.

"That's what I'm going to find out."

"Do you not think we should tread more lightly? Get some more details?"

"There is only one person who is going to give me the information I need."

"Do you really think barging in on them like this is a wise idea, V?"

"Steph Anderson is hardly going to turn me away, Rab. I'm just concerned about her daughter, that's all."

"But still... you've made such progress with the pupils at the school. Do you want to potentially throw that all away by making one unwelcome visit?"

"I'm not going to compromise my work just so that a few more people round the village like me, Rab."

"I know V, but is it really worth ruffling feathers? Steph said she'd be back after Christmas. We can just send work home to her. She'll be fine."

"I need to talk to Steph myself. If I need to ruffle feathers then so be it. I would rather that than not see this through."

Rab sighed. "Ok. On your head be it."

***

The Andersons lived in a small house just next to The Cape. The front garden boasted an array of beautiful flowers which had clearly been tended to carefully. A selection hung from baskets at the front door giving a pop of colour to the otherwise plain house. I made my way to the front door, careful not to accidentally tread on the beautiful flowers weaving around the path. I knocked on the door and waited. There was no answer. I knocked again, growing impatient. After a few more attempts, Steph finally answered the door. She did not look pleased.

"It's not really a good time, Mhairi."

"I appreciate that Steph and I'm sorry for the intrusion. I'm concerned about Beth and would feel much better if I could chat to you personally."

She notably softened. "There isn't much to tell, really. Beth has been unwell on and off for a while. We thought she was getting better but then she took a really bad turn at the weekend. We can't get her out of her bed most days never mind to school."

I nodded. "I'm really sorry to hear that."

"Thank you."

"As long as Beth is ok."

Steph paused for a moment. "It's very kind of you to come here, Mhairi. Can I offer you a cup of tea?"

Steph led me into their front room as she made the tea. She returned a few moments later carrying two mugs.

"We understand that Beth is meant to be sitting exams this year." Steph stated, her voice loaded with concern. "With her health as it is, we don't know if that will be a possibility. She's always been a clever girl. We were so proud when she got her results last year."

"She is a studious pupil, that much is clear. Her teachers said the same."

Steph beamed. "That certainly is nice to hear."

"We don't want to put her or you under any additional pressure. We can postpone her exams till next year when she's feeling better. She can stay on at school and finish her qualifications."

"Thank you, Mhairi. That is a massive weight off our shoulders. I'll be sure to tell Beth."

"When did this all start, Steph?"

"Well now…" Steph said thoughtfully, her fingernails drumming the side of her mug. "I guess in August. She told us all about that Morning Assembly, Mhairi. That was the first of her sickness."

"So she was being sick a lot?"

Steph nodded. "Several times a day. When she wasn't vomiting she felt nauseous. It took a lot of effort to get her to eat anything. At least her appetite has returned now."

"So she's a little better than she was?"

"It comes in waves. Some days are better than others."

I nodded, thoughtfully.

"She's just so tired all the time. Getting her out of bed is such a struggle. Some days I just give up. It's so hard seeing her like this. This is not who she is."

"I totally understand. It must be awful for you as a family."

"We are trying to look after her and keep the business going. Nathan Black has been really good at keeping an eye on her when we're in the restaurant. She's so lucky to have him. I don't want to leave her but we have to make a living."

"Yes of course. I understand that." I said, getting to my feet. "I won't keep you from Beth any longer. Thank you for the tea."

"Thanks Mhairi. It really means a lot."

"If there is anything else I can do please just let me know."

Steph ushered me to the door.

As I passed another room, I spotted Beth out of the corner of my eye. She had clearly been listening to our conversation. I acknowledged her presence with a brief nod before she retreated back into the room and out of sight.

Steph's story had all but confirmed my suspicions but after seeing her I knew for certain. All the pieces of the puzzle slotted into place, just as I had worried. Beth Anderson was pregnant.

Chapter Eight

Upon my return to the school, I erupted into the office and slammed the door shut.

Rab, busy guzzling his coffee, promptly spilled it all down himself.

"What the hell, Mhairi?" he shouted, dabbing at his shirt with some paper that had been abandoned on the floor.

"Shhh!" I whispered, pointing at the door.

Rab gave me a stern look. "What the hell?" he said in a whispered but urgent tone, still attempting to clean his shirt.

"Sorry, Rab. I have something I need to tell you but you need to promise not to tell anyone."

"Come on V, like you need to ask…"

"Rab. I'm serious." I interrupted. "This cannot go anywhere."

He gave me a quizzical glance and eventually sighed. "Yes. Absolute discretion. I shan't say a word, boss. Scouts honour."

"Please be serious, Rab. Just this once."

He looked at me expectantly, folding his arms which were now coffee stained.

"We have a bit of a situation…"

I explained everything that had happened at the Andersons' house, including Beth and my conversation with Steph, whilst frantically pacing round the tiny office. I felt like a caged animal hungry for certainty in an altogether fragile situation. Once I had finished, I stopped pacing and turned to Rab.

"Well?" I said, eager to hear his response. "What do you think?"

"Are you sure of this, V? Can we really be sure she's pregnant?" He was sitting with his mouth half open, the colour drained from his face.

"I am certain of it. I had my suspicions before and everything that Steph said all but confirmed it. I saw her with my own eyes."

Rab sighed thoughtfully, drumming his fingers on the table. "Right. *If* this is the case (and I say if because it was not confirmed by Beth or Steph) what do you propose we do?"

"For the time being we carry on as normal. We cannot let this news get out for as long as possible. Steph obviously didn't want me to find out so I highly doubt she will want the rest of the village to know."

Rab nodded thoughtfully, still drumming his fingers.

"Word will get out eventually. We just need to manage it when it does. I assume the direct family already knows and likely Nathan Black as well."

Rab stopped drumming his fingers. "Nathan Black? Does that mean Iris knows?"

"Something tells me Nathan Black wouldn't be in a rush to let his Grandma in on the secret."

"Fair point."

I began pacing again. "This has village scandal written all over it. These types of secrets have a way of getting out so we will re-assess when that becomes the case. Beth's well-being is the most important thing at the moment so we must respect her wishes to keep this quiet."

Rab nodded, staring at his shoes.

I sighed. "These things happen, Rab. Our job is to support our kids when they do happen."

"Not in this village, V. I don't think I've ever heard of something like this happening in Allaban."

"Well. There is a first time for everything." I cleared my throat. "Right. My visit at least shed some light on the mystery. Maybe just keep an eye on Nathan for the time being."

I turned my attention to my computer screen but my focus was anywhere but on my work. I felt so sorry Beth. She was a young girl trying to make sense of a very grown up problem. I could very much relate.

***

After a long and largely unproductive day, I was glad to be finished. I decided that, instead of working late, I would go home and cook dinner for Steven. It was the least I could do for him. I went home via the local Spar to pick up some ingredients for Spaghetti Bolognese. A novice like me could not go far wrong with a good spag-bol.

As I browsed the aisles for all the ingredients I'd need, I bumped into Iris. She had changed into denim dungarees and her wild, white hair had been tamed into a messy ponytail. She beamed at me, her blue eyes glistening.

"Good to see you out of the school building at a reasonable time, Mhairi!"

I laughed nervously. "I try my best. Thought I might cook Steven dinner for a change. Would be nice to have some real food instead of microwave meals."

"You need to spend more time taking care of yourself, Mhairi. That school can work just fine without you spending every waking minute there."

I shot her a defensive look. "I'm not there all the time."

Iris raised an eyebrow. "A likely story. I'm just getting some more food for Nathan. The amount that boy puts away! It's a wonder he is still a beanpole. I wish I could get away with eating that much!"

I laughed. "Teenage boys, eh?"

"Absolutely. Sleeps all weekend, eats all the food in the house and barely says two words to me. The joys!"

"Well he will grow out of it... eventually."

"If he grows any more I'll need to take down the ceiling." She laughed whole-heartedly. "How are you settling in?"

"It feels like I've been here for months and not weeks, Iris. I guess that's always the way with schools."

"You'll be in with the brick work like me before you know it! You need to let your hair down and enjoy it."

"Yes well. When I have time."

"Aww c'mon Mhairi! You and Steven need to see the boat. I'll invite some other folk and we can have a Boat party. How does Saturday sound? Give you a chance to meet more of the village."

"Iris, I…" I began, trying desperately to concoct an excuse.

"Mhairi, I insist. It's about time you relaxed a little. You will come on Saturday night and you will not bring your car. I will not take no as an answer."

"I really don't know if that's a good idea."

"It's not a good idea- it's a great idea. You can thank me afterwards." Iris touched my arm affectionately. "It'll do you good, Mhairi. Nothing beats a drink in the sea air."

I sighed. "Sure." There was no point in protesting. It was clear I wasn't getting out of this one.

"Excellent." Iris beamed. "I best be off. I can't keep the hungry teenager waiting! Looking forward to Saturday already! See you at school." With that, she was gone.

It certainly seemed that Iris had no idea about Nathan and Beth's predicament. If she did, she was making a good show of hiding it. It was hard enough raising her grandson on her own… how would she cope with helping him raise a baby?

When I arrived back at the cottage, Steven was nowhere to be seen. He was probably still at George and

Emily's. I set to work on the Spaghetti Bolognese. I was glad of the distraction. I pushed thoughts of Beth Anderson to the back of my mind and began chopping the onions. I wasn't convinced the tears I shed were because of them.

"Mhairi… are you cooking?" Steven said in surprise as he entered the cottage. He surveyed the chopped onions. "Are you feeling ok?"

"I just thought I'd treat my fiancé to a home cooked meal."

"Wow, Mhairi. What is the occasion?" He gave me a peck on the cheek and plucked a beer from the fridge. "You've not cooked since… I can't even think."

"I'll try my best not to poison you." I continued preparing all of the vegetables and the meat. I was exhausted. This was why I didn't cook often.

"So how was your day?" called Steven from the comfort of the couch.

"Eh… I've had better."

"Care to elaborate?"

"Sorry I can't. Confidential stuff."

"Well I'm sure it'll all sort itself out soon."

I scoffed. It would certainly come to an end… one way or another. "Iris from school has invited us to a Boat Party on Saturday." I said, changing the subject.

Steven looked up from the couch. "A boat party? Sounds awful fancy."

"I think it's just an excuse for a piss up."

Steven laughed. "Sounds good to me."

I wrestled with the carrots. "What about you? How's the work going?"

"Aww Mhairi it's great. It's looking like we will be renovating the whole house at this rate. It's so exciting. George has a real eye for stuff. I'm learning a lot from him. I can't believe I'm getting paid for this!"

"That's great. They seem to be keeping you plenty busy."

"You can say that again. George has a list as long as his arm." Steven rose from the couch and made his way over to me, taking me in his arms. He kissed my forehead. "Things are good, Mhairi. Really good."

I forced a smile. If only he knew.

Chapter Nine

It was finally Saturday night and the evening of the Boat Party. I wasn't particularly looking forward to it. The party at the Campbell's had left a sour taste in my mouth However, Iris had insisted on our attendance and Steven was like an excitable puppy. I attempted to keep up appearances for him. Iris had been so supportive since I arrived in Allaban... I just couldn't say no to her. All I had to do was turn up. Enjoyment was entirely optional.

I lay on the bed reading whilst Steven tried on an array of ties.

"What do you think Mhairi?" he said, holding a plain royal blue tie in-front of his white shirt. "I thought blue and white would complement the nautical theme."

I couldn't help but snigger from behind my book. "Steven, we are going to a party on a boat. You are acting like we are going to the Oscars."

"Just making an effort. I want to make a good impression."

"I don't think many people will notice your nod to the nautical theme."

"Mhairi, you're not even looking."

I glanced at him for a couple of seconds before returning to my book. "It's nice."

"That is not an answer!"

I put my book to one side and rolled off the bed. Plucking the tie from Steven's hand, I threw it on the bed. I undid the top button of his white shirt and pecked him on the cheek. "Perfect."

Steven sighed. "So... definitely no tie?"

I pulled him close. "Definitely no tie."

"If we turn up to this thing and I look underdressed I will blame you."

"I take full responsibility, Mr Smith."

Steven held me for a moment before looking me up and down. "Mhairi, you're not even dressed yet."

I looked down at my baggy t-shirt and grey joggies. "What does it matter what I wear?"

"I'm pulling out all the stops here, Mhairi. Smart casual doesn't mean I dress smart and you dress casual."

"Wow Steven. I had no idea." I said, my voice laced with sarcasm.

Steven raised an eyebrow. "I don't think we are going to Iris's to watch a movie."

"Shame..." I crooned, sliding my hands under Steven's shirt and around his waist.

"This tactic is not going to work, Mhairi."

I looked at him innocently. "What on earth are you talking about?"

"I'm talking about you being all sexy and distracting me."

"I thought you didn't approve of my ensemble."

"I'd approve of you in any clothes, Mhairi."

I tilted my head to one side. "What about no clothes?"

Steven studied my expression carefully. "That I could definitely get on board with." He whispered, pulling me to him. He kissed me fiercely and I ran my hands to his torso. An unwanted memory flashed before my eyes. I sprung away from Steven, a knee-jerk reaction.

He looked at me, puzzled. "Everything ok?"

I blinked. "I just realised the time… I really need to start getting ready." I was shaking wildly but attempted to hide this from Steven.

Steven glance at his watch. "Shit." He whispered, heading quickly for the bathroom.

Once he was gone, I sank onto the bed, breathing heavily. I focused on my breathing while my mind was engulfed with flames. Slowly, the flames began to smoulder. I stopped shaking. My face was damp with tears and perspiration. The flashbacks were happening more and more frequently. It seemed being back in Allaban was uprooting them. I sighed, once again pushed the ugly recollections from my mind and set about getting ready.

Steven and I arrived at Iris's boat at 8pm. Had it been up to Steven, we would have arrived an hour earlier. There were a few people milling about the Harbour as we approached.

I don't know what I expected Iris's boat to look like but I hadn't expected what was sitting in front of us. The boat itself was painted a bottle green with "Wanderer" written on both sides in white, curly writing. It certainly looked like it had been wandering for a long time- the paint was flaking away from the body and rust was gathering at its edges. The mast had a large white sail, slightly discoloured and boasting a few holes. It ebbed in the wind, seemingly without a care in the world.

"Mhairi!" A familiar voice called. Iris rushed over to greet us wearing a long green maxi dress. It was as though to match with her vessel. Her blue eyes twinkled with mischief as they darted between Steven and I.

"So you must be Steven." She said, pulling him into a hug. "Lovely to finally meet you."

"Yes, it's great to finally put a face to a name." Steven said enthusiastically. "Thank you so much for inviting us. I've never been to a party on a boat before."

"Welcome to the Booze Cruise!" Iris exclaimed, throwing her hands in the air. "You two are far too sober for a Saturday evening. What can I get you? Wine? Beer? Cider?"

Steven beamed. "A beer would be great."

"Gin and tonic if you have it, Iris. Thank you." Iris winked before going in search of drinks. Steven and I followed.

"I've got a cooler in the back of my car." She said. "Just hop on the boat and I'll bring them to you."

I was immediately glad I'd decided to wear sandals. The boat was secured to its moorings with a partially rotten rope and a thin plank of wood bridging the gap. Steven crossed first and then extended his hand to me. I tentatively made the transfer.

"Come on, Mhairi. It's perfectly safe." Said Steven, loosening his grip on my hand. I grasped him tighter. I successfully boarded the boat without careering into the loch.

"I'm not known for my sea legs, Steven." I said through gritted teeth.

Iris appeared with our drinks, nimbly crossing the plank. "Here you are." She said, handing us our drinks. She then leapt down from the plank and landed gracefully on the boat.

Steven looked around admiringly. "It's a beauty, Iris."

"She's my pride and joy. Got her from a fisherman a good number of years ago now- he was trying to pawn her off so I got her for a brilliant price. The joke's on him. My neighbours thought I'd gone mad. She needed a little TLC but now she's good as new."

"Must have been an amazing project!" Steven said enthusiastically.

I smiled weakly, the scene swaying before my eyes. I had clearly left my sea legs at home. I drank my gin and tonic greedily, hoping it would steady my nerves.

"You alright there, Mhairi?" asked Iris, looking concerned. "You're starting to look a little green."

"I'll be fine." I said breathlessly. "Not used to being on the boat yet, that's all."

"The waves can have that effect. Just try to focus on the horizon. You'll get your bearings."

Iris spotted another group of guests arriving and went to greet them. Steven and I found seats on the top deck and gazed at the waves.

"You sure you're alright, Mhairi?" asked Steven, taking my hand. "We can leave if you don't feel well."

"I'll be fine once I've had this gin and tonic." I whispered. I downed my drink in one long gulp. A warm feeling spread through my throat. "I feel better already."

Steven laughed. "Take it easy, lightweight."

"Mhairi! Steven!" called a familiar voice from the edge of the boat. The voice belonged to Rab. Standing by his side was Tom. My eyes widened. It seemed sea sickness was the least of my worries. My heart sank. Perhaps falling off the plank and into the loch would have been the preferred option.

After scaling the edge of the boat, Rab and Tom sat down across from us. I tried to act casual, all while avoiding Tom's gaze. He seemed to be doing the same.

"How's things?" said Steven, taking a swig from his beer.

"Fine, fine. This one is burying me in work." Rab raised his own beer bottle in my direction. "I take it Mhairi has told you about our most recent predicament?"

Steven turned to me. "I don't think so."

My eyes widened. "Rab. Not here."

Rab looked taken aback for a moment but then once again sipped his beer. "Anyway. Enough work chat. How are you settling in? Mhairi driving you mad yet?"

"No more than usual."

The boys laughed.

"Someone has to keep you two in line."

Rab tutted. "You often forget I'm older than you, Mhairi."

"In years only, Rab. I've met six year olds more mature."

Rab looked at Steven with faux hurt in his eyes. "See what I need to deal with? V supplies me with my daily ego bashing to accompany my morning coffee."

Steven chortled.

Tom sat quietly, a silent observer in the conversation. I stole glances of him and then scolded myself for doing so. I was not going to make the same mistake twice.

As Rab and Steven chatted, the sun dipped behind the horizon, leaving the village basked in an ominous glow. I was hypnotised until something on the shore drew my attention.

A figure came into view, coming towards the boat. Nathan Black stumbled around the pier, swinging a six-pack of beer. I caught sight of Iris's face. It was clear that Nathan had not been on the guestlist.

"Excuse me." I said, putting a hand on Steven's shoulder as I left the group. Steven gave me an inquiring look before catching sight of Nathan zigzagging towards the boat. Iris reached Nathan first and I wasn't far behind her.

"Nathan what are you doing here? You're making a spectacle of yourself." Hissed Iris, snatching the six-pack from his hand.

"I'm here to join the party. Isn't that obvious?"

"You are embarrassing yourself and me."

"Lighten up, Grandma. I'm just bringing some life to this party."

"You will leave. At once."

Nathan suddenly went an acute shade of green and promptly vomited all over my sandals. Stunned reactions echoed from the guests on the boat. Iris gasped.

"Mhairi I…" she began, trying desperately to find the words. The bright and confident woman had vanished.

"I'll watch Nathan if you want to go and get a bucket, Iris? I'll find somewhere a little more private in the meantime."

Iris nodded and left. I propped Nathan up, his drunken stumbling becoming more exaggerated with every moment. We made our way behind one of the old Harbour buildings, now concealed from the view of the boat. At least we no longer had an audience to worry about. Nathan slumped onto a barrel and I knelt in-front of him.

"Better?" I said, looking at Nathan with concern. Nathan attempted to nod but ended up bobbing like a ragdoll.

"They all think it was me." He slurred.

"What do you mean, Nathan?" I tried to meet his gaze but his head lolled around.

Nathan summoned all of his energy to sit up and look me in the eye. "Beth."

"Ah… right." I said.

"I didn't do it. You have to believe me." He said pleadingly. He started to sob uncontrollably.

I put a hand on his shoulder. "I'm not accusing you of anything, Nathan."

"They all just assumed it was me. I see the way her mother looks at me."

"Does your grandma know?"

Nathan's eyes grew wide with anger. "You're not listening to me. It's not mine." He promptly threw up again, narrowly missing my feet this time.

"It's ok…" I soothed, patting his back. Just then, Iris appeared with a bucket and a towel.

"Here you go, Mhairi. Sorry about your feet." She handed me the towel. Her tone became deep and angry as she addressed her grandson. "As for you, Nathan Angus Black…

you are in for a world of punishment tomorrow. Prepared to be grounded for a very long time."

Nathan groaned, hunched over the bucket.

***

The party didn't last long after Nathan's drunken display. Steven, Rab, Tom and I were amongst the last to leave and it was still early. I felt sorry for Iris but decided she'd rather be alone to deal with Nathan. My mind revisited his confession- did drunken thoughts really speak sober minds? I carried my vomit-stained sandals as I made the journey home on foot. Steven wanted to carry me home but I declined. My feet were pleasantly numb from the alcohol so didn't hurt a bit. Once we were on solid ground, my sea sickness disappeared as quickly as it had arrived and ambling home was very enjoyable. The sky was bursting with colour, putting on a final display of dazzling warmth before the dusk settled around the hills.

"So what's the deal with that Nathan boy?" asked Steven, his arm draped lazily around my shoulders. "He seemed quite rattled- even for a drunk."

"Being rattled is the least of that boy's worries." Said Rab.

I shot him a look and he immediately became defensive.

"What? I was just stating the obvious."

"We are not talking about this here, Rab."

"Why not? There is no-one else around and the rest of the village will know about it soon enough anyway. It's not like it's a secret that can be kept under wraps for long…"

"What are you two talking about?" Steven asked, interrupting Rab's speech.

"That Nathan Black boy knocked up a girl in the High School. Beth Anderson."

I took one of my sandals and promptly smacked Rab over the head with it.

"Ow! What was that for?"

"You know fine well." I hissed.

"He was going to find out anyway!"

"Not from us he wasn't!" I said, lifting my sandal high, ready to strike Rab for a second time.

"Hey! Watch where you swing that sicky sandal, V."

"Hey! Mhairi! Calm down!" Steven plucked the sandal from my grasp. "It's not like I'm going to tell anyone."

"That's not the point, Steven. This is a confidential matter. It has nothing to do with you."

Steven looked a little hurt but refrained from comment.

Rab rubbed his head where my sandal had struck. "Come off it, Mhairi. Lighten up a little."

"This is a girl's future, Rab. She and Nathan are going through a rough time. This isn't a laughing matter. Show a little compassion for a change."

We reached a fork in the road- the Campbell Croft in one direction and the cottage in another.

"Fancy coming to ours for afters?" Steven asked. "I have a bottle of whisky I've been saving for a special occasion."

"Are you sure that's a good idea, Steven?" I said, suddenly concerned.

"Oh I could go for round two. What do you think, Tommy?"

"Not a good idea, Rab."

"Oh come on. Why? It's only just past midnight. The night is young."

"I just don't think we should."

"Why not? What secrets are you hiding?"

"I just need to be up early in the morning so..." Tom's eyes met mine briefly before he looked away. "...not a good idea."

"Spoil sport. You're far too sensible to be a Campbell man." Rab playfully ruffled his brother's hair. Tom swatted him away.

"Oh well. We best be off, I suppose. See you on Monday, V."

***

I arrived in school on Monday morning, entered the office to find Rab already sitting at his desk, cradling a cup of coffee with his feet propped up.

"Steph Anderson phoned." He said, giving me a knowing look.

"What about?"

He shrugged and returned to his coffee.

I sighed, picked up the phone and punched in Steph Anderson's phone number. The phone was answered on the first ring.

"How could you?" Steph hissed.

I was entirely caught off-guard. "Steph I... are you ok? What's going on?"

"Beth told me you saw her and by Sunday night the whole village knew... bit too much of a coincidence if you ask me."

My heart sank. "Steph, I did not tell another soul. You have my word."

Steph scoffed. "Well who else blabbed then? Beth? Nathan?"

I was silent.

"Yeah, I thought as much. I really thought I could trust you, Mhairi. You seemed like a genuinely nice person."

"Steph I..."

"Do us all a favour and leave. You did it once, after all. I'm sure you'll have no remorse doing it again."

The line went dead. I stared at the receiver. "Steph Anderson thinks it was me."

Rab looked up from his coffee. "What?"

"Steph Anderson thinks it was me." I repeated. "She thinks I blabbed."

Rab stared at me. "Oh shit."

"Yeah oh shit. Now you see why I was keen to keeps this under wraps. Now the whole village thinks it's me that let the cat out of the bag."

"Surely the whole village won't think you're behind this, V."

"And why not? The girl that very recently moved in and just so happened to visit right before word got out?"

Rab sighed. "Point taken."

I slumped in my chair. "Our first priority is Beth Anderson. Can you check in with Steph, Rab? She won't talk to me but maybe she will talk to you."

Rab nodded. "Not a problem."

I smiled weakly. Steph thought I had spilled the beans and there was nothing I could say to change her mind. Protesting my innocence would only make me seem more guilty. I shook this thought from my mind and tried to focus on what was important... who was important. I decided to leave to office to get some fresh air. I needed to distance myself from my thoughts and figure out a plan. I just needed to calm down first. I walked past the front desk catching a glimpse of Donna. It was clear she had recently been crying. I stopped dead in my tracks. "Donna?" I whispered.

Donna spun round in her chair, busying herself with the filing cabinet at the other end of the front desk. "What do you want?"

"I just... I wanted to check you were ok."

Donna turned to face me, a quizzical look on her face. "What does it matter to you?"

We both stared at each other for what seemed like an eternity before Donna broke down into guttural sobs. "My Dad..." She whispered, tears running freely down her cheeks.

I reached a hand across the desk and put it on Donna's shoulder. "Whatever it is Donna... go home."

She looked surprised. "No. I couldn't possibly do that."

"I would much rather you were at home with your family that worrying about it here."

Donna gave me a long, hard stare.

I removed my hand, feeling awkward. "We can take care of everything here. Go home."

Donna sniffed. "Why? Why are you being so nice to me?"

"You're upset. I'm worried about you."

"Worried? About me?"

"Yes, I am. I really do think you should go home, Donna. Your family needs you just now. We can keep things going here."

She blinked at me in surprise. "Ok." She said quietly, as though trying not to disturb the tears lingering in her eyes. "Thanks."

I nodded and made my way to the front entrance. I could feel Donna's eyes on me long after I shut the door.

The school building sat right on the loch. It still baffled me how beautiful it was. It was a crisp winter morning and the light danced on the cool water like diamonds. Although the air was icy cold, it's touch brought a warmth to my cheeks. The water rippled in the breeze as I walked by the loch. Halfway round, I spotted a familiar figure. It was Bill Rodgers. I waved in his direction. He smiled and waved back.

"A little early in the day for you, eh Mhairi?"

I shrugged. "Needed to get out of there for a bit."

"Yes. I hear what the village has been saying."

"Bill, I…"

"Relax, Mhairi. I don't believe a word of it."

I smiled gratefully, falling into step beside him.

"I remember all the things they said about me when I first moved here. Not the friendliest of folk in this village. People always want someone to blame and we are an easy target."

"It's hard, Bill. If I were to profess my innocence it would make me look more guilty."

"When people are angry or upset, they are blind. It is only our actions and not our words that people can see."

"I can't imagine anyone hating you, Bill."

He chuckled. "I wasn't like this six years ago, let me tell you. Time brings perspective."

I sighed. "I don't think I'll ever be accepted here."

"It's not about being accepted by everyone, Mhairi. It is about knowing who our real friends are. Those are the people you hold onto with both hands."

"How will I know who those people are?"

"You'll know, Mhairi. You will reach a time in your life when you'll reach rock bottom or close to it. Some people will desert you but others stay and support you. A fine few."

"I just feel so much pressure to get everything exactly right. The eyes of the whole village are on me all the time. It's exhausting."

"We are only under as much pressure as we allow ourselves to be. They hate you right now, sure. That won't last. They will move on. Have faith."

"But what if they don't?"

"They will. What do you do when there is a rope dragging you to the edge of a mountain?"

I pondered this for a moment. "I... I don't know..."

Bill chuckled. "It's simple, Mhairi. Just let go of the damn rope."

I felt better after speaking to Bill. It was nice to have the company of someone who understood what I was going through. Someone who knew what it was like to not belong. We walked the rest of the way in silence, content in each other's company. I hoped Bill was right, but Steph's words weighed heavily on my shoulders as I wandered back towards reality.

Chapter Ten

I had lived in Glasgow pretty much my whole life and knew I didn't fit in. Arriving in Allaban as a child had been like entering a house after being outside in the bitter cold- a flood of warmth overwhelming my senses, slicing through the frost. I returned to Allaban in search of that warmth. My body ached for the inviting glow of the hills. However, upon my return, it was clear the frost had spread. I didn't belong anywhere. When Grandma died, the light had left, taking all the warmth with it.

As the school came into view from the other side of the loch, I pushed those feelings down, drowning them in reality like a lost dream. Bill smiled as he turned off in the direction of the grounds. I made the rest of the journey alone.

As I entered the school building, Rab greeted me at the door. "Mam phoned. Dinner tonight?"

"What?" I said, confused.

"Dinner at the Croft. Tonight."

"Yeah. Yeah, that's fine." I whispered.

Rab gave me an intense stare. "You alright? You seem a little... lost."

I forced a smile. "Yes. Sorry."

"There's only so far coffee can take you, V. Mary'll fix up a nice meal and you'll feel right as rain. You'll see."

He gave me a reassuring look before darting down the corridor. Going to The Croft would be a welcome distraction

127

from everything that was going on. It would force me to concentrate on something else. I'm sure Steven would relish a change from the rotation of ready meals.

When we arrived at the Croft that night, Mary was already at the door to greet us. Her brown hair was tied back in a messy bun. It was peppered with grey, mostly disguised by the red bandana tied neatly behind her ears. She wore a long, yellow dress I recognised from years ago, still as vibrant as it had always been. Her smile radiated warmth.

"Lovely to see you, Mhairi." She said warmly, pulling me into a hug.

She smelled of fresh flowers and oatmeal, just as I remembered. As a child, when I was really cross with mum, I used to say I was going to live with Mary. She had always been more of a motherly figure than my own had ever attempted.

"And you must be Steven. Please, come in, come in." She ushered us inside. Rab was in the living room, ready to greet us.

"Good to see you both. V, you remember Dad?"

Alan Campbell looked up from his newspaper, irritated by the interruption. My whole body prickled. He was a shadow of the man I remembered. His once plump face was haggard and gaunt, wearing years of ill health and struggle. His brown hair was combed to attempt to hide the bald patches all over his scalp. He sported a 5 o-clock shadow which sprouted messily on his jaw and neck. He wore thick rimmed brown glasses but still didn't seem to fully register Steven and I. His dark brown eyes were dim, lost in a prison of their own making. I struggled to recognise him.

"Alan, it's me, Mhairi."

Alan's eyes looked like they were about the glaze over.

Rab put an arm around me. "He barely says two words these days, Mhairi. Not really been the same after the stroke." He turned to his Dad. "Mhairi Sinclair, Dad. Sadie's granddaughter."

A dim light flickered behind Alan's eyes. There was a chilling silence in the air.

"Tom not joining us?" I asked carefully.

"He'll be in soon. Finishing up on the farm."

Mary shuffled into the room. "Dinner's ready. We're eating in the dining room."

Rab whistled. "It must be a special occasion. It is Christmas already?"

"Stop your joking Rab and help me set the table."

The dining table had been pulled out and placed in the heart of the room. It donned a yellow table cloth and matching yellow napkins. It was clear that yellow was the theme of tonight's dinner. I took a seat between Steven and Rab with Alan sitting at the head of the table.

Mary entered with a large serving dish containing sizzling roast potatoes. "It's a "help yourself" dinner tonight.

Take what you want and leave what you don't. Rab, can you help me with the other dishes?"

Rab dutifully left the table to assist his mother. I heard the back door of the kitchen opening and closing.

"Tom," Mary called from the kitchen. "Give Rab a hand, will you?"

Alan, Steven and I sat awkwardly at the table whilst the bustle in the kitchen continued. I suddenly became very interested in my yellow napkin. After what felt like an eternity, the rest of the party joined the table. It was stuffed with mis-matching casserole dishes, filled to the brim with an array of home cooked dishes. The dishes took part in an intricate dance as they were passed around the table.

"So, Mhairi." Began Mary, stretching across the table to pass a plate to Rab. "What's it like being back here?"

"Yeah. It's good." I said, smiling awkwardly. I stole a glance at Rab, trying to gauge whether he had told his mother about Beth Anderson. He gave nothing away. "School is quite busy at the moment but things are starting to settle. Steven's doing some work on George and Emily Harris' house. It's all pretty good."

Mary nodded enthusiastically. "So you're a tradesman, Steven?"

Steven nodded. "Joiner. George wants a lot of the house re-modelled so that's keeping me busy."

"Oh how exciting."

"Yeah it's great being able to see everything come together."

"Tom here has a habit of starting projects and not finishing them. He's still footering around in that old barn."

"I'm restoring it, Mum." Tom interjected before taking a large bite of chicken.

"Aye, you've been saying that for months, Tom. Still looks like the same old barn to me. Maybe if we got Steven on board to help it might be finished this side of the century."

Tom rolled his eyes as Mary giggled.

"That old barn holds so many memories. The three of them used to hide in there as weans. They thought we didn't know." Mary let out a hearty laugh. "Tom said he caught you out there on the night of the party, Mhairi."

I nearly inhaled a roast potato and Steven began patting my back. Mary didn't seem to notice.

"Old habits die hard, I guess." She crooned.

"Yes." I whispered. "I guess they do."

"So. Mhairi. How are you, pet? It's been such a long time."

I smiled, feeling the warmth radiate from her eyes. "I'm fine, Mary. I've been a teacher for ten years now. I've taught in a few schools in and around central Scotland until I got the job up here."

"Rab said. I was so shocked to hear you were coming back after all these years. Your Grandma would have been thrilled."

"Yes I think she would have."

"What do you make of Allaban, Steven?"

Steven paused as he finished a mouthful of mash potato. "It certainly is a beautiful place. I'd never been further north than Aviemore until we moved up here. Aviemore is certainly more densely populated."

"What did you make of Mhairi getting the job up here?"

"I was... very proud of her. She's always been ambitious and I'm happy to hang on her coat tails." Steven took my hand. "She is a marvel."

I blushed. "Steven, stop."

"And modest too!" Mary cooed. "The boys were ever so sorry to see her go. Tom in particular really missed her."

Steven dropped my hand.

I cleared my throat. "So what about you, Mary? What have you been up to all these years?"

"Och nothing really, Mhairi. Just keeping busy with the farm and such. Alan's health hasn't been the best as you know so... we've all been working hard to lighten the load."

I nodded. "Of course."

"We were all so proud of Rab when he got his job and the High School. His promotion was just a bonus."

"Well I was never gonna be much help on the farm." Rab joked. "Tommy is the farming prodigy in the family."

"Well if he could tidy the place up a bit that'd be nice. The place is a pigsty- no pun intended."

Tom shook his head but refrained from comment.

"You love clearing up after us, Mum. Don't lie."

"I don't have much of a choice, Robert Campbell so just as well I don't mind."

It was lovely to see Mary but it was clear that Alan remained the elephant in the room. I just didn't know how to act around him. His presence made me feel uneasy. Mary had always been devoted to her husband. He was dying slowly from the inside out and his dutiful wife was forced to sit and watch.

***

We arrived back at the cottage and Steven turned off the ignition. I made no move to leave the car.

"You coming in, love?" Steven said.

"Give me a minute Steven." He shrugged and got out of the car.

As he closed the door, I sighed. He was blissfully unaware of the war taking place in my head. Was it finally time to tell him about Tom? Sitting between the two of them at dinner had been purgatory. What had happened the night at the beach had been a mistake, that much was clear. It was his right to know about it. The thought of telling him made me feel sick. However, much like nausea when unwell, you always felt a little lighter when you let it go. My mind was made up.

I got out of the car and made my way to the cottage, ready to unburden myself of the lie that had been consuming me over the past few months. I took a breath and entered the front door, psyching myself up for the fateful feud that was to follow. To my surprise, when I entered the cottage, Steven was hunched over on the sofa, his head cradled in his hands. The wind left my sails as I stood in the doorway, unsure what to do or say.

"Steven?" I said, confused. I began approaching the sofa but my eyes were drawn to a brown envelope left abandoned on the kitchen worksurface, crumpled and dog-eared. I stopped dead in my tracks. It had Steven's name on the front and had been ripped open. I picked up the envelope carefully, as not to further rip it and spill its innards. I studied the contents and my heart stopped, my eyes unable to fully absorb what they were seeing. It seemed that I'd had my opportunity to share the truth with Steven myself but that time had well and truly passed. Inside was a picture of Tom and I from that fateful night at Feic beach, locked in our condemning embrace.

I saw my relationship with Steven crumble before my eyes, seeming in slow motion but happening in an instant. In the end, I had no defence- the evidence was there in black and white and I had kept it from him. There was nothing more than could be said. I had squandered my opportunity to repent. When I had played out the scene in my head, I had imagined an explosive fight. In the end, Steven barely said two words to me, his voice scarcely above a whisper. His eyes were dark. He went upstairs, packed a bag and left. He had a friend who lived in Inverness so decided to move there for a while. I sat on the sofa, looking for signs of the devastation I had created. All I could see was a cold and empty home. I slumped onto the sofa, ready for an eternity of pain and guilt.

***

After a long time, there was a knock at the door. Emily Harris stood there, Steven's toolbelt in her hand.

"Steven left his belt and I thought I'd..."

A wave of tears came before I had a chance to stop them. The alarm on Emily's face was apparent.

"Mhairi..." she whispered, unsure of what to say.

I stared at her, my eyes puffy and red.

"can I... come in?"

I nodded. I attempted to tell her what had happened but instead began crying again. Her eyes caught sight of the discarded photo on the kitchen counter. She gathered me in her arms. "Oh Mhairi."

I erupted into broken, guttural sobs.

She guided me over to the sofa. "You need a cup of tea."

I clung to one of the purple tartan pillows whilst Emily made tea. We sat in silence for a long time. I clung to my mug of tea like a lifeline but largely didn't drink it. My jagged breathing eventually began to regulate to occasional snatches of breath. I was emotionally exhausted and had nothing left to give.

"Right." Said Emily, trying her best to sound firm but supportive. "You need to tell me the whole story. From the beginning."

The entire account came flooding out. Emily listened carefully, digesting everything word. She waited patiently for me to finish, absorbing every detail. After I stopped speaking, we sat for a while in silence.

"So…" Emily began, treading carefully. "Steven is… gone?"

I nodded. "Inverness."

"Right."

I looked at Emily through red-rimmed eyes. "I'm an awful person, aren't I?"

"No, no, no, Mhairi. You're human. We all make mistakes."

"As far as mistakes go this one is huge, Emily."

"Ok, you kissed Tom. Not your finest moment. However, you realised your mistake."

"Not quickly enough." I said bitterly, still clinging to my cold cup of tea.

"Ok, yes. You could have acted quicker. There's nothing you can do to change that now. However, the reason you didn't tell Steven about it was because you knew how hurt he was going to be."

"I should have just told him though, Emily. Him finding out like this is a hundred times worse."

"It's not the best situation to be in but it's not irreparable."

I scoffed. A new wave of tears escaped down my cheeks.

Emily took my hand. "Mhairi, Steven clearly adores you. He followed you from Glasgow all the way to Allaban for goodness sake. Not a day would pass in our house without him waxing lyrical about how amazing his fiancée was."

I smiled through the tears.

"However."

I blinked.

"From everything you have just told me, it is clear that Steven loves you unconditionally." She paused. "However... I'm not sure if his feelings are requited."

I was puzzled. "What do you mean?"

"Mhairi... do you love Steven?"

I was motionless. Steven had always been my safety blanket. He had been there for me through every big moment of my life. He had supported me in everything I did but... did I love him?

"I think that's your answer, Mhairi." Emily said. "He is a wonderful man but is he the right man for you?"

"No." I whispered. I had known the answer for a very long time but had always been afraid to say it out loud. Love was reckless, fragile and vulnerable. Not matter how hard I tried, I had never felt that kind of love about Steven. There was never any reason for me not to love Steven… but love shouldn't be built on reason. I cared about him deeply but didn't love him. I had fooled myself into thinking I loved him for all these years. It took moving to Allaban to realise that.

"It doesn't make you a lesser person, Mhairi. We don't choose who we love. You need to make decisions that are right for you and no-one else. Steven will be hurt for a while but he will move on. Your job is to let him."

I nodded, my eyes welling up again.

"Come here." Emily pulled me into a hug.

I sank into her, hoping to dissolve into nothing.

"I think you should move in with George and I… at least for a few days. Until everything has settled."

"Ok." I whispered, still firmly wrapped in her arms.

"Go and pack a bag and I'll meet you down here."

***

I ended up staying with Emily and George for some time. In that time, Emily was a brilliant friend - she would listen if I needed someone to talk to or stay out of my way if I wanted to be alone. I spent most of my time on auto-pilot, going about my day without any sense of joy or despair. I was being forced to contemplate life in its everyday monotony, stripped down to its meaningless skin, the frills all but forgotten. I felt numb. It was like I had used up all of my emotions that night at the cottage. After a few days I began to feel better so decided I should call Steven. I dialled his number but it went straight to voicemail. Steven was clearly not ready to talk. Who could blame him?

I went about my school days in a similar fashion. The pupils acted as if nothing had happened but it was clear that the news had escaped. The majority of the staff avoided me when they could. Donna was still absent from school whilst looking after her Dad so at least I didn't need to face her judgment. I did what I do best- buried myself in work as not to drown in my emotions. After a week or so of ignoring Rab, he plucked up the courage to speak to me.

"Mhairi?" he whispered, treading lightly.

I ignored him, but he spoke again.

"V?"

I whirled round in my chair. "What?"

"I just want to check that you're ok."

"What do you think?" I turned back around in my chair, attempting to focus entirely on my computer screen.

"You can't just shut me out, V. You're the one that said we are a team."

"When it comes to school matters, yes. I agree."

"I'm your friend too, Mhairi."

"I appreciate your concern, Rab, but this is something I need to deal with on my own."

"I understand that Mhairi but this is the most you've spoken to me in the best part of two weeks."

"So?"

"So… we don't do this. We talk, we argue… we work through it."

"I need space, Rab."

"We don't have that luxury." He said, eyeing up the cramped office. "If it's any consolation… Tom didn't tell me anything. I had no idea what had happened until now."

"Tom is a better person than I will ever be."

"I don't think that's true, Mhairi. Surely you don't believe it either."

"It doesn't matter, Rab. It should have been a conversation between Steven and I- not a picture in an envelope. I failed. This is entirely my fault and I will get through it. Alone."

Rab sighed. "I phoned Steph Anderson, by the way." He whispered.

I once again whirled around in my office chair, eyeing him expectantly.

"It wasn't a very long conversation, in all honesty. Beth's keeping the baby. Steph doesn't know if she will even return to school and didn't sound especially happy about it."

"Did she mention Nathan at all?"

"Nope."

I nodded. After Beth's pregnancy became public, Nathan's attendance had been patchy at best. When he was in school, he often looked hungover and dishevelled. I had tried to have a conversation with Iris about it but she ignored me. Like the whole village, she suspected I had leaked the information about Beth Anderson's condition. I still hadn't told Rab about our discussion at the Boat Party. I knew what I had to do.

"I'm going to speak with Nathan Black."

***

Nathan Black arrived at the office looking anything but calm. His eyes were wide with panic, blood-shot from lack of sleep. He avoided my gaze and instead stared at the floor with such intensity that I wouldn't have been surprised if he bore a hole in the carpet. Although he was fully grown, he seemed smaller than he had before. He was hunched over and his hands were glued to the insides of his pockets. Not a confident boy to begin with, the whole situation with Beth had already taken its toll.

I gave Rab a loaded look. He left the office, eyeing up Nathan as he left.

"Please have a seat, Nathan. You're not in any trouble."

Nathan hovered in the doorway and continued to stare at the carpet.

"I was wondering if you could help me."

Nathan looked up from the carpet, a confused expression on his face.

I gestured to the empty chair at Rab's desk. "Please. Have a seat."

He sat down cautiously, looking anywhere but directly at me.

"As I said, I didn't call you here to give you into trouble. I just want to talk. You and I had a conversation at your Grandma's Boat Party. Do you remember?"

Nathan's eyes returned to the floor. He nodded.

"Okay. Do you remember what you said to me?"

He offered no response.

"I know this is difficult for you, Nathan. I know you've been through a lot recently. However, I need you to know that you can trust me."

"You won't call me a liar?" mumbled Nathan, still averting his gaze.

"Of course not, Nathan. I trust you to tell the truth."

After a long pause, he exhaled. "Ok."

"Take your time, Nathan. I'm not going to rush you or interrupt you."

Nathan looked at me, blinking. Behind those eyes was a scared little boy, unsure of who to trust. He was clearly unsettled and although we were sitting side by side, he was trapped in his own anxiety and I was just the helpless onlooker. I felt a pang of familiarity.

"I..." he stuttered. "It's not mine. Everyone... just assumed it was mine. Even Gran. They look at me differently. They... don't really look at me anymore. I'm there but... it's like... they're just looking through me. I tried to tell them but... they wouldn't listen. They don't want to talk about it. They want to focus on Beth. I want to help Beth but it's hard.

142

She won't talk to me. She… she won't tell me who… who the father is."

I looked at Nathan trying to keep my face as neutral as possible.

"She told me before anyone. She was crying a lot. I didn't know what to do so I just held her. She said she was… pregnant. I was confused because we never… so I asked her. She said it was a secret. It was their secret. She couldn't tell anyone or he would get into a lot of trouble. No one else would understand. She told me she… loved him. She told me he understood her. He listened to her. I got angry. I started yelling at her because I was confused. She said she was sorry and that we couldn't be together anymore."

I picked up a box of tissues and placed them next to Nathan. He took one and quickly cleared his eyes.

"I asked her to tell me who he was. She refused. All she told me was that they would be in a lot of trouble if anyone found out. We stopped talking about it after that. I still go and see her but we don't talk anymore."

Once it was clear he was finished, I lay a hand on his arm. "You've been really brave to tell me all this, Nathan. Thank you."

He nodded, tears threatening to escape again.

"If you ever need to talk to me I'm here. I believe you and I'm here to support you. Ok?"

Nathan nodded briskly, fidgeting with his handkerchief.

"You can sit here for a while longer or you can go back to class. The choice is yours."

After a brief pause, Nathan stood. He looked at me for a moment and then left without a word.

My head was spinning. The bile began to rise in my throat and I used all of my energy to suppress it, my memories consuming my consciousness. It was all too much. Beth had convinced herself that she loved this man. This man had raped Beth and she was protecting him. I had successfully buried my feelings for so long but today it was not working. They returned from their shallow grave, suddenly buoyant. My skin was hot.

At that moment, Rab entered the office and came to an abrupt stop. "V? Mhairi? Are you ok?"

I could hear his voice but wasn't registering anything he was saying.

"Mhairi, you really don't look well."

I needed to escape the building. I grabbed my car keys and headed for the exit. Rab called after me but I was already gone.

I couldn't go back to Emily's. She'd be too full of questions I couldn't answer. I couldn't go back to the cottage. It was still drenched in memories of Steven. I knew I had to go to the one place I felt safe. I drove to the beach, barely registering the scenery as I flew past. I needed my Grandma. I needed her to wrap me in a warm embrace and tell me everything would be ok. I drove to Feic beach. The beach itself lay calm and quiet, undisturbed by the turning of the tide. I breathed in the calm, letting it consume me. I ran across the beach, seeking solace on the tired wooden bench. When I finally reached it, I lay down, pulling my jacket tighter around me. The bench was cold and wet, coated in a layer of sea salt. I lay there for a long time, the salt in my tears mingling with the sea-stained bench. The constant undercurrent of stress that had threatened to overwhelm me slowly retreated. I let the roaring of the waves carry me away from myself.

A violent ringing in my pocket shattered my illusion of calm. I answered.

"Hello?" I whispered, my voice hoarse with emotion.

"Mhairi? Is that you?"

I closed my eyes. "This really isn't a good time Mum…"

"Darling I have not heard from you in over two weeks. A mother worries, you know."

Tears streamed down my cheeks. "You know how it is Mum. Work is busy."

"Work is always busy. You don't live in the school building, do you?"

I sighed. "No."

"Exactly. I'm not asking for much, Mhairi dear. I just like to be kept in the loop. I was just rooting around some old boxes and I came across something I thought you'd be interested in. Can you guess what it is, Mhairi?"

"No, Mum. I have no idea."

"What, you're not even going to try? Fine. I came across a letter that must have been sent not long after your Grandma passed away. I can't even remember receiving it. Isn't that so bizarre?"

"A letter?"

"Well." she cleared her throat in anticipation. "After your Grandma Sadie passed, we were inundated with flowers and cards... you know. Very nice of people to do but it can be rather overwhelming. I distinctly remember our house looking like the Amazon Rainforest for the best part of two months. Anyway, that is by the by. Someone sent me a letter telling me they were dedicating a bench to your Grandma Sadie. That one you found at the beach, remember?"

I fingered the golden plaque fixed to the heart of the bench.

"Well. You will never guess who it was, darling. I thought it was a bit bizarre myself, to be honest."

"Who was it, Mum?"

"It was Alan Campbell, Mhairi darling. Can you believe it? Rab and Tom's father. No mention of his wife Mary or the boys either. Just Alan. I wonder if Mary and the boys know it exists. He must have known your Grandma very well. Such a thoughtful but very strange gift. Is that not bizarre? Hello? Mhairi, dear? Are you still there?"

My phone lay abandoned in the sand a few feet away. My mind barely registered as it flew from my grasp, instinctively shutting out the pain. I stared at the plaque, tears fizzing in my eyes. I began pounding at the bench, wood splintering my skin until my knuckles blead and my throat dried from screaming. I thrashed that bench for the years I had lost to that man, to the years of my childhood that were permanently tainted with that face. I thought I had buried the memories in the abyss of my mind but they stung with a raw, new fire. I could feel his lips on mine, drunk with desire. I wanted to vomit but instead collapsed in-front of the bench, sobbing quietly. Memories were flooding my consciousness, threatening to drown me in the past. I clung tightly to the bench and kept my eyes screwed shut. I couldn't let my memories overwhelm me. Being in the place where time stood still, I could see the shadow of the past at every turn. This time, I didn't have my Grandma's embrace to shield me from the storm. Instead, I sunk into a sodden pit of despair. I wallowed in the deep abyss of my mind, unsure if I'd ever resurface.

Chapter Eleven

It had been a beautiful day in Allaban that fateful day fourteen years ago. The cool summer evening warmed the trees as I made my routine journey to the Campbell Croft, the leaves catching in my long tangled hair as I ran through the streets. Rab and Tom would be waiting for me and we would spend our time lounging in the abandoned barn, lazing away the long summer nights. Grandma had warned me so many times to stay away from them. I ignored her until she gave up trying to stop me. I had always been a stubborn child and I was determined to do what I wanted.

It was only a couple of days after the fight in the barn and things had been tense. I hadn't spoken to Rab and Tom since that night. I had decided to give them some breathing space to sort things out between them. They had gotten into fights before but nothing like this. Hopefully everything would be back to normal and we could forget it had ever happened.

I arrived at the Campbell Croft and something felt different. I couldn't quite put my finger on it but the Croft felt ominous. Smoke wasn't rising from the chimney in the main house and everything was altogether too quiet. I ignored my feelings, entered the front gate and I ran up the path to the main house, chapping loudly on the door, making my presence known. There was rustling and then a jangling of keys in the door. I was expecting the warm embrace of Mary but instead Alan Campbell stood in the doorway, stoic and unwelcoming.

Alan used to be a very intimidating man. He was the one that laid down the law in the household and the boys were terrified of him. He usually spent his days working around the Croft so I didn't see him much. When I did see him he barely acknowledged my presence, maybe grunting in my direction if he felt inclined. I never knew how to behave around Alan. His stony face was often difficult to read. The only exception had been the night of Tom and Rab's fight. Mary's ready excuse had always been that he was tired from work. When I asked Grandma about him, she swiftly changed the subject, not wanting to colour my opinions of him and share her thoughts with his sons. I just thought he was a disagreeable old man and was often proven right.

That day, his mood had been different. Something about him was off but I couldn't put my finger on it. I was still too young to appreciate what Alan was. He had been so amiable that day. He said the rest of the family were at a local market and would be back soon. He said I was welcome to wait for them in the house.

He spoke lazily, the words oozing out of his mouth. As the conversation flowed, I caught sight of the bottle of Whisky tucked behind his chair. He put a hand on my knee and tucked my hair behind my ear. His hoarse whispers reeked of intent. I was frozen. Rab, Tom and Mary never did come home- I later learned they were staying overnight in

149

Inverness. My Grandma was wrong- it wasn't the Campbell brothers I should have watched out for.

When I finally escaped the house, my body was dripping with sweat. I wanted to cry but the tears wouldn't come. I went home and Grandma knew something was wrong. The truth spilled out like bile but it was her face that drained of colour. She took me in her arms and rocked me. I don't know to this day who the one seeking comfort was. I made her promise not to tell anyone what happened-including Mum. She kept that promise till the day she died.

The next day, she phoned Mum. She said I was very unwell and needed to go home. I heard their arguments as Mum probed for more information. She could sense something was wrong but Grandma did not budge. When Mum eventually arrived to pick me up, she could not deny that I was unwell. Grandma had said that I'd feel better in time. She said I'd be able to come back next summer. My Grandma said a lot of things. That was the last summer I had spent in Allaban. Grandma said that I was outgrowing the place and there was no need for me to visit. Allaban was no place for a girl of my age. I didn't realise it would be the last time I'd ever see my Grandma.

"Mhairi. V." I was suddenly aware of a voice over the rush of the waves. "Mhairi. You need to sit up."

I was curled into a ball, propped up against the wooden bench, seemingly unmoved by my violent outburst.

I must have fallen off with the weight of the wind. The air was cold. I was shivering.

"Mhairi you need to listen to me. You need to move. You'll catch your death out here."

There was a blanket wrapped around my body, scratching at my skin. I opened my eyes. Tom was looking down at me, his eyes wide with panic.

"Mhairi if you don't answer me I'll need to go and get help. I can't move you. You need to help me."

I slowly got to my feet. My bones felt rusty. Tom supported me as we approached his truck. I was moving slowly but he didn't rush me. We sat in silence for a while. Tom turned the heat up in the truck and it slowly worked its way into my bones. I sat with my eyes closed and focused on breathing. Eventually Tom sighed and drummed the steering wheel. "V, you're scaring me. This is the second time I've found you in a stupid situation. You could have died."

I sat motionless, barely unravelling Tom's words.

"I'm not always gonna be here to save you, Mhairi. You need to take some responsibility and stop pulling these stupid stunts. We aren't teenagers anymore. We need to grow up sometime."

"I know. I'm sorry."

"Why do you keep doing this, V? What is the point in these dangerous escapades?"

"Steven knows, Tom." I whispered. "There was a picture."

Tom sighed, the wind escaping his sails. "I know, Mhairi I... I'm sorry. I didn't tell anyone. I swear."

I exhaled. "It doesn't matter, Tom. He knows. He left."

"That's still no reason to... you need to..." He started half a dozen sentences before giving up in frustration.

"I should never have let it happen, Tom. I should have told him while I had the chance. This is my mistake."

"*Our* mistake." Said Tom.

"I'm the one with the fiancé, Tom."

Tom ran his hands through his hair in irritation. "I really am sorry, V. I acted impulsively."

I smiled weakly. "So did I. Anyway, the damage is done. He's gone. Steven's better off without me. I'm a little bit of a mess."

"For what it's worth, I don't think you're a mess. I think you've got a lot going on and you're trying to deal with it. You're just going about it in a really reckless way. You need to stop pulling these stunts. You need to talk to someone, V. I'm not saying it has to be me but you need to get these things off your chest. It's no good keeping them all bottled up."

"I know."

There was a pause.

"If Steven doesn't forgive you he's an idiot."

"Thanks Tom."

Tom hesitated, choosing his words carefully. "Please promise me you'll talk to someone, V. Please."

I sighed. "Ok. I will."

Tom raised an eyebrow. "Promise me. I'm serious."

"I promise."

Tom looked at me for a few more seconds, analysing my gaze. "Okay." He whispered, satisfied. Tom put the car in gear and drove in the direction of civilisation. I looked out the window and watched my Grandma's beach disappear.

Tom drove me back to Emily's house. I asked him to drop me at the bottom of the road but he insisted on taking me to Emily's front door. I caught sight of my reflection in the car's dark windscreen. My hair was matted with sand, my clothes were drenched from the sea air and my skin was hollowed and dark. Tom helped me out of the truck. He knocked on the door and Emily answered almost immediately. She was taken aback and gave me a sideways glance before turning her attention to Tom.

"Sorry for the intrusion, Emily." said Tom apologetically. "I just wanted to make sure Mhairi got back safely."

Emily looked me up and down, a worried expression on her face. "I appreciate that Tom."

Tom gave her a curt nod and turned back to the truck.

Emily bundled me inside, shutting the door. "What on earth, Mhairi?" she whispered, her eyes darting towards the kitchen. "You can't just disappear and not tell anyone."

I looked at her sheepishly. "I'm sorry Emily. My head's just been a little all over the place today."

"Well we can speak about that later. You have a visitor."

I gave her a puzzled expression. "A visitor?"

"You better go upstairs and change. Quickly."

I rushed upstairs. I put on some fresh clothes and rinsed the sand out of my hair as best I could. After a few minutes, I hurried into the kitchen. Emily was awkwardly entertaining my guest in my absence. She was sitting in the kitchen with the last person I expected to see- Donna. I stopped abruptly in the doorway, staring at them both. Donna was sitting awkwardly on one of the bar stools, clutching a mug of tea.

"I better go check on George." Said Emily. She gave me a knowing look as she left the room. I remained in the doorway, frozen to the spot and staring at Donna.

"Hi Mhairi." Donna said carefully, her eyes dotting between me and her mug of tea.

"Hi." I said, my expression bewildered. I was suddenly very aware of my bedraggled appearance. I folded my arms over my chest.

"I guess you're wondering why I'm here."

I nodded.

"This might be a little less awkward if you sit down."

I looked at her for a moment before edging over to the breakfast bar. I took the seat furthest away from Donna. We looked at each other uncomfortably, a heavy silence falling between us.

"So Mhairi... I've got something I need to tell you... ok?"

I nodded, shifting in my chair.

"Ok." Donna paused, collecting herself. "I'm sure you're well aware that we didn't get off to the best start at the school. There is a reason for that, aside from me immediately taking a disliking to you. The previous Headteacher was a very good friend of mine. When she left, not on the best terms, my loyalty remained with her."

I bit my lip, reserving comment.

"Anyway, I had decided from the outset that I didn't like you. When you left the first time, it wasn't right. I thought you would be the same daft girl you were all those years ago. I already had you pegged before you even arrived. That was my first mistake."

I waited, intrigued.

"My Dad is really unwell. He had cancer a few years back. He was given the all clear but the treatment hit him pretty hard. He has these turns sometimes which he usually snaps out of quickly enough. This time it was a really bad one. It lasted for a week." Her eyes began welling up. "I had decided that you would never give me the time off to take care of him so I came into work. I was a bit of a wreck and very annoyed with you. Not fair, I know. You were so nice to me that day and… I couldn't believe it. I completely misjudged you, Mhairi. I'm sorry about that."

I give her a puzzled look.

"I should never have judged you based on a memory from fourteen years ago. We were both kids then and you probably don't even remember me. It was a very childish thing to do. I'm sorry. When my friend, the other Headteacher, left the village, it hit me pretty hard. She and I were very close. I had no one left that I could talk to. No one else really understood about Dad."

I nodded, listening intently.

"Anyway I'm avoiding what I came here to tell you. You have to understand… it was a means of self-preservation. I thought if I exposed you for the outsider you are, you might leave and everything would be as it was. This was a really stupid notion. Basically… it was me. I was on the beach that night. I saw you and Tom. I took the picture."

Donna removed something and pushed it across the table to me. It was the picture. My stomach flipped.

"I only made one copy, I swear. That was the one I sent to Steven. I'm so sorry."

I was taken aback.

"I took the picture that night and, in a flurry of rage, decided to deliver it to Steven. I had already posted it by the time you sent me home that day. It was too late- the damage was done. I had come to my senses but there was nothing I could do to stop it. It was a petty and selfish thing to do,

Mhairi. To me, it was the ultimate revenge for stealing my friend's job and... Tom."

I squinted in surprise. "Tom?"

Donna sighed with frustration. "I like Tom, ok? He only ever had eyes for you, Mhairi. Even when we were kids. I couldn't get anywhere near him- he was always running around after you. I was jealous. I thought I had gotten over it but seeing you both on the beach... that was enough for me."

"Donna I... didn't realise."

"Well of course you wouldn't." she scoffed.

"Tom and I were just friends in those days, Donna. Nothing was going on between us."

"Well I don't think Tom saw it like that."

"I didn't know. I'm sorry I hurt you, Donna. It was never my intention. What you did was wrong but... what I did was wrong too. I was too much of a coward to admit that to myself, never mind Steven."

"I'm sorry I retaliated, Mhairi. After you were so nice to me that day, I realised my mistake. I'm just sorry I realised it too late."

I smiled weakly. "I guess we've both done things we regret."

"That's why I'm here, Mhairi. I need to make this right. There's something I need to tell you. Something I should have told you before now."

I gave her a puzzled look.

"All of the phonelines in the school are connected, Mhairi. I sometimes pick up the receiver and someone else is on the phone. Last week, I was going to make a routine group-call. I picked up the phone but it was already in use. It happens. I usually just hang up but for some reason I didn't that day." Donna shifted uncomfortably in her seat. "This conversation was different. They were clearly in the middle of an argument. One of the voices sounded familiar but I couldn't place it. The things they were saying… I was so shocked. Then… I realised who it was. I didn't tell anyone. I wasn't sure who to tell. I was afraid of what might happen if I did."

My stomach dropped. Suddenly all of the pieces of the puzzle fell into place. I couldn't believe it had taken me this long to figure it out. "Donna… who was on the phone?"

"It was… Rab Campbell and Beth Anderson."

"And they were talking about…"

"Beth's baby. Their baby."

***

Donna made her excuses and left. I was glad- it gave me time to process everything she had said. It was overwhelming. She had liked Tom, she had taken the photo, she had sent the photo to Steven, she knew about Rab… Rab. The thought winded me for a second time. A part of me had always suspected but I drove the suspicion away. It couldn't be him. Not Rab. I had pushed the thought down like a float in a swimming pool and, at my least suspecting moment, it

158

had hit me full force in the face. I didn't know how to feel or what to think.

Emily lingered in the doorway.

"I'm assuming you heard that entire conversation." I whispered.

She looked at me guiltily. "I'm sorry Mhairi. The walls in this house are paper thin."

I ran a hand through my hair in exasperation.

"Do you... want to talk about it?"

I shrugged. "You know everything anyway."

"Yes but talking it through can help... do you know what you're going to do about it?"

"Well normally I would go to Rab for advice..." I snorted. I put my head in my hands, attempting to shelter it from the blow.

I felt Emily's hand on my back. "You couldn't have known, Mhairi."

"I should have known, Emily. It's my job to know these things. I should have worked it out. I need to deal with this in a professional manner but... Rab? How on earth am I going to speak to Rab?"

Emily sat for a while, choosing her words carefully. "This could all be a big misunderstanding, Mhairi. You've only got Donna's words to go on. You need to speak to Rab with an open mind. Innocent until proven guilty."

"Rab is my friend, Emily. I've known him since I was six years old. How am I supposed to talk to him about this?"

"You've just got to be patient with yourself. You're not talking to him as his friend. You are talking to him as his Boss. You're doing this for Beth Anderson, remember. You're giving that wee girl a voice."

My eyes filled with tears.

"Everything you do has to be for that wee girl, Mhairi. She needs you. You can't let her down."

I nodded soberly. My life would have to be put to one side. I needed to focus on my job more than ever. I was giving Beth Anderson the voice I never had. I rose from the stool and went in search of my jacket.

"Mhairi, where are you going?"

"I'm going to the Campbell's Croft before I lose my nerve."

"Do you not want to talk it out first, Mhairi? I think you're too emotionally charged at the moment."

"If I don't do it now, I never will. I need to confront Rab. I need to know the truth once and for all."

The journey from Emily's house to the Campbell croft, although in reality it only took a few minutes, seemed to take an eternity. In that time, I played through every scenario I could think of. Would he be angry? Sad? Defensive? I had no idea how he would react. I just hoped I would be able to have a rational conversation with him. I couldn't let my temper get the better of me.

The Campbell Croft looked so still in the evening glow. The sun was close to setting, casting a tapestry of light across the house. It looked so calm and quiet. The Campbells remained unaware of the violent storm that was going to tear them apart limb from limb. The reality of my actions came to the forefront of my mind. How could I do this to the Campbells? I had known them for most of my life. They were family. Tears began to gather in my eyes but I brushed them away. I had to think of Beth Anderson. I was doing this for her.

I knocked on the door with confidence I did not possess. My heart was pounding in my ears. A minute stretched into forever. Eventually, Tom answered the door.

His eyes were hollow, red raw. In just a matter of hours, he had aged tenfold. He stooped, his frame exhausted with effort as he leaned against the door. The wind had been taken from my sails.

"Tom?" I whispered, searching for answers in his empty expression. "what's the matter?"

He continued to stare at me. I could hear the muffled sound of crying from inside the house. He moved to one side, indicating that I should go in. There was no sign of life in the living room. The inaudible cries continued, coming from one of the rooms upstairs. I turned to Tom.

"Where is Rab?" I asked, sounding braver than I felt.

"He's upstairs with Mum."

I sighed. It was all too clear what had happened. "He told you then." I whispered.

"What?"

"About what happened. I'm assuming Rab told you."

Tom looked puzzled. "Mhairi, what are you talking about?"

I paused. "About Beth Anderson."

Suddenly, a flurry of footsteps erupted from the stairs.

"Tom, who was that at the-" Rab stopped when he saw me. "V. What are you doing here?"

"Rab I need to talk to you. It's urgent."

"Mhairi, this really isn't a good time."

"Is there really ever going to be a good time to talk about this, Rab?"

He looked perplexed for a moment but then the penny dropped. He looked at me with absolute horror. "Mhairi I... we can't talk about this now. This is not a good time."

"Rab you can't just-"

Tom erupted. "Dad is dead, Mhairi!"

I stopped abruptly and turned to look at Tom.

"Dad died, Mhairi." He said more gently, his eyes locked with mine. "a couple of hours ago."

I opened my mouth to say something but the words would not come. I looked from Tom to Rab and back again. "I..."

"As Rab said, this is not a good time, Mhairi." Said Tom, quietly but firmly. "Whatever you need to say can wait."

My sense of purpose had vanished, leaving me floundering.

"We need you to leave, Mhairi. Please." Tom tried to be firm, but his voice broke with emotion.

Rab continued to stare at me, a panicked expression on his face.

I cleared my throat. "Right. Yes. I'm… sorry for your loss." I left, not daring to look at Tom or Rab. I left the house as quickly as I had come.

As I walked down the path, a voice called from behind me.

"Mhairi, wait."

I stopped in my tracks. It was Rab.

"Mhairi… V…"

"What?"

"…about Beth."

I stared at his face long and hard and then exhaled. "Your father has just died, Rab. Go and be with your family."

"But I have to explain-"

"Any explaining you need to do can be done tomorrow."

"Please don't tell anyone, Mhairi. Please."

I stopped in my tracks. "Do you really think that little of me, Rab? Do you really think I would wander around the town like some demented minstrel sharing the news of your exploits?"

Rab winced. "That's not what I meant."

"Your father is barely cold and you're more interested in self-preservation."

"V, come on. That's not fair."

"Oh we are talking about fair now? Is it fair for Beth Anderson? Is it fair for your family?"

"Mhairi, please stop."

"Oh I'm sorry. Is the truth not pretty enough for you?"

Rab sighed. "Who told you?"

"That doesn't matter, Rab."

"But what if they…"

I shot him a look and he stopped mid-sentence. "They've kept silent for this long, Rab. They had the sense to come to me with this. Unlike you."

"What was I supposed to say?"

"Anything! Anything at all! This whole time you've let me play detective in a mystery of your own making. You've wasted so much time, potential… but most of all you have wasted the life of a sixteen year old girl."

"It wasn't like that, V. If you could just give me some time to explain-"

"It's no use, Rab. The damage is done. Your family needs you right now."

"Mhairi I…"

"Go and be with your family. Mourn the loss of your father."

"Can we talk about this tomorrow, V? I will explain everything. I promise."

I nodded gravely. "The truth has a way of finding its way to the surface, Rab. Remember that."

Chapter Twelve

It had been peaceful in the end for Alan Campbell. He had come into the house during the day, complaining of a sore head. Mary had convinced him to have a lie down to see if he could sleep it off. When he hadn't emerged hours later, she went to check on him. To most observers, he looked like he was still sleeping. After a long battle with ill health, he had finally found peace. However, this peace had rocked the very foundations of the Campbell family.

I had mixed emotions about Alan's death. On one hand, I hated to think that Mary, Rab and Tom were suffering. I didn't like to see them in pain. However, I couldn't help but feel a sense of relief. A part of my agony had died with Alan and a great weight had been lifted from my shoulders. I had no remorse at his passing. I would go as far to say that I was glad. Due to these feelings, I felt I couldn't support the family the way I should. Rab's potential guilt was merely another spanner in my altogether muddy mind.

***

On Monday morning, I went into school early. I had to prepare myself for my conversation with Rab. I hadn't contacted him over the weekend. It thought that would be too cruel given the circumstances. I wanted to give him a couple of days before bringing in the next shit storm. I owed him that much.

The minutes ticked past, fast approaching the beginning of the school day. There was still no sign of him. I grew concerned. Although he was sometimes disorganised, Rab had never been late for a day of work since I'd started at the High School. When the school bell rang, I dialled through to Donna.

"Hi Donna. Have you heard anything from Rab this morning?"

"I thought he had told you, Mhairi. He's taking two weeks of compassionate leave."

"Oh. Yes of course." I was a little taken aback. It wasn't surprising after our confrontation at his house he hadn't wanted to talk.

"The funeral is next week."

"Right. Yes. Thank you Donna." I quickly hung up the phone.

After everything that had happened, could I bring myself to attend the funeral? I didn't relish the thought of paying my respects to Alan. It was another trial for another day. My mind was awash with noise and I could not bear yet another difficult decision. I busied myself with emails until there was a knock at my door.

"Come in." I called absentmindedly.

"Can I have a word?"

I whirled round in my chair. Iris stood in the doorway. I stared at her for a moment, trying to gauge her expression. I hadn't spoken to Iris for a few weeks now. To begin with, I attempted to make conversation with her. Latterly I hadn't bothered.

Iris stood awkwardly, fidgeting with her watch. "I wanted to chat to you about Nathan. He has been going through a rocky patch of late. Things have gotten quite tense at home."

I sat still, not daring to say anything.

"He's always been a socially awkward boy but lately he hasn't been speaking to me at all. I am so worried about him. That episode at the boat really frightened me. I have never seen him like that before."

"I understand, Iris. It's been really difficult for you both."

"Nathan mentioned he had spoken to you."

I paused. "Yes. Yes he did."

Iris hesitated. "So he told you the baby isn't his?"

I exhaled. "Yes."

"And you believe him?"

"I don't think Nathan would lie about something like that, Iris. So yes, I believe hm."

Iris nodded. The silence in the room was deafening. "I guess what I'm trying to say is… thank you. It really means a lot that he had someone to confide in. Not many people are being as kind."

"I'm sorry, Iris. I'm sorry you've had to go through this."

She smiled weakly, her eyes filling with tears. "Yes well. What doesn't kill you makes you stronger... or something like that. For what it's worth... I didn't believe that you would spread the gossip about Beth. Just didn't sit right with me."

"The problem with professing your innocence is that it often makes you look more guilty."

"Yes I guess that's true. Anyway, I best go. Thanks again, Mhairi. It means a lot."

"Any time."

Iris gave me one final look before leaving the office.

I was relived she didn't speculate over who the father was. I hoped the rest of the village didn't find out about Rab until I had the opportunity to speak to him myself. I needed to know the truth. I had jumped to the worst conclusion and until I heard his side of the story I would find it difficult to believe anything otherwise.

***

I worked late into the evening, sorting the last of the boxes in the office. It was a different room from when I first arrived. The trail of coffee cups which once adorned the office like mismatched decorations had vanished. The piles of paper were no longer scattered haphazardly around the room like jenga towers. The dust that once decorated the shelves and surfaces had vanished. There was a new sense of order and structure, with old documents filed and everything else culled. I looked around, admiring the work I had been steeped in since my arrival. It had taken the best part of five months but I could finally see the fruits of my labour. Things in the school were finally beginning to take shape. Just as, ironically, the rest of my life had fallen apart.

I left the school building searching for a breath of fresh air. I took my usual route round the loch, gazing at the peaceful village that lay at the other side. It was hard to believe the turmoil occurring in the village from this still scene. Suddenly my phone vibrated in my pocket. I answered it automatically.

"Hello?"

"Mhairi?"

My heart stopped. A rush of memories and emotion accompanied that voice. "Steven? Is that you?"

The line crackled with the wind. "Yeah, it's me."

"I've been trying to call... it went straight to voicemail."

"I actually turned my phone off."

"Ah, I see."

"I just needed some time, you know?"

"Yes. I get that." I paused. "How are you? How are things?"

"Good, yeah. Still in Inverness."

"Good, good. That's great."

"What about you? How are... things?"

"Yeah things are... things are ok."

There was a pause as we both drew breath.

Steven was the first to speak. "I've been thinking a lot, Mhairi. I needed the time to think."

"Yes, I understand that."

"I've thought a lot about everything that's happened and about us and what we want."

"So… what were your thoughts then?"

"Well… we've been together a long time, you know? Getting engaged and married seemed like the next step really. The only thing is… I'm not sure if that's right anymore. I've always wanted to get married, Mhairi. More than anything. I've always wanted to have a family to look after and stuff. I wanted all the things my mother took from me when she left my father. That's always been the end goal for me. I think I had convinced myself that you wanted all of that too but… now I'm not really sure. When we moved around with your work I always thought we'd eventually stop and settle down. You applying for that job… it surprised me. I had thought we were finally on the same page and suddenly you were ready to move again. You were always ready to move on."

I sighed. "Honestly…I'm not really sure what I want, Steven."

"I think you do, Mhairi. Deep down, you know exactly what you want. You just don't want to admit it to yourself. I guess… actions speak louder than words, Mhairi. Looking back at everything that has happened… that's what stands out to me. Moving around, not wanting to get married, that stuff that happened with Tom…" his voice cracked a little. "That was really hard at the time. I was really upset. But then I started to wonder if maybe…"

"Maybe what?"

"Maybe it was the thing that would put an end to the game we're playing."

"Game?"

"We've been pretending, Mhairi. Pretending we both want the same things. That is a fairy-tale and it's time for us both to wake up."

My eyes filled with tears. "I'm sorry Steven."

"You're very ambitious, Mhairi. You always have been. I had tricked myself into thinking you'd change or settle or finally be satisfied but it was never going to happen. We want different things and I think it's time I accepted that."

I exhaled, the tears rushing down my cheeks. "You deserve better, Steven."

"Yeah well… I don't know about that. Bye Mhairi."

The line went dead. I clutched my phone to my chest and continued walking, dusk settling around the hills.

The conversation I had with Steven made everything seem so final. Our relationship, which had lasted the best part of two decades, was over. I had clung to Steven for all those years because it seemed like the right thing to do. I hadn't broken up with him because I didn't have a reason to. He was my rock, my safety net. He was always there when things got a little too tough. One slip had frayed the safety net. What was once my worst nightmare was now a reality… and the world did not end.

My love for Steven had changed, I couldn't deny it now. My emotions subtly shifted over the years and I was unaware until I was forced to face them. I loved Steven but not in the way that constitutes a marriage. He was woven intricately into the tapestry of my life but it was finally time to move on and let that part of me go. Our love was merely a memory, a chapter written and read in a book. It was time to move on, to blaze a new trail. Steven deserved a better love than me.

I don't know why but I instinctively returned to the cottage instead of the comfort of Emily' house. I only realised when I opened the door, face to face with my recent past and once destined future. It felt like Steven was everywhere. Being in the place we shared was an odd sensation- I felt comforted but also uneasy. I was dancing on the knife edge of my emotions. I felt like I was already a different person than I was two weeks ago. The ground underneath my entire life had shifted.

I called Emily and told her I'd be staying at the cottage again. I said I would pick up my things in the morning and thanked her for her hospitality. I had felt bad intruding on Emily's kindness for so long and relished the thought of being in my own space. She had been an unbelievable friend to me in the wake of disaster and I had done nothing to deserve it. Instead of showering me with blame, she took my hand. I recalled what Bill Rodgers had said some time ago-in the face of adversity, you find out who your real friends are.

My first night back in the cottage was the best night's sleep I'd had in a long time. I was free to sleep exactly as I liked- right in the middle of the bed with my limbs hanging off at each corner. I stretched and tossed and turned to my heart's content.

As I busied myself getting ready for work, my mobile rang. I groaned when I saw a familiar name flash up on the screen.

"Mum, Hi."

"Mhairi darling, it's good to speak to you. I was worried when our last call ended so abruptly."

My thoughts returned to that evening at the beach. "Yeah sorry the signal... dropped."

"You'd think they'd have improved the signal up there by now. In an age with fibre broadband you'd think they'd have mastered a simple telephone connection."

I grunted in response as I finished getting ready for work.

"So what's new with you, Mhairi? You didn't really tell me much the last time we spoke."

"Same old, Mum. Work is still busy."

"That's always the answer I get when I phone you, dear. What else has been happening? Surely your entire existence isn't based on your job?"

"That's what being a Headteacher is, Mum."

"Even someone who works as ridiculous hours as you do needs a little downtime with her fiancé."

I sighed.

"You never tell me anything, Mhairi. Any news I need to squeeze out of you. I am interested in your life, darling. I care."

"I know, Mum." I said unenthusiastically.

"What about the rest of your life, hmm? What about Steven, dear? How is his business going?"

"Fine, I think."

"You think? Do you two not talk about these things?"

I hesitated. "Actually Mum... Steven and I aren't together anymore."

The gasp at the other end of the line was very audible. "What? What do you mean 'not together'?"

"We broke up, Mum. These things happen. Steven is in Inverness."

"Is that it? You're not going to talk to him Mhairi? You've been together forever, darling. You can't just throw that all away."

"We have spoken, Mum. We were both in agreement. I really do think it's for the best."

"Steven is a catch, darling. You can't just let that one get away."

"Mum, it's over. It's been over for a while."

"Relationships aren't smooth sailing, Mhairi. They must be worked at. You must persevere. That's what makes a long lasting relationship."

"Steven and I weren't destined to be together, Mum. Our relationship was twenty years too long it seems."

"I'm thinking only of your best interests, dear. I'm worried you're making a mistake, that's all."

I sighed. In Mum's eyes, Steven was the golden boy. He was a beacon of hope. "I know what you think Mum but I've made my decision."

"You're so stubborn, Mhairi Sinclair. Just like your father."

"I know what I want. Surely that isn't a bad thing?"

"I knew your move was a mistake."

"That has nothing to do with it, Mum."

"It has everything to do with it, Mhairi. You and Steven were happy in Glasgow."

"Our relationship would still be over if we stayed. I needed to move here for me, Mum. Glasgow had nothing to do with our relationship."

There was a silence on the other end as Mum chose her words carefully, like an archer preparing his killing bow. "Well. You lost your chance at happiness, darling. Was Allaban really worth it?"

"But Mum I wasn't actually happy."

"Yes you were. You were very happy in Glasgow with Steven."

I groaned, exasperated. "You're not listening, Mum. You never listen. I wasn't happy with Steven. I've never been truly happy with Steven. It wasn't fair on either of us if we stayed together."

"I am your Mother, Mhairi Anne Sinclair. I am just trying to be the voice of reason here. I know you. You're letting your stubbornness cloud your judgement, darling."

"Thank you for your opinion once again, Mum." I hissed and hung up the phone. This was why I chose to keep Mum in the dark. She often muddled my feelings with her own agenda.

The day at work dragged. My brain was all over the place and I was having trouble pining it down. I needed to focus. The school day had been uneventful which I welcomed. It was nice to escape all the drama even if it was only for one day.

Suddenly, my phone screen lit up. It was a text from Rab:

"Meet me at the Loch?"

I sighed. I had been trying to phone Rab for days but it went straight to voicemail. I had texted him a dozen times but they had all gone unanswered... until now.

I replied: *"Yes. Be there in ten."*

I grabbed my jacket and headed out into the cool night air. Darkness had settled onto the hills and I hadn't noticed. I began my usual walk around the loch but with a renewed sense of vigour. I could see him at the far end, a silhouette against the dark sky. He looked at me sheepishly as I approached. He was no longer the confident man I had known for most of my life. I had never seen this side of him before. We stood in silence and stared at each other for a long time.

"Rab..." I began, unsure of what to say.

"So you know."

I nodded soberly.

"How long have you known for?"

"A few days now."

"Who told you?"

"As I said before...that doesn't matter."

Rab sighed. "I guess I knew this was going to happen eventually. I had just hoped you wouldn't be the one to find out first. It's not what you think, V. I know you think the worst of me but it wasn't like that. I need you to hear the real story, Mhairi. For me. Let me tell you everything before you judge me."

It had started during the summer. Rab had not long escaped another relationship and was feeling pretty low about it. He had decided to take an evening stroll around the village with a bottle of whisky as his companion. The drink was starting to do its work when he ran into Beth Anderson. Her face had been full of worry as he tried to maintain his composure. She ended up walking with him while he poured his heart out. It wasn't one of his finest moments. He woke up the next day full of regret and shame. He called Beth and apologised profusely for his actions. She had been so understanding and they ended up chatting on the phone for a long time. She was so easy to talk to. She seemed far older than her years. They started texting a lot and Beth eventually suggested they meet up again. Rab had been nervous at first but convinced himself it was a harmless get together. He was attracted to her but Beth didn't see him in that way. He was wrong. He hadn't meant for it to get so out of hand. Their relationship remained a secret. Rab knew that it was wrong but he couldn't help himself. He was drawn to her. They were always very careful not to be caught but there had been a few near misses. One night when they had been dangerously close to being found out, they had fought about it. Rab could lose his job and any prospect of future employment. He ended it and Beth was devasted.

When Beth ran out of the Morning Assembly, he knew something was wrong. They couldn't talk at school so instead met up that night. Beth had told him that she'd been feeling sick for a few days and her period was late. A pregnancy test only confirmed what she already knew. Rab wanted to support Beth and his baby. He knew they couldn't be together but he said he'd give her money. He wanted to look out for her. When the news broke, the village suspected Nathan. As long as that lie was in circulation, he could keep his job and support Beth. They talked about running away together.

Rab looked at me expectantly. My whole body was numb with the cold but I barely noticed. I tried to see Rab as the boy I had known all my life. I tried to have an open mind. The anger fizzed beneath my burning skin. "She is a child, Rab." I whispered, unable to look him in the eye. "How could you do this to a child?"

"I love her, V. I know you don't believe me but I really do love her."

"She is sixteen, Rab. You are thirty-nine. That's twenty-three years of an age gap. Can you not hear how deluded you sound?"

"I know how it sounds, Mhairi. Why do you think I've kept it a secret for this long?"

"Maybe because you're a coward who is in a relationship with a sixteen year old girl?"

I could see the pain in Rab's eyes. "You're my friend, V. I need you to listen to me."

"I am your friend, Rab. However, I am also your Boss. It seems I am the only one acting professionally here." I took a deep breath and tried to compose myself. "Here is the deal. I will go to the police about this. That is my job."

Rab looked at me with alarm, his eyes pleading.

"I will go to the police… in two days. That gives you two days to come clean yourself. You can talk to Beth and do what you have to do before turning yourself in. That's all I'm giving you, Rab. Two days." I left before I could hear his reply.

Chapter Thirteen

In the end, I had given Rab four days. I wish I had a better reason but, ultimately, I found it difficult to turn him in. As much as I wanted to deny it, Rab's story had hit a nerve. It really did seem that he cared about Beth Anderson. Also, even after everything that had happened, Rab was still my friend. I couldn't deny that this man was a big influence in my life. It felt like a betrayal. To me, he was still the boy who I teased, fought with and loved like a brother. Losing him would be like surrendering a piece of my childhood.

I had sat outside the police station for at least an hour, arguing with myself. To any passing car, I must have looked crazy… and perhaps I was. I had two voices in my head competing for attention. I fitted perfectly into the 'crazy' category. I just hoped that Rab had beaten me to the police station. I clung to this hope with both hands.

I had to physically drag myself out of the car and into the station. I had seen the village policeman around but, thankfully, had never had any dealings with him. He was a pleasant enough man. Despite his tired appearance, he listened to me attentively and took copious notes. He asked for every intimate detail of my story, picking it apart and stitching it neatly back together again many times over. I attempted to detach from it but failed miserably. We had to stop the interview a few times as I tried to compose myself. He waited with patience and kindness. He kept offering me cups of coffee which I accepted but started to make me jitter.

"Thank you very much for your time today, Miss Sinclair. I can appreciate that coming here was not an easy thing to do."

"No problem."

"Your statement today will remain completely anonymous. I will be in touch to make some follow-up enquiries. If you don't hear from me for a while, be assured that this case is being taken very seriously. I will follow every line of enquiry. This may mean it will take some time before I speak to you again."

I nodded solemnly.

"In the meantime, if there is anything you would like to add to your statement that you've forgotten, please do not hesitate to give me a ring. Here's my number." He slid a card across the table. "Thank you again for coming here today. That took a great deal of courage."

Courage? I felt like a coward. Not only had I reported one of my closest friends to the police, it had taken me four days to do it. Neither of the voices in my head were particularly happy with me.

***

I went into work the next day, my head still fuzzy. The school had been transformed overnight, covered from head to toe in Christmas decorations. Was it December already? The calendar on my computer confirmed it, suspending my disbelief. Silver tinsel lined the corridors, looking sparse and a little sad. I was relieved to see that my office had not been affected by the sudden eruption of holiday cheer. There was a tentative knock on the door and Donna popped her head in.

"Hi Mhairi. Sorry to disturb you."

I raised my head from my paperwork. "No problem Donna. What can I do for you?"

She carefully closed the door and assumed Rab's seat. "I just wanted to ask…" Donna twitched nervously. "…if you had heard anything from Rab?"

"The situation is well in hand, Donna."

"Yes, of course. I understand. You just hadn't mentioned it so I wanted to check everything was ok."

"I can't share any other details about the matter but be rest assured that it will be taken care of."

"Ok. I'm glad. I understand it puts you in a very difficult situation."

"It all comes with the job."

There was an awkward pause.

"So…" Donna began, attempting to fill the awkward gap. "Are you ok?"

I gave her a bemused look. "Yes. I'm fine. I assume you're coming to the Christmas Concert this week?" I was desperate to change the subject. Discussing my personal life with Donna was not high on my priority list.

"Yes, I'll be there. I'm always in charge of the raffle. It's a really good night, actually. It's very well attended by those in the village."

"That's good."

"How is Sophie getting on with the organising?"

Sophie, our resident Music Teacher, was anything but calm about the Christmas Concert. She had started rehearsing the acts in October and seemed to come to me on a daily basis on the brink of a meltdown.

"Yeah it's all going fine. Sophie is very organised."

"She is indeed."

***

After everything that happened, my work/life balance was non-existent. When I wasn't in the school building, I was at home sleeping or eating a microwave meal. I knew this wasn't healthy but I couldn't help it. Throwing myself into my work was my way of coping. It always had been. My personal life was crumbling all around me and there was nothing I could do to stop it. All I could do was simply watch the devastation unfold. My only friend was Emily.

"Donna seems to be making more of an effort, Mhairi. That's nice." Emily said as she sipped her gin and tonic and I poured out my soul.

"I guess. It's just so awkward."

"Give it a little time. Things will settle. If I'd told you a couple of months ago that you and Donna were on speaking terms you would never have believed me."

I shrugged. "True."

"Have you heard any more from Steven?"

"He is still in Inverness as far as I know. He is coming up at some point to collect the rest of his stuff though I don't know when."

Emily smiled sympathetically. "How are you feeling about that?"

I let out a dry laugh. "I feel like I should be lying on a chaise longue with a pack of tissues in my hand."

"Oh I'm sorry."

"Don't be. I've never had a therapist who gave me gin on arrival."

"Don't worry- I'm charging it all to expenses."

We both laughed.

Emily looked at me thoughtfully. "Seriously though... how are you?"

"I'm fine. Breaking up with Steven was for the best. I feel more like myself than I have done in a long time. It's just quite new and I'm still getting used to it."

"It's amazing what time can do."

"Yes it is." I took a thoughtful sip of my gin. "I meant to ask... are you coming to the Christmas Concert this week?"

"I usually do."

"It would be really nice if you were there, Emily."

Emily smiled. "In that case, I wouldn't miss it for the world."

The Christmas Concert was the last place I wanted to be. However, as Head Teacher, it was an expectation that I attended. It would be a good distraction, I guess. On the day of the Concert, Sophie was running around the school like a headless chicken. The Assembly Hall had been transformed for the occasion- multi-coloured Christmas lights donned the ceiling and decorations were dotted on the walls. A modest Christmas tree stood in the corner, littered with ornaments hand-crafted by the pupils. The room was awash with performers for the entire day, an eclectic mix of ensembles filling the rickety wooden stage. I approached Sophie tentatively as she organised the chairs and music stands on the stage like an intricate game of Jenga.

"Anything I can help with?"

She gave me a strained smile. "Everything is under control. Just having final rehearsals with all of the ensembles ahead of tonight. The lighting is sorted, the stage is set, the raffle is set up... and I'm exhausted."

"There are plenty of people on hand if you need help, myself included."

"Thanks, Mhairi. I really appreciate it."

"Don't do everything by yourself, Sophie. Let some other members of the faculty help. Lighten the load a little."

"Yes. I will."

"I was planning to say a few words before the concert if that's ok?"

"Yes that's fine. I'll get the orchestra on the stage after you're finished."

"Excellent. Again, if you need anything, you know where to find me."

Sophie flashed me a strained smile before returning to her task. She reminded me a lot of myself in the early days- full of ambition and determination, wanting to blaze a trail on her own. The thought made me smile. It already felt like a lifetime ago.

I decided to stay at work until the concert- it gave me an opportunity to tackle the mountain of paperwork on my desk. As I worked, Rab's face floated into my mind. I hadn't heard anything from him since our meeting at the loch. I was worried about him. I pushed his face from my mind. I had done the right thing- I had to remember that. I couldn't keep his secret any longer.

***

The concert didn't start till 7pm but a lot of the village appeared at 6pm. This was apparently normal- everyone wanted a good seat in the Assembly Hall as the acoustics were terrible. I stood shivering by the front entrance, attempting to warmly greet guests as they arrived. My heart stopped when I spotted Mary and Tom in the crowd. I caught Tom's eye but he turned away, making a beeline for the hall. Mary waved, bustling through the crowd to greet me.

"Lovely to see you again, Mhairi." She said.

"You too, Mary. How are things?"

"Oh, you know. We are muddling through. Nothing else for it. What about you? Rab said you'd practically moved into the school building."

"Having a work/life balance was never one of my strong points, Mary."

"It takes a little practice, Mhairi but you need to be willing to work at it. You need to put yourself first sometimes."

"I'll bear that in mind. How is Rab doing?"

"Just working away as usual. You know what he's like- needs to work through his emotions. He's away down South buying some new equipment for the farm at the moment."

I nodded. "Of course. Things must be really busy for you."

"As far as the farm is concerned it's still business as usual. The cows and sheep don't know anything is different."

"Well I appreciate you making the time to come tonight. It's great to see you."

Mary smiled, her eyes filling with tears. "You too, Mhairi." She pulled me into hug, holding me tight. After a while, I reluctantly let go and she made her way into the Assembly Hall.

I wasn't surprised that Rab hadn't shown up. It was a sensible decision. It would be safer for him to stay away. However, after speaking to her, it also seemed that Mary was still in the dark about his relationship with Beth Anderson. I hoped he would tell her before the news broke. Mary deserved to know the truth but I wasn't going to be the one to tell her. It was Rab's burden to share.

There was a storm brewing outside and it whistled periodically through the open doors, hitting me with a fresh blast of cold night air. The sky had a dark purple hue, threatening to spread it's ripples of rain. Oliver rushed in from the cold evening, clutching tightly to his tweed jacket and hat. He rushed past and into the warm Assembly Hall. I smiled. Not even Oliver Stevenson could stay away from the highlight of the school calendar.

As I approached the dimly lit stage, a hush fell over the audience. I tapped on the mic to make sure it was on but also to silence the murmuring of the crowd. My eyes were drawn automatically to Tom, who was sitting near the front of the crowd. I smiled in his direction but he consciously adverted his gaze. I was suddenly aware that he was sitting beside Donna, holding her hand. Donna was neatly nuzzled into his neck. My heart broke, but I ignored it. I turned my attention to the spotlight burning from the other side of the room.

I cleared my throat. "Good evening, ladies and gentlemen. It is a great honour to be standing here as Headteacher of Allaban High School. As usual, it has been a very busy term and this is the perfect way to end it. We are about to be thoroughly entertained by our young people who have worked extremely hard in preparation for the concert. Rehearsals began as early as October to showcase the best of what Allaban High School has to offer. I would like to take this opportunity to thank each and every one of them for their time and talents this evening." I paused and applause rippled through the crowd. "A school also couldn't function without the dedication and hard work of its staff. As for this event, there is one member of staff I need to thank above all others. Sophie Turner has put on this event pretty much single-handedly. That takes a massive amount of work, creativity and patience. We are so lucky at Allaban that the staff go the extra mile for our pupils and Sophie Turner is no exception. Last but certainly not least, I would like to thank all of you. Our pupils are performing to a full house tonight. That couldn't be possible without your support as parents, guardians and friends. I feel lucky to be involved in a village community that supports and cares for one another."

My eye was drawn to the double doors leading out of the room as they swung open. The policeman I had spoken to a few days previous stood at the back of the hall.

I smiled a warmly as I could muster to the audience. "Thank you all. I now have the pleasure of introducing the talented young people of Allaban High School." The hall erupted with applause as the first act made their way to the stage. I slinked to the back of the hall towards the policeman.

"Can I have a word?" he whispered.

I nodded and we both stepped outside. I did not want to give the audience another show.

"Can I help you, officer?" I said, drawing my arms around my body as it adjusted to the cold night air.

He sighed. "It seems the enquiry you raised with me a few days ago has taken an unprecedented turn."

I looked at him in surprise. "What do you mean by that?"

"I have been following many lines of enquiry since our meeting, Miss Sinclair. We were making good progress until the case changed unexpectedly. In light of this, I must collect another statement from you. It is crucial for this investigation."

"I appreciate that but... I don't understand. What new turn are you talking about?"

"When you first approached me, this investigation was purely a suspected rape. However, since we last spoke, the perpetrator in question has been unavailable for questioning."

All the colour drained from my face. "Are you telling me that…"

"We have reason to believe that Mr Campbell has fled the village following the beginning of this investigation, Miss Sinclair. It is now imperative that I collect a fresh statement from you in order to determine his whereabouts."

"Of course, officer. Anything I can do to help."

"Thank you, Miss Sinclair. You are very obliging. If you could come to the police station immediately I would be very grateful."

"Yes. No problem. Can I just ask… who else is aware of this situation?"

"No one that I know of… at the moment. This is a very small village, Miss Sinclair. Word travels fast."

In spite of the cold night, I broke out in a fierce sweat. "Yes. Yes it does."

Chapter Fourteen

I ended up having to abandon the Christmas Concert. I sat in the station for what felt like an eternity, going over and over my final encounter with Rab. Did we argue? What was his state of mind at that time? Did he mention wanting to run? I attempted to recall but the memory had become faint. I left the police station unsure if I'd been any help at all.

Rab had well and truly vanished. He had left for a farmers market the morning of the Christmas Concert, promising to return later that evening but he never came back. I had tried to call him dozens of times but they all went straight to voicemail. Rab's reason for leaving the village, as far as the locals were concerned, was shrouded in mystery. Many people suspected the worst but no one mentioned Beth or the baby. Rab's secret was still safely tucked away. With any luck, it would stay that way. As far as I knew, the only people who knew the truth were Beth, Donna, Emily and Me. The rest of the village were blissfully unaware. A few people had probed me for answers but I'd managed to deflect them. They suspected I knew more than I was letting on but I stayed silent.

Rab's disappearance hit the Campbell family hard. Mary had not long come to terms with the death of her husband when her eldest son had vanished. She and Tom worked tirelessly to look after the farm and prepare for the funeral. A tall order without the mixture of grief and worry.

I had almost gone to the Croft a few times but decided against it. There would be too many questions and I didn't want to paint myself into a corner. It would be better than Mary and Tom thought I didn't care rather than caring too much.

The whole situation made my stomach churn. Rab's disappearance was my fault. Had I not confronted him that day maybe he wouldn't have fled. I replayed the scene over and over again in my head, hoping to see myself in a better light. In the end, I was still the villain in my own memory.

"You couldn't have known, Mhairi." Said Emily, reassuring me. We both sat in her kitchen drinking gin. I was there so often that George had joked about me helping with the mortgage.

"I just wish I hadn't been as hard on him, Emily. Maybe if I'd been more understanding he would still be here."

Emily shrugged. "He's a grown man. He can make his own decisions whether we perceive them to be right or wrong."

"I'm so worried about Mary and Tom. They're having to run the farm and organise a funeral at the same time. Alan's body is barely cold and she has lost her eldest son too."

"He'll turn up, Mhairi. Either the police will find him or he will come to his senses. Let's just hope it's the latter."

"It's been a week, Emily. Do you not think the police would have found him by now?"

"Maybe they have. We don't know that."

"In this village? We would know. I just think if he was going to come back he would have by now. His father's funeral is tomorrow."

"Are you going?"

I shrugged. "I don't know. I don't think the Campbells would want me there."

"Of course they would. You're practically family."

"The last time I went to the Croft, I picked a fight with Rab while Alan was lying dead in other room. Not my finest hour."

"Mhairi." Emily put a hand on my shoulder. "You need to stop beating yourself up about this. You weren't to know about Alan. They don't hate you for that. You said yourself that Mary hugged you at the concert."

"That was before I had to leave to give a fresh statement to the police about her son's disappearance."

"We are going round and round in circles here. You should go to the funeral. You'd feel awful if you didn't."

Emily was right. I would never forgive myself if I didn't support Mary and Tom in their time of need. Tom. I recalled seeing him and Donna looking very much together at the concert. I neglected to mention this part of the story to Emily.

"It's just a quick service at the church. You don't even need to go to the Allaban Hotel afterwards. Just show face. I'll come with you."

I smiled weakly. "You are far too nice to me, Emily."

"That's what friends are for. Who else have I got to indulge my gin addiction?"

***

The morning of the funeral was the coldest of the year. Frost dusted the grass surrounding the church, giving the morning a more ominous feel. It crunched icily under my feet as my made my way to the building. My warmth breath felt laboured with effort, shocked by the freezing air. The sky was bright and clear over the village, seemingly unaware of the sorrow which hung in the air. I hurried up the path with only a couple of minutes to spare.

The church was full to the brim. The Campbells were a well-liked and respected family in the village, although I was unsure how much of that was because of Alan. I clocked Emily waving, sitting in the back pew. I slid in beside her, grateful of the company. It would normally be Steven I would be sitting next to. His presence alone always made me feel more calm. I did not like funerals. Every one I attended reminded me too much of my Grandma.

The service was very short which I was grateful for. The minister said a few words about Alan, his life and his family. I tuned out and instead focused my attention on Mary and Tom. I could see Mary's shoulders shaking in the front row, subtly at first but soon becoming heavy and laboured. Tom put his arm around her, attempting to settle her sobs. She was a woman who was grieving twofold- for the death of her husband and her missing son. The guilt sat in my stomach like a stone. At the end, a large red drape was drawn in front of the coffin. Suddenly, the reality struck. All of the pain and suffering from my childhood was laid to rest behind a velvet curtain. In that moment, it still felt very much alive, burning in my stomach, eating my contentment whole.

The congregation exited the church row by row from the front. I ducked my head as Tom and Mary walked past. I told myself this was a sign of respect but in reality I couldn't bear to look at either of them. Emily and I were among the last to leave the church, waiting until all the other rows had emptied.

Emily touched my hand. "Come to the hotel. Just for a little bit."

"I really don't think that's a good idea."

"Come on. I pulled the short straw by driving. At least you can have a drink."

"What if I have to speak to Mary? Or even worse… what about Tom?"

"They'll be too busy making small talk with the rest of the village. We can sneak in and out undetected."

"Ok fine."

As we arrived at the hotel, we were ushered into a small room towards the back. It smelled faintly of whisky and tobacco. An array of tables were squished into the tiny room, making it feel even more cramped. A table was set out at the far end boasting a small selection of soft drinks. I could see Tom in the far corner of the room, talking quietly to Donna.

"Drink?" asked Emily.

I nodded and Emily disappeared. I was suddenly alone in the bustling crowd.

I was glad Emily had convinced me to make an appearance at the funeral. Mary had been so good to me over the years. However, I was glad I had managed to avoid speaking to the Campbells. I had no idea what I would say, especially to Tom.

"Mhairi?" called a voice. My thoughts disintegrated. Tom was standing in front of me.

I was taken aback. "Tom. Hi."

"Can we talk?"

"Yeah of course."

He looked around. "Not here."

Tom took my hand and lead me out of the room. We went through a labyrinth of corridors until we came to a set of double doors leading to the back of the hotel. Tom threw them open, the cool air welcome on my face. The back yard was empty and sad, with only a cluster of kegs beside a dustbin. Tom sat on one and began searching his pockets.

"What are we doing out here, Tom?"

"I wanted to talk to you and I didn't want an audience." Tom pulled a pack of cigarettes from his pocket and a small orange lighter. "Sorry. Do you want one?"

"No thanks."

Tom lit up and exhaled deeply, loosening his black tie. "The attention in there was smothering."

"Yeah I can imagine."

"Was it like that at Sadie's funeral?"

"I can't really remember. I was so young."

Tom nodded thoughtfully, taking another drag. "We need to talk, Mhairi."

I looked at him intently.

"That night at the Croft... when Dad... you wanted to speak to Rab."

I nodded. "Yeah it was just school stuff. It wasn't important."

"See... that was the story I got from Rab. I didn't believe him and I don't believe you." My palms were sweaty so I thrust them into the pockets of my jacket.

"You were angry, Mhairi. Why would you be so angry about 'school stuff'? Why did you come to the Croft to confront him about it?"

I shrugged. "I can't really remember, Tom. Whatever it was can't have been that important if I can't remember."

"Stop lying, Mhairi." Tom whispered, his anger bubbling. "You show up and a few days later Rab goes missing. You're keeping something from me just like Rab did. I'd like to know what that secret is."

"It was nothing, Tom."

Tom exhaled, exasperated. "There you go again. I keep trying to talk to you and you keep shutting me out."

"I'm not shutting you out, Tom."

"Oh yeah? What is this then?"

"I'm trying to protect you."

"That ship has sailed, Mhairi. My Dad is dead and my brother is missing. I'm sure I can handle whatever else is thrown at me."

"It has nothing to do with you, Tom. It doesn't matter."

"If it didn't matter so much, why are you talking to the police?"

I remained silent, trying to steady my breathing.

"I saw that policeman at the concert. How do you plan on explaining that one?"

"I need you to trust me, Tom."

"I can't trust you when you keep lying to me, Mhairi!"

"Why can't you just leave it alone?"

"Because I'm worried!" Tom was shouting now.

"I'm worrying you? Who is the one that's shouting? Jesus, Tom."

"You keep pulling these stupid stunts and insist nothing is wrong. Is this another stupid stunt, Mhairi? What have you done this time?"

"I told you. It's nothing. Just try and forget about it."

"I'm scared, Mhairi. I am so scared for you, every single day."

"Well you have a funny way of showing it." I bit back, turning my back on him.

"What is that supposed to mean?"

"I don't know. Maybe you should ask Donna. You two are certainly close these days."

"Forgive me for trying to move on with my life!" Tom exhaled, trying to calm down. "I try to move on but you keeping sucking me back in with your dramatics. It's hard. Do you have any idea how broken I was after you left the first time? It took me years to get over that. Just as I begin to move on in my life, you come strolling back into it. It's been nothing but heartache and drama since you turned up."

I turned to face him. He looked exhausted.

"I can't believe after everything that has happened you don't even have the decency to tell me the truth. This is Rab, Mhairi. He is my brother." He made no attempt to hide the tears. "Just do me a favour… leave me alone. Leave

Mum alone. Go back to Glasgow. Do whatever you like but from now on I'm staying out of it." Tom flicked the butt of his cigarette onto the ground and left.

I sat outside the Allaban Hotel for a long time. I didn't dare go back inside and face Tom again. It had been a mistake to come in the first place. Tom had made it very clear that I wasn't welcome. I had lied to him for so many years. He didn't understand that I was doing it for his own good.

My phone buzzed in my pocket. It was Emily.

"Mhairi! Where did you go? I went to get you a drink and you'd disappeared."

"It's a long story, Emily. I ended up having an argument with Tom."

"Oh no... are you ok?"

"Not really."

"Aww Mhairi... I'm sorry. I'll meet you at the car and we can leave. Okay?"

"Yeah that sounds good to me." I ended the call and sighed, slumping onto a keg. Not telling Tom the truth had been difficult. I had done it to protect him but it ended up tearing us apart.

Emily drove us back to her house. The heavens opened and torrential rain smacked violently against the windscreen. Emily drove cautiously through the winding country roads, rain sloshing on the car roof.

"I don't know what this big secret of yours is Mhairi but… I think you need to tell him."

"What? Are you mad?"

"It just sounds like protecting him from the truth hasn't really worked. It's ruining your relationship."

"I'm just worried that if I tell him the truth it will drive him further away."

"The boy just told you to leave his family alone. Could he be any further away at this moment?"

I sighed.

"You're not kids anymore, Mhairi. You're both grown-ups. Maybe it's time you treat him like one. Whatever your secret is I'm sure he can handle it. It will help you both get past this."

"The truth is really going to hurt him though."

"It'll hurt for a moment but maybe it will heal whatever is keeping you apart."

"I don't know."

"I'm just giving you advice, Mhairi. It is your decision at the end of the day."

"Even if I wanted to tell him the truth… he asked me to stay away."

"Those were words spoken in anger, Mhairi. You cannot take them to heart. I'm sure he didn't mean it. Why not write him a letter? It gives you time to get all of your thoughts down on paper. You can finally tell him how you feel."

I hesitated. "I'll think about it."

We made the rest of the journey back in comfortable silence. Emily was just trying to look out for me but she didn't know about my past. Could Tom and I ever recover the friendship we had lost? Would my secret bring us closer together or drive us further apart?

***

"When should I expect you, darling?" I gathered things from around the cottage to put in my suitcase as I precariously balanced my phone between my ear and shoulder. It was the start of the Christmas holidays and I was going to stay with Mum. She had insisted and I didn't have a good enough reason to refuse.

"I'm hoping to be on the road in the next hour, Mum. It just depends on the traffic. I'll phone you from Perth."

"I just need to know when to put the dinner on, Mhairi darling. You wouldn't want to be having it cold, would you?"

"Just eat without me, Mum. I'll grab something on the way down the road."

"My only daughter is coming home for Christmas. You will have your dinner here."

I sighed. "Fine."

"Make sure to text when you leave, darling. Safe travels."

"Will do." I hung up the phone and continued with my erratic packing. Leaving Allaban for a while was probably a good idea- it would give me a chance to clear my head before the start of the new term. It would be strange leaving Allaban for the bright city lights of Glasgow. I had gotten used to the village. However, I was sure a lot of people would be glad to see the back of me for a while. I had dutifully kept my promise to stay away from Tom and Mary but it was hard. I really missed him. Rab was still nowhere to be found. Where was Rab? I attempted to push these thoughts from my mind and continue packing but my thoughts drifted back to Tom. Why not just tell him the truth? What did I have to lose? Before I had the chance to talk myself out of it, I picked up a pen and some paper and began to write.

Dear Tom,

I've started this letter so many times over the years. I can only apologise that it's fourteen years too late. When we last spoke, you said I was keeping things from you. You're right. I have fourteen years of secrets and lies. It breaks my heart to keep things from you but please know that I did it with good intentions. I didn't want to hurt you or your family. It's important for me to say this now because what I'm about to tell you will change everything.

The final summer I spent at Allaban was not a happy one. I had never intended it to be the last time I saw you but I didn't have a choice. I have never disclosed what happened that summer because I was too ashamed. I could barely admit it to myself- never mind to you. Instead, I spent the rest of my life running from the truth. It was always going to catch up with me in the end.

One afternoon, I came to visit you and Rab after the incident in the barn. I had left it a few days because I wanted you both to work things out. I was a complication so I stayed away. You weren't there. Your father said you'd be home soon and invited me in. I should have said no. Hindsight is a wonderful thing.

He had been drinking. I could smell it on his breath as he spoke. He started touching me in ways I didn't want him to. I begged him to stop but he didn't. Once he'd had his way with me, he let me go and I ran all the way home. My grandma Sadie was there to pick up the pieces.

At the time, I told Mum I was sick and wanted to come home. She didn't believe me but didn't argue. I had to get as far away from Allaban as possible and shut the door on that painful memory. I thought I had successfully buried the past. The only person that knew was Grandma. She never told another soul. I thought I was ready to return to Allaban as Headteacher of the High School. I was wrong.

I'm sorry I didn't tell you this sooner. I was afraid you wouldn't believe me and it would tarnish our relationship forever. Even if you did believe me, how could you look at your father in the same way ever again? I never wanted to leave you or Rab but I had to stay away. This secret has been detrimental to our relationship and for that I am truly sorry. Those are precious years I will never get back.

As far Rab... I can't tell you about that. It's Rab's secret to tell. He will come to you when he is ready, I'm sure of that. I cherish his friendship too much to betray his trust. I hope you can understand that.

After spending years keeping the truth from you, I discovered I had hidden another truth from myself. I love you, Tom. I have always loved you and I always will. I've been too wrapped up in my own mess to realise it. I thought leaving Allaban would alter my feelings for you but they are the same as they've always been. They confused me for a long time but I have come to realise that I cannot bear to be without you.

I hope this letter has shed some light on the past. I'm sorry that it had to come out this way. I'm sorry I have hurt you so much on account of what happened back then. Hopefully now you will understand why. In spite of this, every single time I have fallen, you've always been there to catch me.

I've always been yours.

Mhairi.

I suddenly realised that I had been crying. The ink had gathered in pools of water on the paper. I brushed the tears away. I needed to begin my journey back to Glasgow. I grabbed an envelope and scrawled Tom's name and address on the front. Before thinking it through, I went out to the post box at the end of the street and posted the letter. I resolved to forget about it until my return to Allaban.

As I made my way back to the cottage, my phone rang.

"Sorry to bother you, Miss Sinclair. We need you to come to the police station right away, if possible. It is a matter of urgency."

"Yes of course. I'm on my way." I was puzzled. I had not spoken to the police officer since the evening of the Christmas concert. Had there been a breakthrough? I threw the rest of my things into the car and locked up the cottage for the last time in a while.

"Thank you for attending so promptly, Miss Sinclair." The police officer said as he lead me through the station's maze of corridors. "There's been a development in the case and we needed you here so we could begin the next steps of our enquiry."

"What do you mean by next steps?" I asked.

"All will become clear soon. Follow me." He lead me into a small interview room with only a table and two chairs at either end. A large mirror filled one of the walls. He indicated that I sit and I obliged.

"What is going on?" I said anxiously.

"We just need your co-operation for this next stage of the investigation. I need to record your response for our records."

"Yes of course. Happy to help."

The policeman plucked a tape recorder from his pocket and place it flat on the table. He pressed the record button and muttered some information I didn't understand.

"… Interview with Mhairi Sinclair on 18 December 2019 at 1304 hours. Thank you for being here today, Mhairi. I must ask that you answer these questions honestly and to the best of your knowledge. Can you verbally confirm that you understand?"

"Yes." I said quietly.

The policeman went through many of the questions he had asked me the first evening I reported the crime. I went into as much detail as possible, trying not to distort the memories from the evening I met Rab. The policeman nodded thoughtfully as I gave a brief account of everything I knew.

"…thank you for that information, Mhairi. I am now going to ask you to look at the mirror on the other side of the room. All you have to do is identify the individual on the other side. We will be able to see them but they cannot see us."

I nodded and rose from my chair, edging towards the mirror at the rear of the room. In an instant, a light came on, turning the mirror into a clear panel, not dissimilar to a viewing window at a zoo. He was barely recognisable and yet I recognised him in an instant. I was shocked by the pallor of his appearance, his once full face brimming with life now haggard and gaunt. Had he not been breathing as I watched, I would have assumed him dead. His once well-kept appearance looked jagged and erratic, with more than a five o'clock shadow sprouting from his skin. His clothes were matted with sweat and needlessly clung to him. He sat hunched at the other side of the glass, resigned to his impending fate by his own hands. There was nothing I could do to help him now. My validation of his identity would confirm what the authorities already knew.

I stared at him before exhaling deeply. "That is Robert Campbell."

Chapter Fifteen

"Mhairi darling, you've barely touched your dinner."

It was Christmas Day and I was feeling anything but festive. It was very odd being at home alone with Mum. I had grown so accustomed to Steven being there. He certainly made staying with Mum more bearable. He was the golden boy. I looked at Mum, gave her a brief smile and continued pushing my brussel sprouts around my plate.

In the space of a few months my whole world had been turned upside-down. After I had confirmed that it was indeed Rab in the police station, the policeman had let me go. I rushed to Glasgow in a bid to escape my guilt and arrived at Mum's house after barely pausing for breath. It was only when I finally pulled into her driveway that I realised my feet had gone into cramp and my back had completely seized up. Mum had to help me out of the car. I felt like I was on the brink of emotional collapse. My months in Allaban had stripped me of all of my reserves. I tried and failed to push thoughts of Allaban from my mind. That evening I stumbled to bed, desperate for sleep to carry away my troubles. As desperate as I was it also evaded me. Every time I shut my eyes, all I could see was Rab's weather-beaten face staring back at me through the glass.

I thought leaving Allaban would give me time and space to collect my thoughts. I thought being away from the village would, even for a few days, put my emotional turmoil to rest. It was no use. Being away seemed to make it worse. It was worse not knowing. The whole village would surely know Rab's secret by now. How would Mary and Tom cope with the allegations? What would be the reaction from the Anderson family, their daughter hell-bent on protecting her attacker?

"Mhairi!"

I shook myself free from my thoughts. "Huh?"

Mum was giving me a cold stare. "We are trying to have a nice family meal and all you can do is stare vacantly into space. You've barely said two words to your own mother. Your turkey is getting cold."

I smiled wearily. "Sorry Mum. I'm just tired."

"Have you been taking your vitamin D tablets? I told you to take one a day, darling. We don't get enough natural sunlight in this country."

"It's nothing to do with vitamins, Mum. The first term at school was really exhausting. I think I'm still recovering."

"Why was it so exhausting? What happened?"

"It's a long story."

"Well it would be a welcome change from you staring into space for most of the evening."

"No, I shouldn't. It's confidential and will put a big downer on the Christmas celebrations."

"Now you simply must tell me, Mhairi. You know a good bit of gossip is my weakness. I shan't tell a soul. These lips are sealed."

"There's been a bit of an incident."

"An incident? Sounds very serious."

"Yes well... it is."

"Go on. What happened? What is the big village scandal?"

"One of the girls at the high school is pregnant."

"Pregnant? How old is this girl?"

"She's sixteen. She's a sixth year."

Mum gasped. "Sixteen? My goodness."

"Yes. It's been quite a difficult situation."

"You can't be expected to be involved in this, Mhairi dear. You should definitely not be thinking about it over the holidays. The molly-coddling schools have to do these days. It has nothing to do with you- it is up to the young girl and her parents."

I shifted awkwardly in my seat. "Well actually... the school has to be involved."

Mum raised an eyebrow. "Oh really? And why is that?"

"The father is... a member of staff."

Mum choked on her turkey. "An adult? A teacher?" she spluttered.

"Yes."

"How horrific. Who? Was it that Campbell boy?"

My silence gave the game away.

Mum started at me, aghast. "I knew it. I told you, Mhairi. A leopard cannot change its spots. That Robert Campbell was a disaster from the beginning."

"Now Mum, that's not fair."

"The man took advantage of a pupil. How can you defend him, Mhairi? After all that he's done?"

"You don't know-"

"He knocked up a sixteen year old girl! It's perverted! It's sick!"

"Mum it's-"

"That man has always been a monster. Anyone with a brain can see that. That stupid girl should gotten rid of the evidence while she had the chance."

"Mum!"

"Nothing good can come from something so perverted."

"How can an innocent baby-"

"Innocent? Anything born out of a twisted relationship like that will never be innocent. That girl got what she deserved for being so foolish."

My fist collided with the table as I erupted with anger. I stared at Mum in disbelief, my eyes filling with tears.

"Why are you getting so upset about this Mhairi darling? It's not your fault, dear."

I sniffed and attempted to wipe the tears away. "You don't know the whole story, Mum. You cannot just jump to conclusions-"

Mum put a hand on my arm. "I think I know what's going on."

I looked at her, puzzled. How could she possibly know?

"This is about Steven, isn't it?"

I rolled my eyes, shrugging her arm away.

"Don't roll your eyes at me, Mhairi Anne Sinclair."

"We have had this conversation so many times, Mum. My relationship with Steven is over. It has been for a long time. It has nothing to do with this."

"There's been a change in you Mhairi and it's not a positive one. I think that, deep down, you still love Steven. You've been together for the best part of twenty years. How could you not be suffering?"

In her eyes, Steven was a golden beacon in the darkness of my life. He would rescue me. What if I didn't need rescuing? What if I needed to learn to jump without my safety net? "Just because we were together for so long doesn't mean it was right. In all honesty I should have ended it years ago."

Mum gasped. "Mhairi you're not thinking clearly."

"I'm actually thinking more clearly than I have for the past twenty years. Allaban has been good for me, Mum. It was the right move for me even if it was the wrong move for my relationship."

"You are a shadow of your former self, darling. You cannot truly believe that moving to that remote village was the right decision."

"I do."

"I care about you, Mhairi. It hurts me to say this but moving to that village has done you nothing but harm. You're exhausted and alone. You'll regret it, darling. It may not be soon, it may not even be a year from now but one day you will regret it. I just hope you see sense before that day and leave."

I took a deep breath, attempting to contain my anger. "Do you remember what you said to me when I told you I was moving to Allaban? You said that it's my life. *My life.* I get to decide which path I take. If I make a few mistakes along the way, that's my choice too."

"I'm just trying to guide you, Mhairi darling. I only have your best interests at heart."

"I appreciate your concern Mum but, frankly, it is none of your business." I turned my attention to the unappetising turkey and attempted to eat it. Mum looked at me for another few seconds and then sighed. "This argument between you and Steven doesn't have anything to do with those Campbell brothers, does it?" she whispered ominously.

I averted my gaze. "No."

Mum always thought she was looking out for my best interests. Truthfully, she had always muddled these with her own agenda. Dad's death had taken a massive toll on our family. Mum had done everything in her power to give me a normal childhood with the same opportunities as other children. She wanted me to succeed regardless of our situation. However, pushing so hard had pushed me away. Our relationship had been fractured, broken under extreme stress. It had healed over time but never fully and never the same again.

"Can you help me clear the table?" Mum said, her tone notably frosty. There was no way I could tell her about everything that was happening in the village. It would only add fuel to her fire. It was much easier to keep her in the dark. I wondered how Beth was coping. Was she getting the support she needed from her friends and family? Was she still planning to keep her baby even if Rab was likely to go to prison? She was just a child. She had her whole life ahead of her. Rab's selfish and careless actions had stolen a little bit of her life from her. She would never get that time back.

My thoughts returned to Tom. Had the letter been delivered? Had he opened it? It had already been a few days since I posted it. My mind drifted through the possibilities. The thought set new butterflies free in my stomach. After dinner, I quickly retired to my bedroom, complaining of a sore head. The truth that I really didn't feel like celebrating. I fell into a fitful sleep, wrapped up in the all-consuming drama of Allaban.

***

I left Mum's house very early on the 27th. I didn't waken her to say goodbye. I told her I wanted to miss the traffic but truthfully I just needed to escape. I think she knew I was lying but chose to believe me in that moment. The truth that her only daughter needed to escape her was not one she wanted to accept. Mum had always been intense when I still lived at home but, when I left, it seemed to get 100 times worse. I don't know if it was because I'd grown accustomed to her smothering ways over the years. Maybe I'd just adjusted my breathing space. Either way, it was a relief to be leaving her house behind and making the long drive home with only the darkness to keep me company.

I found myself missing Steven's company. It was odd making the journey alone. I was merely in love with the idea of being in love- I knew that now. Although I knew I didn't love Steven, I missed the security of him. It felt like a tightrope walk without a harness- although I had walked the walk many times before, the fall was suddenly a lot more perilous. After almost twenty years of him, I guess it would be something I'd eventually get used to. However, throughout the whole journey, I found myself glancing at the passenger seat, continually surprised he wasn't there.

I spotted a coffee shop and decided to pull in. My head was pounding from the early start and I relished the thought of a warm cup of coffee to ease me into the day. The coffee shop was unassuming- just a little spec from the road. I could have easily driven right past it. If I blinked at the right moment I would indeed have missed it. However, almost half way through a six hour drive, I was glad I didn't. It was clearly a family run business. Family pictures donned the walls as well as rustic decorations. The décor was so busy it took a moment for my eyes to adjust. I approached the counter, ordered poached eggs and a black coffee, sat at a table by the window and pulled out my book, grateful for a moment of peace and quiet after the Christmas rush. That moment of peace ended up being very short-lived.

"Mhairi? Is that really you?"

The voice struck a nerve. I glanced up from my book wondering if I was awake or just dreaming. Was Steven really talking to me? I stared at him dumbly.

"Hi. Mind if I take a seat?"

"Not at all."

He sat across from me and I put my book down slowly. I began drumming my fingers nervously on its spine. I tried to summon the words but they just wouldn't come, floating helplessly above my head as I sat in a dumb daze.

He cleared his throat. "So… what brings you here?"

"Just on my way back up North after staying with Mum."

"Ah nice one. How is she?"

"She's fine. Just her usual… inquisitive self."

Steven smiled faintly. "That's great. I was gonna give her a call but… you know."

I folded my arms. "Yeah of course. Don't worry about it. How are your family?"

"Yeah fine. Went to Dad's for Christmas Eve then Mum's Christmas Day. Had a job starting today so came back last night."

We looked at each other for what felt like an eternity. A million words were lost in the space between us.

"I'm glad you're doing well, Steven." I finally said, the words failing to express how I really felt.

Suddenly, the bell above the entrance rang. I whipped my head round in surprise. A blonde woman entered the café looking irritated. She wore a black fitted dress dripping with sparkle. She teetered around in red high heels. It was a wonder she could keep herself upright- and yet she floated through the café with elegant ease. Her blonde hair tumbled over her shoulders, perfectly styled. Everything about her appearance was effortless- a woman who demanded the attention in every room without so much as lifting a finger. She looked like something out of a black and white movie.

She spotted Steven and glided over to the table. "Steven! We have to go! I'm going to be late." As she looked at me, she put a hand on his arm.

Steven's face turned red. "Sorry, love… I actually ran into Mhairi."

The blonde gave me a cold stare. "Oh… so this is Mhairi?"

I smiled awkwardly. "Hi. Sorry to keep Steven back."

She didn't respond.

Steven's eyes darted nervously between the two of us. "Oh sorry, I didn't introduce you. Mhairi, this is Lucy. Lucy, Mhairi."

It was so odd seeing Steven with someone else. He was, of course, entitled to move on but I hadn't thought he'd do it so fast. "It's a pleasure to meet you, Lucy." I said as warmly as I could muster.

"So you are the ex that works in the tiny village school in the middle of nowhere?"

"Em... yes."

She looked me up and down with obvious displeasure. "Charmed." She said dismissively. "Steven, I'm going to be late for work. Let's go." And with that, she grabbed Steven by the arm and steered him out the door.

Steven turned, giving me a final wave. I raised my hand in response.

***

The rest of the drive to Allaban was beautiful- the sun was shining gloriously in a cloudless sky. It was a clear but cold day, frost still crisp on the grass. The trees were bare and exposed to the brilliant sunlight. The village was still sprinkled with festive cheer, seemingly frozen in recent festivities. Glittering fairy lights lined the streets with ornate snowflakes fixed to the lampposts. All was quiet as the families of Allaban enjoyed the peace of the season. Everything seemed normal... and yet it wasn't.

I entered the cottage. It had grown cold in my absence. I quickly threw a few logs in the burner, hoping to pump some heat into the empty cavity. I pulled my jacket tighter around me as I investigated the bundle of mail left on the doormat. I flicked through every letter. There were a few Christmas cards, bills... but there was nothing from Tom. It had been well over a week since I posted the letter. Was he angry at me? Did he not believe me? My stomach twisted with fear.

After unpacking, I decided to visit Emily. Perhaps she could shed light on the situation in the village.

"I've not heard anything, Mhairi. There's been no mention of Rab anywhere." she said as clutched her mug of hot tea. "It's possible the Andersons and Campbells are keeping things quiet- it's barely been any time since the news of Beth's baby got out."

"Gossip like this always finds its way to the surface in Allaban, Emily. Surely the Andersons would want the village to know about Rab?"

Emily shrugged. "It's the Christmas holidays, Mhairi."

"I suppose. Have you heard anything from Tom?"

"I saw him at the shop a couple of days back. I didn't stop to chat but everything seemed normal. Why?"

I sighed. "I took your advice. I sent that letter, Emily. I told him everything."

She beamed. "That is great news, Mhairi. How do you feel about it?"

"Honestly… I feel sick to my stomach. He hasn't replied yet."

"When did you post it?"

"Just before I left for Glasgow."

"It's still early days yet, Mhairi. You've got to give the boy time to wrap his head around it."

"I just thought I would have heard something from him by now."

"You'll hear from him soon enough. He will be in touch when he's ready." Emily placed her hand on my shoulder. "I'm really proud of you, though. It took real guts to send that letter."

I smiled wearily. "I don't feel very brave."

"It takes real bravery to be vulnerable, Mhairi."

Chapter Sixteen

The holidays had officially come to an end and the sprinkle of Christmas magic had all but vanished. It was the first Monday morning back at work after the break. I wasn't sure what to expect. I was walking in blind, unsure of the situation that greeted me at the other side of the door.

It was an in-service day so no pupils would be in. It was nice to have an extra day before the pupils returned. I always found these days more productive because there weren't as many interruptions from students. However, in light of recent events, I suspected this not to be the case. I decided to call a staff meeting first thing to confront the unknown head on. I needed to know the lay of the land in order to assess the magnitude of damage. How odd it would be to lead a staff meeting without Rab, one of my few allies. I always felt more at ease with him next to me.

Returning to school was clearly a shock to the system for the majority of the teachers. The only person who looked fully awake was Sophie who, as usual, sat eagerly with a notepad and pen, taking notes. The meeting hadn't started yet so what notes she could possibly be taking I had no idea. The final members of the faculty staggered to the table, a steady drone of noise filling the room.

I scanned the table, trying to get a sense of the atmosphere. "Good morning everyone. It's great to have you back. I hope you all had a relaxing Christmas break with friends and family."

A hand was raised at the back of the room. It belonged to Oliver Stevenson. He slowly stood from his chair, waiting until he had the undivided attention of everyone in the room. "What's happening with the Campbell boy?" he bellowed.

A few nervous glances were shared between the staff.

"What do you mean, Oliver?" I said, keeping my expression neutral.

"You know fine well what I mean."

"That is confidential business, Oliver."

"So you didn't think you should share it with other staff in the school? Is that not your professional responsibility as Head Teacher?"

People around the room started talking animatedly.

"Ok, ok." I said with a raised voice, waiting for the buzz of chatter to stop. "I am obligated by law to keep it confidential, Oliver. This is an ongoing investigation. All you need to know is that everything is well in hand."

"How are we expected to trust that? We've been working with the man for years. You've been working with him for about five minutes and turns out he's been fiddling with a student."

"Oliver, that's enough." I said sternly.

"How are we supposed to look out for these kids? How are they supposed to feel safe here now? You let a predator roam the halls for months."

"I said, that's enough." I snapped.

Oliver held my gaze.

"When the allegations came to light, I followed the protocol. I was not going to tarnish the reputation of a well-respected member of our faculty without just cause. The matter has been reported to the proper authorities. All we can do is carry on as normal until told otherwise. Our job is to protect our young people. We must carry on as normal for their sake."

Iris raised her hand. "I understand that Mhairi," she said, "but I have to agree with Olly on this one. I can't understand why you didn't tell us sooner."

"At the moment, it is an ongoing enquiry that remains confidential. I cannot tell you anything else about it while this is still the case. It was never my story to tell. I don't know how this information became public knowledge. However, that does not enable me to share the case with you. I will inform you if that situation changes."

Oliver gave me a long, hard look. His reaction didn't surprise me. If anyone was going to argue it was going to be him. This was his chance to finally topple the young and inexperienced management team, to prove that he was right and I was wrong. The staff felt betrayed. They had heard this information on the grapevine rather than from me. I was fighting a losing battle. I felt powerless.

I returned to my office feeling deflated. It had felt like a game of Whack-a-mole as I attempted to dart and dodge any inquisitive questions. I slumped in my office chair and instead sifted through my emails. Suddenly, there was a knock on the door.

"Come in." I called.

"Mhairi?"

I turned round in my chair.

Iris was standing in the doorway, her arms firmly folded. "It's about Rab."

I nodded and waited for her to continue.

"You knew everything that was going on with Nathan... why couldn't you set the record straight? This has been unbearable for him. You said in there about protecting the pupils... what about Nathan? What have you done to protect him in all of this?"

I sighed. "I'm sorry, Iris. I didn't know until the end of term and even them I wasn't sure. I had to know the facts before I went around accusing people. I'm sorry that Nathan was collateral damage in all of this."

"Collateral damage? He's a wee boy, Mhairi. Not a statistic."

"I just mean that he was inadvertently dragged into this mess through no fault of his own."

"Exactly. None of this was his doing. He was dragged into this mess through no fault of his own. The poor boy is traumatised. He didn't even feel like he could turn to his own grandma for help."

"He's had an awful time of it, Iris. I totally understand."

"I don't think you do, Mhairi. That child has been crying himself to sleep for months whilst you were out playing Miss Marple. He thought the whole village hated him even though he'd done nothing wrong. Nobody believed a word he said. He's a teenage boy, Mhairi. That time in life is traumatising enough."

"I'm sorry, Iris."

Iris looked at me sternly, unmoving.

"I've done everything I could. My hands are tied. If I reveal confidential information, it might cause personal bias and jeopardise the case. I can't do that."

"Even a heads up would have been nice, Mhairi. That's something a friend would do. I thought we were friends." Iris, turned to leave but hesitated. "I better go home and deal with the collateral damage, eh?"

She slammed the door as she left, knocking an empty mug onto the floor which proceeded to burst into a million pieces. I buried my face in my hands. I did not close my eyes but instead tried to seek solace in the absolute blackness of my palms. Hiding from the world brought me some comfort. Part of me wondered if I stared long enough I could bring clarity to an altogether muddy situation. I felt like I was trailing the swampland, alone and unaided. I was up to my waist in marsh, attempting to cross but only succeeding in dragging myself deeper and deeper into the bog.

The phone on my desk began to ring, making the table shudder. I snatched it in a wave of shock.

"Hello?" I whispered, panicked.

"Mhairi, it's Daniel Pearson here."

I drew a sharp breath. Daniel Pearson was the Direction of Education for the local council. I hadn't had any dealings with him until the Rab incident. After that he had felt like a pen pal.

"Daniel, Hi."

"Been meaning to phone sooner than this, Mhairi. Sorry for the delay."

"No problem. Have there been any developments?"

"Not as many as I'd like, truthfully. The whole case is currently buried in paperwork. Until a formal hearing, Robert Campbell's teaching registration has been revoked. Once the case has been closed formally, the Teaching Council can decide on a suitable outcome."

"Is there anything else you need at this stage?"

Daniel sighed. "Not at the moment. You may have to testify in court but that is up to our judicial system to decide. At the moment, as an authority, there is nothing else we can do."

Testify? In court? "Is there any indication of how long this will take?"

"Off the record Mhairi… I have seen cases like this before. More than I'd like to admit. This process can take years to sort itself out."

Years?

"Our hands are tied until the court sorts this one out. However, from what you've told me, it doesn't seem likely that Robert Campbell will keep his registration for much longer."

I knew this would be the eventual outcome. However, having the truth uttered aloud made it so fiercely real. Rab's life was ruined.

"With that being said," Daniel said, interrupting my thoughts. "you need to get an Acting Depute Head Teacher in post. The sooner the better, I'd say."

"Surely it's better to keep things as they are a little longer?"

"On the contrary… parents always wanted action to be taken. They can't see the business that goes on behind the scenes. They need proof that real steps are being taken to move on. You cannot be seen to be doing nothing. It will spread the storm cloud."

I ruminated this before replying. "Daniel… is it possible to make this an internal appointment? I don't think it's a good idea to bring an outsider into the equation."

"Yes, fine. We can always go external if the candidate isn't the right fit."

"Perfect. Thank you."

"Sorry I can't give you any more reassurance, Mhairi. It's all a bit of a mess. It probably won't be long until the press get hold of this so be prepared."

The press?

"I'll be in touch."

The line was disconnected. I held the phone for a few more moments. I hadn't even considered the press being involved. Would the rest of the world care about the inner workings of a rural school?

Appointing internally was the best option. The staff and pupils would trust a familiar face. My capabilities as Head Teacher were already in question and bringing in someone new could capsize the boat. I had the perfect candidate in mind. I hoped this would help return the school to some sense of normality.

On my way home from school, I visited the Spar to pick up a microwave meal for dinner. Cooking an entire meal for one seemed like a waste of time and energy and I had neither in abundance at the best of times. I whisked around the aisles in search of a somewhat nutritious meal. In my haste, I almost took out Tom with my basket. I stared at him dumbly, trying hastily to string together a coherent sentence.

I froze. "Tom I... I'm..."

Donna came sauntering up behind Tom and gave him a quick peck on the cheek. I adverted my gaze, uncomfortable with the open display of affection.

Donna looked at me with faux embarrassment. "Oh Mhairi! I didn't see you there." She flashed her most dazzling smile before turning her attention to Tom. "did you find the asparagus, darling?"

Tom looked uncomfortable. "Don't think they've got any left, Don."

"Shame." She turned to me, giving me a knowing glance. "Monday night is our date night. You're awful late, Mhairi."

I smiled curtly. "Just paperwork." Conversing with Donna was like licking sandpaper.

"Tom is exactly the same. You two are just workaholics."

"Comes with the job, I'm afraid."

"You need to learn to relax, Mhairi. Take a night off."

"I'll do my best."

Tom refused to meet my eyes and instead stared intently at the wall.

Donna smiled brightly, seemingly unaware of the awkwardness of our encounter. "Well we best be off. Good to see you, Mhairi. Remember- relax!"

Donna bounded off, Tom in tow. He turned, giving me a final look before he shut the door.

I returned to the cottage and let the emptiness embrace me. My life had crumbled around me and I have nowhere to seek solace. I lay on the couch and let my emotions bear their full weight. I had buried my anxiety for so long that it had started to flower and burst from the ground. I waited for my darkness to swallow me whole. Perhaps then I would finally find some relief. I had shared my darkest and most shameful secret with Tom and he had disposed of me. I had stripped myself of my only armour. I had run out of hiding places so instead took refuge in my darkest thoughts.

Chapter Seventeen

I awoke to the sun streaming through the living room window. I was fully clothed and lying on the sofa, my legs haphazardly draping off the edge. I shifted my body to sit upright and my back groaned. I looked at my phone- 10am. I was suddenly hit with a wave of panic. I was late for school. I scrambled to get off the sofa but in my haste fell backwards onto its arm. My back screamed with pain. I was ready to drag myself up the stairs, ready to frantically change into whatever was clean when a realisation dawned- it was Saturday. The weekend. No school. I breathed a sigh of relief. My heart was still fiercely pumping as I collapsed back onto the sofa, exhausted from the unwelcome alarm.

Last night, all of the events over the last few months hit me like a violent wave. I was the furthest I'd ever been from clarity. As someone who had always been sure of her next career move or life plan, the prospect of not knowing what came next filled me with dread. I screwed my eyes shut. In the wake of a turbulent storm, all I wanted was to be still, even if only for a moment.

A pounding in my head disturbed me from a fitful sleep. I glanced at the clock. 2.30pm. As a teenager, I was always so full of energy. It seemed that supply had finally run out as I lay withered on the sofa, unable to move. The pounding continued and I clutched my head, willing it to stop. It slowly dawned on me that the pounding wasn't actually my head but was instead coming from the front door. Someone was banging furiously. After much exertion, I pulled a blanket around my shoulders and dragged myself to the door.

Standing there was Emily, a panicked expression on her face. "Mhairi! Have you not checked your phone?"

I blinked, adjusting to the fresh sunlight.

"What on earth is going on? I have called you at least a dozen times. It's so unlike you not to reply. What have you been doing? You look…" her voice trailed off.

I stood awkwardly in the doorway. Emily looked me up and down and I adjusted my blanket self-consciously.

"Mhairi… I don't mean to be judgemental but… you look awful."

"Thanks for the pep talk, Emily. Gratefully received." I made a move to shut the door but Emily stopped it with her foot.

"No way, Mhairi. Not a chance. You are not going to shut me out."

"You're the person that just said I look awful."

"I'm just concerned about you, Mhairi. I care about you. I've given you space and I've been there when you've wanted to talk. Now it's my turn."

I opened the door and stared at her. "What on earth are you talking about?"

"One minute you float around like everything is normal. The next minute, Tom shows up at the door with you sodden and covered in mud. The first time, I let it go. The problem is… it keeps happening, Mhairi."

I blinked at her, bewildered.

"Whatever it is, we are talking about it. Now." Emily pushed past me and into the cottage.

I sat uncomfortably on the couch as Emily made tea. She turned occasionally to look at me. I pulled the blanket tighter around my shoulders. She finished brewing the tea and passed me a mug. She sat across from me, her brow knitted with concern. "Mhairi. What is going on?" she whispered.

I picked my fingers. "Have you ever had the feeling of not knowing which direction your life is going to take?"

Emily nodded. "All the time."

"I've had my whole future planned out for a long time and… this is the first time that I've felt totally lost. I've never not known what I wanted. I've always been like that, ever since I can remember. I liked having a plan. It made me feel… like I had… a purpose, I guess. What I hadn't planned was that I'd lose myself somewhere along the way. At some point, I lost myself. I thought I wanted a life with Steven… it was only when we broke up that I realised I didn't really want it. I just thought I did. It scares me not knowing. I don't know what I want anymore. I don't know what my purpose is anymore."

"It's ok not to know, you know. We've all had times when we don't know what direction our life is going to take."

"It's not just that though. I think I was using this purpose and drive as a way to… escape something else. For such a long time, I lived for my next achievement. I thought life was just about getting to the next rung of the ladder… but then I got to the top and realised I've been climbing the wrong bloody ladder."

"That's alright, Mhairi. You're allowed to change your mind about what you want from time to time."

"The thing is… I thought I was just chasing achievements but actually…I've been running away."

"Running? From what?"

"Running from… me. How I feel about stuff. About the past. There's a lot of things that have happened to me that I thought I'd made peace with… but now I'm not so sure. It is becoming more and more frequent."

"Mhairi… what do you mean? What has become more frequent?"

"You're going to think I'm crazy… and maybe I am…"

"You are not crazy, Mhairi."

"How can you possibly know that?"

Emily leaned over and took my hand. "I think you've had a lot of stuff going on. I think you're stressed. I think you work too hard… but I don't think you're crazy."

"It's nothing to do with work. I use work to avoid thinking about it."

"You know you can tell me anything."

"You've got to promise... you can't tell anyone."

"Of course."

I took a deep breath. The words rose like bile in my throat and, before I knew it, came spilling out. I told her about the flashbacks. I told her about the darkness. With every new wave of words, I felt a little bit lighter. The relief of letting the words escape was euphoric. I had clutched them to my chest for so long that I had forgotten how to breathe. It was like tasting fresh air again for the first time.

Emily waited until she was sure I was finished, her eyes not leaving mine for a moment. She leaned in closer. "Listen to me. You have absolutely nothing to be ashamed of. You have been so brave." She paused, still clutching my hands tightly in her own. "I am so sorry for being so heavy handed. I didn't..."

"I should have told you sooner." I whispered.

"I care about you, Mhairi. It's so hard to see you struggling. I had no idea the extent of what you'd been through. It is unforgivable and absolutely not your fault."

I smiled weakly. "Thanks."

"I mean it. To come through something like that... it shows real strength, Mhairi."

"My life is literally falling apart, Emily. I don't think you can call that strength."

"You will piece it back together, Mhairi. I will always be here to help you pick up those pieces."

***

After taking one final gulp of my morning coffee, I returned to my computer screen. Daniel Pearson hadn't been wrong about the paperwork- every second email I received was either from the Police or the Teaching Council. My story had become stale with recollection. It was better that way- I found it easier to distance myself from Rab as it became more distorted. The court date was still unknown and the school hung in a peculiar limbo.

I put the finishing touches on yet another email to Steph Anderson and clicked send. It would likely go unanswered like the other dozen I had sent over the past few weeks. It was odd to think that Beth Anderson was at least six months pregnant. It seemed like a lifetime ago since I visited the Anderson's house. So much had changed since then. I wondered how Beth was coping with it all. I felt so sorry for her. She must feel so cut off from the rest of the world. So alone.

There was a knock at the door. Iris stared back at me from the door way. I gave her as warm a smile as I could muster as she sat in what used to be Rab's chair.

"You wanted to see me, Mhairi?" she said.

"Yes. Thank you for coming. There are a few things I wanted to chat to you about."

Iris looked at me expectantly.

I knitted my hands together nervously. "I'm sorry, Iris. The last conversation we had was not a very pleasant one. I totally understand how concerned you are for Nathan's wellbeing. I am too and I'm sorry if it came across differently. Nathan is not, and has never been, a statistic to me. I want you to know that I'm here to help, support and shield you as best I can. However, there are certain things about this case that I cannot tell to you. My hands are tied. It is, unfortunately, how these matters play out."

Iris had been fidgeting with her hands absentmindedly as I spoke but stopped abruptly when it was clear I had finished. Eventually, she gave a deliberate nod. "Thank you for your apology. I'm sorry I got a little "Mamma bear" about the whole thing. I'm usually quite pragmatic but... I stumbled over that hurdle."

I smiled sympathetically. "It's hard to be logical when it involves someone you love."

"Yes."

"It is a quality I really admire about you, Iris. With that in mind, there is something else I'd like to talk to you about."

Iris shifted in her seat. "What's that?"

"It seems that, due to recent events, we will not have a Depute Head Teacher for the foreseeable future. It'll be temporary to begin with but with everything that has happened... anyway. I was hoping that you'd consider applying."

Iris was taken aback. "Me? Depute Head Teacher? Are you joking?"

I sat forward and took her hand. "Iris. You are the most forward thinking person I've ever worked with. You would be brilliant."

Iris opened her mouth to say something but quickly shut it again.

"At least think about it. The advert will go out at the end of the week so that gives you a few days to mull it over."

"Wow. Well… thanks." Iris said.

"Of course."

I knew Iris was the right choice for the job. She wasn't afraid to stand up for what she believed in. I needed someone unafraid of speaking their mind. Rab's support had been so important but so were his arguments. The compromises we made were the foundation of everything we aspired the school to be. The office seemed emptier without his buoyant personality filling it. I even missed the trail of papers and forgotten coffee cups around the office.

***

I was watching a re-run of an old TV soap and eating the remains of my microwave lasagne when my phone vibrated, making a bid for freedom from the kitchen counter. I managed to catch it before it collided with the stone floor.

"Hello?" I said, still out of breath from the drama.

"Hello? Is this Mhairi Sinclair?"

I glanced at my phone but didn't recognise the number. "Speaking."

"Ah, excellent. My name is Dianna King. I'm part of Mr Campbell's legal defence."

"Right. I see."

"Mr Campbell's trial is currently scheduled for the beginning of next month which is why it was imperative I phone you. Your testimony is imperative to our case. We need you to make a formal statement as part of Mr Campbell's defence."

"What? Like speaking in a courtroom?"

"Not as scary as it sounds, I assure you. Your statement will form the backbone of our whole testimony."

"I don't know if I'd be of much help, Ms King."

"On the contrary. You've known Mr Campbell for a very long time. You know he is of good character. All you need to do is share your story with the court. His relationship with Miss Anderson was a legitimate one built on mutual love and trust. You can help us strengthen his defence. We need you, Mhairi."

"Well… I…" I failed to string a coherent sentence together.

"I'll give you a call in a couple of days to give you time to come to a decision. We can have a proper chat about it then and firm up the details. Thank you, Mhairi."

With that, the call was disconnected. I was taken aback. Could I really stand in front of a courtroom and defend Rab? That evening I sat in front of the TV, attempting to engage with whatever was on the screen. All I could think about was the conversation with Dianna King. It hadn't even entered my mind that I may be asked to speak for Rab's defence. I'd naïvely believed that I'd go to the police, turn Rab in and life would carry on as normal. I was one of the only people outwith Rab's family that had known him for most of his life. I was an obvious choice. However, could I really face a jury and condone what Rab had done? As a Head Teacher, I knew Rab's conduct was wrong. However, as his friend, could I really judge him for pursuing love?

Chapter Eighteen

Iris was the only person that applied for the post of depute head teacher so the application and interview were merely a formality. Having her on board gave me a new sense of vigour. I felt the love for my work bleeding into my consciousness again. As a long standing member of the faculty, she had a wealth of experience of how the school worked. This paired with her innovation and leadership made her perfect for the job. Also, the office lacked a trail of coffee cups on a daily basis which I couldn't complain about.

"I spent all of this time wondering why you worked so much... and now I understand." It had long gone 5 o'clock on Friday and both Iris and I were still in the office, knee-deep in work.

"Tell me about it. One night, I was so late that Bill Rodgers had to physically drag me out of the building, kicking and screaming."

"I can believe it. This school just sucks everything out of you, doesn't it?"

"It surprises me on a daily basis that I haven't turned into a husk of a person."

"It certainly explains why the Spar is regularly out of microwave meals."

I sniggered.

"The work is never truly done, is it?"

"Nope."

"You might have told me that before I took the job."

"Purely a selfish decision. I didn't want to scare you off."

"You know the really scary thing?" Iris paused to look at me, her eyes filled with delight. "I have loved every minute of it."

I beamed. "I told you that you were perfect for the job, Iris."

"Well I don't know about that."

"I do."

Iris laughed. "I take back anything I've ever said about you leaving late. I asked Nathan to start the dinner one night and he nearly fainted. The boy can't even boil an egg! Abandoned by his Grandma."

"How is Nathan doing?"

Iris shrugged. "Better, I guess. He doesn't seem as down-trodden as he used to be. He's still moody but more in a typical teenage boy kind of way."

"That's an improvement, I suppose."

"He's getting there."

"Is he visiting Beth as much?"

"Nathan hasn't seen the girl in months now. To be honest... I think it's been good for him. Supporting Beth took its toll on the boy. It's a fair weight for him to carry on his shoulders. He was emotionally drained by it all and so confused. It's a hard situation for anyone to process never mind a wee boy."

I nodded thoughtfully. "I guess it is easier to distance yourself from the situation when there is physical distance. How is Beth? Have you seen her at all?"

"Nope. Not for a few months now."

"Me neither."

"Steph and Ian are still working full time but I've not seen Beth at The Cape or anywhere else. She must be locked away in that wee house, all alone. Poor wee thing."

"Poor Beth... I do feel for her."

Iris nodded solemnly. "I know. It's hard enough being pregnant at sixteen... but when it's likely the father is going to spend a chunk of time behind bars because of it..." She sighed. "Anyway. No point in thinking about it. Nothing can be done now."

It was clear that Iris did not want to discuss the subject any longer so I returned to my computer screen. Feeling isolated was difficult at any age- never mind as a teenager with a baby on the way. I had tried to reach out to Steph so many times but she blatantly ignored me. Beth was completely alone.

***

That evening, I decided to walk to Feic Beach to clear my head. Although dry, the air was bitterly cold so I bundled on an array of mis-matching layers and walked briskly to warm myself up. The sky was alight with a final spectacle of colours bursting from the horizon before settling down to sleep. Although the winter was beginning to retreat, it was still making its presence known in the village streets. When the sun left, a chill clung to the air. A thin layer of frost dusted the streets like icing on a cake. The houses were illuminated with warmth as I strode past, clinging to the inside of my jacket sleeves in an attempt to keep warm. I was so lost in the spectacle in the sky that I forgot that my hands were entirely numb.

Suddenly, my phone vibrated in my pocket. It was Steven. I answered it before I had the chance to talk myself out of it.

"Hello?" I said in as flippant a tone as I could muster.

"Mhairi, Hi. It's me, Steven."

"Steven, hey."

"How are you? How's things?"

"Fine, fine. School is still busy. How about you?"

"Yeah grand. Everything is ticking over."

Steven cleared his throat. "Listen, Mhairi, I was wondering if I could pop by and pick up some stuff."

"Oh. Yeah. Sure."

"Lucy and I felt it was the right time to pick it up."

I rolled my eyes. I was irritated and had to remind myself that Steve's life was nothing to do with me anymore. "Any time is totally fine. You can always get a key from Emily if I'm not in."

"Actually Mhairi... I'd prefer it if you were in. There's a few things we need to sort out."

"Oh. Ok, sure." I said, the surprise obvious in my tone. "What stuff?"

"Nothing big… just the joint account and stuff like that. It'd be better for me and Lucy when…" he stopped mid-sentence.

"Better for what?" The phoneline crackled. The signal was becoming more and more intermittent as I got closer to the beach. "Sorry Steven, you're breaking up. Just text me when you're coming up and I'll make sure I'm in, ok?"

"Sure, sure. Thanks, Mhairi."

I arrived at the beach and the salty sea air embraced my senses. A warmth spread through every orifice of my body, despite the persistent cold. My last visit to Feic Beach had not been a pleasant one. The past still lingered in the darkness. I couldn't escape it. I took a deep breath of freezing air which caused me to cough and splutter.

***

Everything around the school was beginning to settle into some form of normality. Rab's impending trial was no longer the only topic of conversation amongst the staff. Iris was settling into her new role as Depute Head Teacher. My workload was beginning to settle into a still large but manageable list. Everything was going well. I should have known that it was the calm before the storm.

I decided to take a walk around the loch at lunchtime. It felt like such a luxury to have time. It would be my first walk this year. It was bizarre how fast the time was going. As I made my way past reception, Donna's head popped up from behind the desk.

"Mhairi, hi."

I smiled as warmly as I could muster. "Donna. How are you?"

"I'm good, thanks. Attempting to wade through all this paperwork so I can leave sharp. I have dinner plans with Tom tonight."

"That's great." I said, stretching my face into a smile. I wondered if there'd ever be a time when his name didn't feel like a sharp pain in my chest.

"Yeah everything is going really well." She crooned. "Tom is just... amazing, really. What a great guy."

"I'm glad."

"Yeah me too. It just feels so right, you know? Being together is just so easy."

"Yes... I can imagine."

"I almost can't imagine a time when we weren't together. I know it's only been a couple of months but... it feels like much longer than that in the best way."

"Fabulous." I whispered, my voice laced with sarcasm.

"We are actually having a few friends over to the Croft next weekend- our first big party as a loved-up couple. You should totally come."

"Oh, I… I don't think I can, Donna. Work is just crazy."

"Come on, Mhairi. You're always so busy. You never let your hair down."

"I don't really have much of a choice in this job."

"Nonsense. It's a wee village school, Mhairi. How much work could you really have to do?"

"You'd be surprised. I'll see how things go, Donna."

She beamed. "I will take that as a yes. Looking forward to it already."

I raced for the door. A sob began to rise in my throat but I pushed it down. What was the matter with me?

***

When I re-entered the office, Iris was exactly as I'd left her- glued to her computer screen. "A woman named Dianna King called for you." She said, her eyes never leaving her monitor. "I left a note on your desk."

Dianna had attempted to call me a few times already on my mobile but I always let it go to voicemail. I hadn't made up my mind about Rab and, truthfully, I didn't want to have to make the decision. "Thanks." I whispered and quietly pushed the post-it note into the bin. "Anything else?"

I left school at 5pm that evening- a normal day for most people but a daringly early one for me. Bill Rodgers raised an eyebrow as I made my escape. "It's still daylight, Mhairi. What are you doing leaving?"

"I discovered I wasn't a vampire."

Bill chuckled.

I couldn't remember the last time I'd left so early. It was probably the evening I tried to cook Steven dinner. It was nice to wander outside in the daylight but I felt like I was cheating. As I eased into my car, my mobile rang again. Dianna King.

"Please stop calling, Dianna. I'm busy."

"Mhairi?" Croaked a familiar voice. "Is that you?"

I drew a breath. "Rab."

His usual booming voice hung limp at the end of the line. "It's been a while, eh?"

"It has."

"You have no idea how good it is to hear your voice again."

"You too."

"It's weird. I'd kinda forgotten what you sounded like."

"Well it has been a few months, Rab."

There was silence. All I could hear at the other end of the phone was Rab's shallow breathing. "V. I need your help. Please."

I sighed. I had successfully distanced myself from the events surrounding Rab's arrest but I turned to butter when I heard his voice on the phone. "Rab. I need to think about this."

"I know, V. I know it's a big ask. I'd owe you forever. You could be my ticket out of here."

"Rab it is really for a jury to decide…"

"If you testify, they'll see that I'm not the monster they've made me out to be. I'm not a monster, V. I just made a mistake, that's all."

"I understand that Rab but a jury is not going to see it that way."

"You can make them see it that way, V. That's your superpower. I'm depending on you. Please."

Speaking to Rab broke my heart. At this point, I did not imagine Rab as the almost 40 year old man. I saw the timid wee boy I was friends with. The boy that rode down the hill with me on our bikes. The boy that pulled me out of the mud when I got stuck. The friend that was always there for me no matter what. "Alright."

"Really? You mean it? You'll do it?"

"Yes, Rab. I'll do it."

"Mhairi you have no idea… this means… thank you. Thank you from the bottom of my heart."

"I'll call Dianna first thing in the morning, ok?"

"I'll let her know. Thanks, V."

I ended the call and slumped into my car seat. It was probably Dianna's idea that he call to pull on my heart strings. The nerve of that woman. Speaking in Rab's defence… it sent a very public statement. It showed the world who's side I was on. I thought of Beth and her unborn baby. Would she be happy I was speaking on Rab's behalf? Or had she woken from love's young dream facing the ugly reality of what he had done? In that instant, I resolved that I would tell the whole truth. I would lay Rab's actions on the table and let the jury decide if he was right or wrong. He was a kind hearted man who had behaved recklessly in pursuit of love. Just because what he had done was wrong did not mean there wasn't any right within it.

***

"You've just got to tell them the truth, Mhairi. No sugar coating."

I was sitting in Emily's kitchen, cradling a glass of gin. "It's just so hard Emily. I'd want nothing more than Rab to go free but... he did a really bad thing. An inexcusable thing."

"I know."

"I couldn't live with myself if my testimony resulted in him being behind bars forever... but I don't know how I feel about him being released either."

"You've got to trust that a jury will make the right choice based on the evidence, Mhairi. You won't be the only one making a statement. You can't keep putting pressure on yourself over this."

"What will the rest of the village think?"

"It doesn't matter what the rest of the village thinks. What do you think?"

I took a moment to ponder this question. "I need to do it."

"There you go. You know it's the right thing to do. You know you have to share your story."

I nodded soberly.

"Now tell me more about Donna."

I rolled my eyes. "I thought I couldn't like her any less and yet…"

"She started dating Tom."

I smiled weakly. "Am I that transparent?"

"Yes."

"Great."

Emily chuckled softly, shaking her head.

"I wish I never had to see her again but it's hard to avoid someone when you work in the same school."

"It's hard to avoid anyone in this village, believe me. Before George and I were dating, he wandered around after me like a lost puppy."

"That worked out though."

"Yes, it did. Things always have a way of working themselves out."

"I don't believe you."

"You'll see, Mhairi. You'll get your happy ending."

"My fairy tale isn't due yet, Emily."

"It never will be if you keep talking about it like a train timetable."

I scoffed.

"You are a catch. Don't ever forget that."

"That's your opinion."

"It'll be everyone's opinion when we get you all dressed up for Tom and Donna's party next week."

I groaned. "Not a chance of me going to that. I can barely tolerate love's young dream at work."

"If you don't go, you're giving people a lot of wiggle room to talk about you."

"No-one knows about me and Tom."

Emily raised an eyebrow. "No-one has spoken to you about you and Tom."

"Do you really think they know?"

"This is a small village full of gossips and nosey neighbours, Mhairi. You seem to forget that sometimes."

I sighed.

"You will go, show your support for Tom and Donna and look drop dead gorgeous in the process. Simple."

"Simple? You are having a laugh."

"It may not be simple but you've got to make it look simple, Mhairi. It's the only way to put those rumours to bed."

"Let people talk. I can't be bothered with village gossip anymore. Count me out."

"Don't be such a party pooper, Mhairi. I am fantastic company, after all."

"I'm not in the party mood."

"The only way to get into the party mood is to dress up, make up and show up!"

I laughed. "Good luck with that one."

"Once I'm finished with you, Tom won't be able to keep his eyes off you."

"I don't know about that."

"Well I do. The boy clearly fancies you, Mhairi. All we need is a posh party frock and he will be helpless to resist. We need to show that boy what he's been missing."

I smiled wickedly. "Bring it on."

Chapter Nineteen

We were in Emily's bedroom, attempting to get ready for the party at the Croft. The party didn't officially start until 8 so I was horrified when Emily told me to be at hers for 5.

"This kind of beautiful takes time, Mhairi." She said.

"I can honestly say that I had never spent more than an hour on my appearance. This includes when I was a bridesmaid for my friend's wedding in May last year." It wasn't that I didn't care about my appearance- I just didn't have the time or the patience to indulge in it. I went to the hairdressers as rarely as possible as sitting in a chair for an hour was my idea of torture.

"Aww come on, Mhairi. It'll be fun. We will drink wine and the time with just fly by. We cannot rush art."

"Surely we don't need three hours to create art."

"We'll do your hair, make-up, outfit, drink wine…"

"Surely we can squeeze that all into an hour, Emily."

"I will see you at my house at 5pm. Don't be late." There was no arguing with Emily. After all, she knew where I lived.

There was a tentative knock at the door and it gently opened a crack. George timidly poked his head around the door.. "When am I dropping you off, Emily?"

"We will be ready at 8.30pm, George love."

"Oke doke." George shut the door gently.

I turned to Emily, confused. "Emily that's still an hour away. What more could we possibly have to do? My hair and make-up are pretty much done."

"We still have to pick an outfit for you and that bottle of wine is not going to finish itself. We need to find something absolutely perfect." Emily glided over to her wardrobe and surveyed the contents carefully. She flicked between the hangers, pulling out an assortment of dresses and throwing them on her bed.

"Emily I'm sure-"

"Shhhhh!"

After studying the bundle intently for a few moments, Emily picked a purple dress from the bundle and thrust it into my arms. "I like this one for you. Go and see what you think." I stumbled into the en-suite bathroom and slipped the dress on. It fit like a glove. I turned to look at myself in the mirror. The dress was full length and covered in tiny sequins which sparkled as they caught the light. The sleeves were made entirely of lace, hugging perfectly to my arms. It had a plunging neckline and a slit on left hand side from the bottom to just above the knee. I swished from side to side, feeling every bit like a princess.

Emily chapped the door impatiently. "Everything ok in there?"

"Emily I can't wear this. It is far too revealing."

"Oh come off it, Mhairi. This isn't a school function. Live a little!" Emily stormed into the bathroom but stopped dead when she caught sight of me.

I looked at her apologetically.

"What is that face for? You look unbelievable."

"I don't think I can pull this off, Emily. It's not something I would usually wear."

"All the more reason to wear it. You look stunning, Mhairi. Tom will not be able to take his eyes off you."

"I don't know about that." I blushed. "I think I need another glass of wine."

We ended up leaving at 8.45pm, which had unsettled my already restless disposition. Seeing Tom at a party was already too much for me and we hadn't even arrived yet. I sat in the back of George's car, my palms sweaty. We pulled up to the Croft which was already bustling with people. Guests spilled onto the porch and the surrounding garden. My stomach churned. Sensing my uneasiness, Emily grabbed my arm.

"You are beautiful, Mhairi."

"I don't feel beautiful."

"Fake it till you make it. You are gonna walk into that house like you own the place and Tom won't believe his eyes. You can do this."

George stopped the car. "Enjoy ladies. Just give me a shout when you want picked up."

"Thanks George, love." Said Emily. She turned to face me. "Ready, Mhairi?"

I breathed in and out as slowly as I could muster. "Ready as I'll ever be."

I opened the car door and Emily lead me to the front door.

"Breathe, Mhairi." She whispered in my ear.

I entered the house with an air of confidence I didn't possess. The living room was packed full of people and yet I couldn't see one familiar face.

"Emily! Mhairi!" it was Sophie Turner, the Music teacher. She staggered towards us. "So good to see you both. Mhairi I'm so happy you're here!" She hugged me tightly, her breath perfumed with wine.

"Yeah, me too." I patted her back gently, waiting for the awkward embrace to be over.

She beamed. "I think we are the only people from school here. I don't recognise anyone else."

I scanned the room and saw a few familiar faces from around the village. However, I couldn't put a name to any of them.

Sophie gasped. "Mhairi. Your dress is… wow!"

"Thanks. It's Emily's."

"Your hair and make-up too… you look amazing."

"So do you!"

"Aww I don't know…" Sophie mumbled shyly. "Do you guys have drinks? I'll get drinks!" With that Sophie was off, merely a blur as she raced through the crowd.

Emily leaned into me. "She is more enthusiastic than normal… I didn't think that was possible. Let's see if we can find Tom." Before I had a chance to object, Emily steered me through the crowd of people in the living room and into the kitchen. The room felt like it was swaying as we weaved between people.

"Donna!" shouted Emily, waving.

Donna was in the kitchen deep in conversation with Tom and a few others. She turned, a plastic smile on her face.

"So lovely to see you."

"Emily! It's been a while. I'm so glad you both could make it." Donna said breezily.

I forced a smile. "Wouldn't miss it." Whilst scanning the room, I clocked Tom. My heart pounded.

"Mhairi I love your dress."

Emily nodded in approval. "I know, right?" she said as she winked.

Sophie appeared at my side, three wine glasses balanced precariously in her two hands. It was clear she'd already succeeded in spilling some of the contents down her dress. "Here you are ladies." She said, passing the glasses to each of us.

Emily raised hers in the air. "Cheers." She said, taking a large gulp. I did the same and felt the warm liquid slip down the back of my throat.

"Thanks so much again for coming ladies. Tom and I are thrilled that so many people could make it." The familiar stabbing sensation hit my chest. "It's nice that so many people could come to our first party as an official couple. Everyone has been so supportive."

Emily smiled. "Yes it's a great party."

"It is, isn't it? I organised it myself- Tom has been a little busy. He runs the farm himself now. He's putting the finishing touches on a barn conversion out the back. It is amazing. My Tommy is so talented."

"Yes." I said, trying to hide the venom in my voice.

"Anyway ladies I better go and mingle. Can't keep our other guests waiting. Enjoy the party!" with that, Donna disappeared back to her original group. She linked her arm in Tom's and gave him a peck on the cheek.

"Mhairi, you need to work on your poker face." whispered Emily as she took another large gulp of her wine. "the temperature plummeted as soon as Donna came over."

Sophie gasped. "I thought it was because of me. No one likes me."

"No, no Sophie." Emily and I fussed.

"I just hate her swanning around acting like the Queen Bee." I whispered.

"She loves the attention, Mhairi. Always has."

"She's a bit of a bitch isn't she?" said Sophie, a little too loudly.

Emily and I burst out laughing and began shushing Sophie.

"Not so loud!" said Emily, still sniggering. "The Queen Bitch might hear."

This set me into another fit of the giggles.

Emily, Sophie and I chatted long into the night with Sophie periodically disappearing to refill our drinks. The room was spinning pleasantly and the conversation flowed. With every drink, I felt more and more relaxed. What was I so worried about? Partying was so much fun. Suddenly, my palms became clammy again. I felt the colour drain from my face. Emily gave me a concerned look.

"Mhairi? Are you ok?"

"Yeah fine. I think I just need some fresh air." I zigzagged my way through the crowd and towards the door. This made me feel more sick. I escaped the house and the cold air hit me like a slap in the face. The crowds outside the house had vanished. What time was it? I removed my heels and stumbled towards the barn, the fresh air intoxicating me more and more with each step. I found myself spinning with my head upwards, making the sky dance with light. The night became a glorious discothèque of colour as I swirled round and round, my dress only adding to the shimmer and sparkle on show in the night sky.

The barn had been completely transformed. It was no longer the derelict building with a large hole in the roof. The roof, in fact, had been entirely replaced, the exterior painted and the surrounding foliage tamed. It was now a charming brick red colour which blushed even in the moonlight. The lamp which once hung precariously at its entrance was replaced with horseshoes holding up a string of lights all around the outer shell. I stopped walking abruptly and gawked.

"This is my hiding place, V. Kindly go and find another one." Tom was at my back, whispering in my ear. I stumbled forward in shock, whirling round to face him. He was swigging from a bottle of red wine. He attempted to steady himself as he issued his ultimatum. I put my hands on my hips, dropping one of my high heels in the process. I scrambled to pick it up whilst Tom sniggered.

"What are you laughing at?"

"You're drunk." He slurred, failing to contain his laughter.

"Oh yeah coming from you that is pretty rich."

"I've not had that much to drink. I'm only half way through this bottle."

"Is that all you've had to drink?"

"Shut up, V. You're not my mother."

I punched him in the arm.

"Ow!" he exclaimed, dropping the bottle in the process. The contents spilled all over the glass, a glugging sound emitting from the bottle as it rolled. Tom sauntered up to me. He reached out towards me slowly, putting his hands on my hips. I shrank back, my heart a flutter. My breath grew shallow. Suddenly, and without warning, he began tickling me. I protested loudly whilst attempting to stifle my laughter.

"Tom! No! Stop! Please!" I pleaded, attempting to catch his hands and pry them from my waist. He ignored me, proceeding to tickle me all over, laughing heartily in the process. I stumbled backwards and tripped, dragging him down with me. We hit the ground in fits of laughter, still entangled in each other.

We lay on the grass, breathing heavily as lazy laughs filled the air. Tom took my hand in his and examined each of my fingers in turn. I turned to face him, tucking my other arm underneath my head.

"Tom?"

"Mmm?"

"Why are you not inside at the party?"

"I should be asking you the same question." He said playfully, a smile escaping his lips.

"I'm serious. Why are you not inside with all your friends?"

Tom took a moment and then shrugged. "Not my scene, V. It's never been my scene."

"Why did you throw the party in the first place then?"

"Donna's idea."

We looked at each other for what felt like an eternity before he looked away.

"Well, for what it's worth, I'm glad you blew it off."

"You seemed like you were having a pretty good time in there."

"Appearances can be deceiving." I whispered, coyly.

"Disappearances can be pretty transparent." He put a finger against my lips. "Don't worry. I will keep your secret... as long as you keep mine."

"My lips are sealed." I whispered.

"I don't think I've ever seen you so dressed up before, V."

I blushed. "It's too much."

"No, it's not that. It's just... different I guess. You look different. Not bad different, just..." his voice tapered off into the windless night. "There is a compliment in there, Mhairi. It's just wrapped up in some inarticulate layers."

I blushed. "Well... thank you."

"I guess what I'm trying to say is... you look good. Really good."

"Thanks. You do too."

He withdrew slightly from me, turning his eyes to the mirage of stars above our heads. "Rab told me, by the way."

"What?"

"About the trial. About you speaking for his defence. Thanks for that."

"Of course."

"No I mean it. I know it's a massive ask. You've come through for him and that means a lot."

I smiled, unsure what to say. "How's he doing?"

"Honestly... not great. I've never seen him like this before. He is just... so small. It's like all of his bravado has been stripped away."

"I'm sorry."

"He did a terrible thing, V. These are the consequences for his actions. It's just hard seeing him like that. After all that has happened, he is still my brother, no matter what terrible things he's done."

"Of course."

"I feel so sorry for him, V. Then I feel guilty for feeling sorry for him. It's so confusing."

"It's hard when everything feels like it's out of your hands."

"It's so frustrating. I'm trying to keep myself busy around the farm so I can forget about it."

"That is totally understandable."

"I'm sorry for harping on like this. Donna is sick of me talking about it."

"He's your brother. Of course you need to talk about it."

"It's annoying though. I get that."

"I don't find it annoying."

"You're just saying that, V."

"No, I'm serious."

"I just... I miss him."

I put a hand on his arm and we turned to face each other. He took hold of my hand and pulled me closer until our faces were almost touching.

"I'm sorry about what went down at the funeral. I was angry. I didn't mean it when I told you to stay away."

"No, I get it. I was keeping something from you and that wasn't right."

"You're entitled to your privacy, Mhairi. I shouldn't have demanded you tell me. I just... I've seen how upset you've been and I wanted to do something, you know?"

"I totally understand that. You were just looking out for me."

"I went the wrong way about it but... yeah. Something like that."

"I'm sorry I kept the truth from you for so long. I hope it all makes sense now. Why I've been acting the way I have." I whispered.

"What do you mean?"

"Everything I've done. Everything that's happened. Why I kept pushing you away."

Tom looked at me, puzzled. "I don't understand, Mhairi. What are you talking about?"

"I hope the letter helps you understand why it has been like this. I hope it makes sense of why I've been lashing out, I guess. I totally understand if you don't..."

"What letter are you talking about?"

I blinked. "The letter I sent you."

"I've not had any letter, Mhairi. What's this all about?"

My face paled. Suddenly all of the pieces slotted together perfectly. "That makes so much sense." I whispered under my breath.

"What makes sense? V, I am confused."

"I'm sorry Tom I... I need to go." I rose from the ground and plucked my high heels from where I'd abandoned them. I stumbled back in the direction of the house, my veins pumping with purpose.

"Mhairi?" Tom called, but I barely heard him. I finally knew why Tom had never responded to my letter. There could only be one reason why Tom didn't ever receive the letter I'd sent.

Chapter Twenty

I erupted into the house, my hand gripping so tightly to my heels that it had gone a brilliant white. I headed for the kitchen, a red mist settling in-front of my vision. How had I not seen it before? Donna had wanted to keep Tom and I apart from the beginning. After our argument surrounding Rab's misdeeds, it was the perfect opportunity for her to swoop in and offer a sympathetic shoulder. Although I had never held Donna in high regard, I didn't think she was capable of this level of deceit. I had actually thought that Donna had changed her ways since we first met. Clearly I was mistaken.

Donna was in the kitchen surrounded by a few guests. She looked so relaxed and happy. That only further fuelled my anger. "Donna." I barked.

Donna whirled round from her delightful conversation. "Mhairi? What's going on?"

"I think we need to talk."

"Is everything ok, sweetheart? What's the matter?"

"You know fine well."

Her face drained of colour. "I have no idea what you're talking about, Mhairi."

"Oh really? Would you prefer for me to enlighten your guests about what you've been up to recently?"

"Let's go outside and get some air." She said quietly, already in retreat.

I stormed towards the door and Donna slinked along behind me. The cold air was abrasive but I could barely feel it. "How could you... you had no right..." I fizzed, barely able to get my words out.

Donna looked at me sheepishly. "Mhairi, I can explain..."

"Oh please do. I'm intrigued."

Donna looked like she wanted to squirm out of her skin. "Things were going so well with Tom and I and... well... I just couldn't stand by and watch you spoil it."

"So instead you decided to meddle in things that were none of your business? How unusual for you to take matters into your own hands."

"Tom was upset after the funeral. I couldn't face him getting hurt again. I was protecting him."

"Protecting him? Or looking out for yourself?"

"He was better off without you, Mhairi. I've heard all about your dramas. Tom shouldn't be the one to bail you out all the time. It's not fair on him."

"Shouldn't that be his decision?"

"Tom is too kind-hearted for his own good. He always wants to help. I was just trying to help him for a change."

"Help him? By reading his mail?"

"He didn't need you back in his life, Mhairi. He didn't need you to mess things up again."

"Tom is free to make his own decisions about his own life. He'd be furious to know you kept this from him."

"Please don't tell him. Please, Mhairi."

"More secrets and more lies, Donna. Is that your answer for everything?"

Donna was silent.

"That letter. Did you read it?"

Donna looked very uncomfortable again.

My stomach churned. "That letter was *private*. How could you..." I hissed. "you are a disgusting, manipulative..."

"What's going on here?" Tom appeared at Donna's side. Donna's eyes brimmed with tears and she began to sob quietly into Tom's shirt. Tom attempted to support her but was unsteady on his feet. "Mhairi? What the hell?"

"Don't ask me, Tom. Ask your bitch of a girlfriend."

This brought on a fresh wave of tears from Donna, who bundled further into Tom's chest.

"Mhairi that is uncalled for. Apologise to Donna."

I scoffed. "Are you kidding? You have no idea what she's done, Tom."

"What has gotten into you?"

My stomach churned, but not from anger this time. Before I could stop myself, I promptly vomited into a plant pot sitting by the front door.

Tom scoffed. "You're drunk, Mhairi. Just go home."

I looked from Donna to Tom and back again. She was clinging to him tightly, her sobs now occasional gasps.

273

"Tom, I know what this looks like but you have to believe me."

Tom held up one hand. "No. I don't want to hear it. I'm surprised at you, Mhairi. I never took you for a mean drunk."

Before I could reply, I threw up again. Tom rolled his eyes as he watched me from a safe distance. I stood hunched over the plant pot as they barged past me. I felt awful so remained hunched over the plant pot, afraid to move.

"Mhairi?" a voice whispered from behind me. "Oh Mhairi." Emily patted my back. "I'll phone George."

***

I woke to the sun spilling through the window of a room I did not recognise. I was suddenly aware of the dull ache in the back of my head and shut my eyes, groping for a nearby pillow to shield them with. An array of images flashed into my mind from the night before. Drinking in the kitchen. Talking with Tom under the stars. Shouting at Donna. I groaned. Shit.

"Good afternoon." Said a voice, too loudly for me.

I grumbled and rolled over. I immediately regretted this as I rolled right off the couch and onto the hard wooden floor. I cradled my thumping head.

"Oooh be careful now. I brought you some coffee." It was Emily. I turned over and opened my eyes slowly. The sunlight was aggressive so I immediately shut them again. "Welcome back."

274

"What... happened?" I said, my voice groggy.

"Wine, mostly. I think you got most of it out of your system though."

I groaned again. "Oh no."

"I've put some paracetamol next to the coffee."

"Thanks." I used all of my energy to smile, still with my eyes firmly shut.

Emily left the room and I immediately fell back asleep, still lying on the floor.

A couple of hours later, I was awakened by voices. One of them was Emily but the other I couldn't place. It sounded oddly familiar.

"... she said I could come over today."

"She probably forgot, Steven."

Steven. I had forgotten that he was planning to drop by and pick up his stuff today. He wasn't supposed to appear until 2pm. What time was it?

"It took me over two hours to get here, Emily. I would appreciate it if I could get my stuff back."

"I understand that, Steven but Mhairi isn't here. She probably went a walk."

"Tell her to text me please."

"I'll let her know."

The front door slammed. My head pounded, irritated from the noise. The door to my room opened again.

"Mhairi?"

I opened my eyes. It was slightly easier that it had been earlier. "Emily?"

"How are you feeling?"

"Better… kind of."

"That was Steven at the door."

"What time is it?"

"Ten past 3."

"3?!"

"Don't worry, I told him you were out a walk. He is none the wiser."

"I promised him he could come over and collect his stuff today. I did not intend on drinking that much."

"None of us ever do."

"How are you not hungover today, Emily?"

"Sophie kept bringing me drinks and I kept leaving them on tables."

"Uhh. Why didn't I think of that?"

"You were pretty worse for wear last night, Mhairi. It's good you've managed to sleep it off."

I groaned. "What happened, Emily?"

She shrugged. "You went outside for a bit to get some air and ended up arguing with Donna."

I flinched.

"I wouldn't worry, Mhairi. These things happen all the time."

"No Emily. It was bad. I remember now." I reached for the mug of coffee, now cold. I drank it greedily and threw the pills to the back of my throat. My stomach gurgled.

"What happened?"

I sat with Emily for some time, discussing what I remembered of the party. I was still clutching my throbbing head. Emily listened intently, letting me relive the highs and the lows without interruption. The evening came back to me in glorious technicolour- much too bright in my hungover state. I cringed inwardly.

"Well. At least you know Tom hasn't read your letter. That's something at least."

"A small consolation from a disastrous evening."

"We've all been there, Mhairi. You were upset."

"I've just given Tom more reason to hate me."

"You can't think like that."

"But he does, Emily. Tom hates me. I embarrassed myself."

"You need to remember that Tom didn't know *why* you were so mad at Donna."

"Like Donna is going to tell him."

"He will find out eventually. Try not to fret."

I shook my head. "I just feel so helpless. And stupid."

"Mmm. Love can do that to a person."

"Does love really make you feel this helpless?"

"I'm afraid so." Emily put a hand on my shoulder. "Just give it time, Mhairi. Now, are you going to see Steven or am I?"

I made the short walk back to the cottage slowly as not to disturbing my throbbing head. The light was still hurting my eyes and the cool afternoon air made me feel somewhat queasy. I immediately went to the bathroom to splash cool water on my face. I phoned Steven while I still had the nerve.

"Steven?"

"Mhairi! Where the hell are you?" his voice boomed through the phone speaker.

My head throbbed. "Sorry… that's me back at the cottage now. Come over whenever you like."

"You sure you're not going to disappear in the meantime?"

I rolled my eyes. "Goodbye Steven."

Steven arrived not long after our conversation. It felt so bizarre seeing him- it felt like just yesterday we had been together and yet a lifetime ago. I barely recognised the man on my doorstep. He had grown his hair so his tattoo was now completely hidden. He had begun growing a beard when he's spent all of his life crisp and clean shaven. I plucked the box from beneath the couch and handed it to him. He thanked me and bundled it into the back of his car.

He turned to face me, a look of uncertainty on his face. "Thanks for that, Mhairi."

I folded my arms. "Sure."

"Mhairi?"

"Yes?"

"Are you hungover?"

I winced. "Just the end of a bad bug, I think."

Steven raised an eyebrow. "Really? Are you sure?"

"Yup. I'm sure."

There was an uncomfortable silence as we both dodged eye contact.

"There's something else I was meaning to tell you, Mhairi."

"Oh? What's that? Is everything ok?"

"Well not really." Steven cleared his throat. "Lucy... Lucy dumped me."

"Aww Steven. I'm sorry." Part of me was relieved. Steven could do so much better than Lucy. She didn't exactly radiate warmth.

"It's ok. For the best I think... she was quite intense."

I tilted my head sympathetically. "Are you ok?"

"Yeah, yeah. I'll be fine." Steven sighed. "Plenty of fish in the sea and all that."

"The right girl will come along, Steven. I'm sure of it."

"But...what if the right girl is you, Mhairi?"

I froze.

"I can't stop thinking about you. In truth, I think Lucy knew that. No-one compares to you, Mhairi. What about giving us another go?"

"Steven... I..." I stammered, attempting to find the words.

"We were great together, Mhairi. We worked. We understood each other. It made sense."

"But... what about love?"

"Love?" Steven paused, looking confused. "Well, that goes without saying, Mhairi."

"I just... I don't love you, Steven."

"It's just been a while, Mhairi. I'm sure you can learn to love me again."

"I don't know if I ever did. It wasn't your fault but... it was never there for me. I see that now."

"You never loved me? Why did you date me, then? Why did you say yes when I asked you to marry me?"

"I don't know. It was wrong of me. It just... made sense at the time, I guess. It was the next logical step. However, I've learned that love doesn't always make sense."

"I just... I don't understand."

"It wasn't you, Steven. You were a great boyfriend... I just wasn't the right one. I know that now."

Steven looked crushed. I just couldn't lie to him again- I'd been doing it for the best part of twenty years and I was exhausted. I'd just convinced myself I loved him. Being with him had been the easy option. I had no reason to leave him. I couldn't let myself fall into that trap again. I had found a part of myself again after ending our relationship. It was liberating and terrifying. I was finally doing what was right for me. It was messy but undeniably me.

Steven put his hands in his pockets. "Well... I guess I better be going."

I smiled at him awkwardly. "Safe journey, yeah?"

Steven nodded in awkward farewell. He got into the car and reversed onto the road, all without giving me a second glance.

"Goodbye Steven." I whispered as his car pulled out onto the road and out of sight.

I went back into the cottage. My headache returned with a vengeance. I took another couple of paracetamol and lay on the couch. This was why drunken nights out were a bad idea. My phone buzzed in my pocket and I pulled it out, glancing at the screen. Dianna King.

"Mhairi, Hi."

I pulled the phone away from my ear, my head reeling at her bright voice. "Dianna."

"I hope you're well. Sorry to be calling at the weekend- urgent business. I hope you understand."

"Mmhm..." I brought the fingers of my left hand to my temple. "How can I help?"

"Well. I just spoke to the powers that be and Rab's trial has been pulled forward. They plan to start first thing on

Monday morning and I was hoping to begin with your testamony. Is that ok? I know it's soon."

My mouth went dry. "Monday? It's so… soon."

"Yes, yes, I know. It's been a bit of a dash for us too. We should be all sorted for Monday though… if you're ready?"

"I… well…"

"I can pop over tomorrow to run some things with you? Just the formalities, really. Shouldn't take long."

"I suppose-"

"Fabulous. I'll be round at 11. Thank you for being so accommodating, Mhairi. Much appreciated. See you tomorrow morning."

She terminated the call. My head was reeling. Was I really ready to speak for Rab's defence?

Chapter Twenty-One

Dianna King arrived at 11 sharp. Her platinum blonde hair was pulled back into a tidy bun. She wore a black suit which had clearly been tailored for her petite frame and a pair of nude Louboutin shoes. She swept into the cottage, coffee in hand. She was polished and emitted an air of importance in her every move.

"Mhairi, hi. Pleasure." She gave me a brief kiss on the cheek before assuming a place at the kitchen table. She opened her briefcase and withdrew a wad of paper, tucked away neatly in a cardboard folder. She also put on a pair of glasses which looked to be the same price as the Louboutin's. "Please have a seat, Mhairi." I found this remark rather ironic. She had been inside all of two minutes and she was already making herself at home. She was clearly a woman who was used to getting her own way. I slowly walked towards my own table and sat down, cautiously eyeing the files she had spread out in-front of her. She took a long, scrutinising look at each piece of paper, as if committing it to memory.

"Ok." She said, looking over her glasses. "As we've already discussed, you are an integral part of this case. You could be the difference between a one year or ten year sentence. No pressure, of course." She reached over and touched my hand. "All we are asking you to do is tell the truth, Mhairi. That's all."

I nodded. "So… what kind of questions should I be prepared for?"

Dianna withdrew her hand as quickly as she'd offered it and plucked a single sheet of paper from the many spread across the kitchen table. She handed it to me. "I've prepared this document for you. These are all of the question I foresee the opposing council asking from you. Nothing too strenuous- just a brief timeline of your relationship with the defendant and your actions after the event in question."

I scanned the piece of paper as she spoke, attempting to take it all in. My brain fumbled over the plethora of information.

"I'm not going to ask you anything you don't already know but the important thing here is how you phrase it. Anything you say can and will be used against you, after all. I'll ask a little about your history, your opinions of the defendant and then your handling of the incident. However." She removed her glasses and gave me an intense stare. "Be prepared for some not very nice questions from the other side… no matter what happens, just keep your cool. They will try and get an emotional reaction from you so that you either compromise your statement or admit something they can use. It petty tactics but that's how the game is played. The thing I foresee them dissecting is your relationship with Rab. You were his friend and his boss… it's quite a grey area. As far as I've read, you've done everything by the book so you should have nothing to worry about. Just don't give them anything they can run with."

"Ok…" I whispered, trying frantically to absorb everything she had just said.

"Don't worry. Everything is detailed in that document. If you have any additional questions I'm just a phone-call away."

I smiled weakly. "Thanks."

"It's my job. Anyway- let's run through your testimony and we can fine tune."

We spent the best part of three hours going over what I would say. Dianna unpicked every sentence as "that is what the other side would do". I became physically and emotionally exhausted. After a while, I wasn't sure if I was even speaking in coherent sentences.

"Ok I think that's enough. I think we've touched on every avenue the opposition could use. Your testimony is airtight now. Do you have any questions, Mhairi?"

"I don't think so…" My head was too busy spinning.

"Excellent. Court starts at 9am sharp. If you could be there for 8.30 and we can have a final briefing. I'm not sure what the order of proceedings will be but I imagine you'll be on no later than 2pm."

I'd have to wait around all day, my nerves knotting in my stomach, to be interrogated all over again? "Ok. That's fine."

"Great." Dianna flashed me a dazzling smile and stood from the table, efficiently packing everything back into her briefcase as quickly as she had withdrawn it. "As I said, call me if you have any questions. Everything we've covered today is in that document so just give it another read. Other than that, you're good to go."

I exhaled. "Ok."

"I'm confident, Mhairi. Just say everything you said to me today and it will be a good outcome tomorrow. For all of us."

***

As soon as she left, I sank into the sofa, my head pounding. I hadn't felt this drained in a very long time. I would take a hangover from hell instead of this any day. Just then, my phone buzzed. I groaned, attempting to get up from the sofa. I plucked my phone from the kitchen table and glanced at the screen, puzzled. The text had come from an unknown number.

Meet me at Feic Beach today- we need to talk. Please.

Who could be messaging me?

Okay… what time?

I stared at the phone screen, willing for a speedy response.

8pm?

I frantically typed my reply.

Okay. See you then.

***

The cold air pinched my cheeks as I made my long-awaited walk to Feic Beach. My stride had a new sense of purpose even if my legs were shaking. My head was reeling with possibilities which made it all the more difficult to focus on the road ahead. I was ready to face whatever was waiting for me on the other side of the hill. Feic Beach was hypnotic at dusk. The waves could barely be seen in-front of the sleepy skyline, the last of the day's colours drained from the atmosphere. The waves were just as boisterous as ever, unaware that the rest of the world was settling down to sleep. As I reached the brow of the hill which overlooked the beach, I was aware something was off. I looked around, unable to place the imbalance. It suddenly dawned on me that something very important was missing- the wooden bench. The bench that sat at the centre of this whole mess. I walked over only to see a gaping hole in the hilltop, the bench uprooted like a cavity. The soil still looked fresh with just a dusting of sand on the crater.

"Hello?" someone said.

I whirled round. As my eyes adjusted to the gloom, I was surprised to see the figure that was standing before me. Her hair hung loose around her face, casting a shadow across her features. She looked so much older than she had just a few months ago. She looked at me with a startled expression, drawing her coat around her. Her swollen belly was very visible beneath her arms.

"Beth?" I whispered.

Beth smiled nervously, catching my eyes before quickly looking away. She clutched her stomach absentmindedly.

"Does your mum know you're here?"

"She and Dad work in the evenings."

"Why did you message me?"

"Rab's trial starts tomorrow."

"Yes."

"He told me you're testifying."

I hesitated. "Yes."

"I needed to see you before you did."

A silence hung in the air.

"How are you?" I asked.

"Better than the earlier days. I'm not throwing up any more but it's difficult to sleep. This one is quite the kicker." Her fingers danced over her stomach.

"How far along are you now?"

"Around 35 weeks, give or take."

"Wow."

She smiled. "Yeah."

"How are you... feeling about it all?"

She paused, considering her answer. "Calm. I thought I'd be really scared about the whole thing. I was at the beginning. As time passed, I... don't know. It's weird. I just feel ready, you know?"

I nodded, staring at the silent sea. In that moment, I looked at Beth and saw my own reflection. Our futures had taken an unprecedented turn at such a young age.

"I was pregnant once." I whispered, my eyes still on the sea. "I was eighteen years old. It... wasn't planned."

"You were? I didn't know. What did you do?"

"I wasn't as brave as you, Beth." I said, looking down at my own flat stomach. "I often wonder what would have happened if I'd kept it. I wish I'd had the courage to find out."

Beth looked at me sympathetically. "I'm sorry."

"Don't be. It was my decision. I just need to live with it. How has your Mum been with it all?"

"She's worried. She confined me to the house but I can't stay in there all the time. It's so... suffocating."

"She's just trying to protect you, you know."

"I know but... I'm not a wee girl anymore."

"You'll always be her wee girl. It's a Mum thing, I guess."

Beth sighed. "There's a reason why I asked you to come here. There's something we need to talk about."

"Yes of course."

"I want this baby to grow up with a Mum and a Dad, Miss Sinclair. Rab and I played equal parts on our relationship. It's not fair that he is the one suffering for it all."

"You're only sixteen, Beth. He's a grown man."

"That doesn't mean I don't know what love is. I know what it feels like. I know Rab and I are meant to raise this baby together. They're not letting me speak at his trial. They say it'll taint the case and it'll be labelled Stockholm Syndrome. There is nothing I can do. I feel so powerless. I'm just so afraid that Rab's going to be gone forever…"

I didn't turn to look at her but it was clear she was crying.

"We need you, Miss Sinclair. You need to tell them that Rab is a good man and deserves to be free. They won't listen to me. To them, I'm just a stupid wee girl."

"I understand. I'll be an honest as I can Beth but… I can't guarantee that Rab will go free. That is up to the Judge, not me."

We stood in silence for a while, trying to find peace from the sea.

"I miss him so much."

I put a hand on her shoulder. "I know." I was more conflicted than ever. Beth was twenty-three years his junior, a lifetime of experiences creating a gulf between them. Logically, it couldn't seem possible but a part of me felt their pain. Could I really rob them of a happy future together?

Chapter Twenty-Two

"It will all be absolutely fine, Mhairi. There is nothing to panic about."

It was 7am and I was already well on my way towards Inverness. The drive from Allaban was just over 2 hours but

I wasn't taking any chances. I had left the house just after 6am. I had barely slept so thought I may as well do something productive.

"How can you possibility know that, Emily?" I snapped.

"Just try to keep calm. It'll all be over soon."

"The attorney said the whole case rested on me, Emily. Not a very calm-inducing statement."

"You've got to do what's right for you, Mhairi. Try not to think about anyone else. Put them all out of your mind."

"How do you propose I do that exactly?" I exhaled, trying to calm myself down. It wasn't Emily's fault- she was just trying to support me. I had spent my entire life appeasing to the needs of others. I even chose a career with that as its core. The very foundation of my beliefs were beginning to rupture, the ground shifting beneath my feet. How could I possibly shut out the external noise to listen to my own thoughts? I had smothered my own voice for so long that gravel had lodged in its windpipe, it's cries barely above a whisper.

"You will know what's right in the moment. Have a little faith in yourself for a change."

As the trial had been moved up, there had been no time to organise a jury. The court would be closed to everyone aside from close family. Although happy with this development, I was concerned that having just a few faces in the crowd would make their disapproving expressions all the more vivid.

"Bye Mhairi. Good luck."

I disconnected the call. I had phoned Emily to gain some comfort but ended up feeling more rattled than I did before. I couldn't quieten the voices in my head and I could feel the coffee beginning to wear off. It was going to be a long day.

All of my experiences of a courtroom had stemmed from American television laced with glitz, glamour and unbelievable drama. The truth was far from the stories shown on television. Everything about the courthouse was beige: the walls; the carpets; the décor... there were all variations on a theme. The reality was much more mundane. There was no camera crew waiting in earnest on the front steps as we approached. There was no defendant's family vying for attention in the lobby. Whatever agony people were feeling was neatly boxed away in their heads as not to disrupt the beige-ness of the building.

I met Dianna King outside, dressed in a different but equally expensive suit. It was clear that she was at ease in the courthouse from the way she held herself to the way she greeted people as we passed. It was the kind of ease that someone could only acquire from sitting on a particular side of the bench.

After we trailed through an endless maze of corridors, Dianna ushered me into a cramped waiting room. This room was also in keeping with the beige theme. The only items in the room were a beige sofa, a brown coffee table and a selection of magazines that were dog-eared and creased.

"Ok." Said Dianna, sitting on the sofa and withdrawing some papers from her briefcase. "This should be a quicker process without a jury. Everything should run to time all going well. I'll come and see you half an hour before and we can run through a few last minute details. Any questions?"

I thought for a moment and then shook my head. I didn't think *Do I have to do this?* would be a welcome question. Dianna plucked her briefcase from the floor and snapped it shut, a bunch of papers still in her right hand.

"Perfect. I'll see you later on. There will be recesses throughout the proceedings so I'll let you know what's happening." What that, she rose to her feet, gave me a curt smile and disappeared.

***

Time dripped past agonisingly slowly. The clock on the wall was almost exactly four minutes slow. I did not want to dwell on what was happening just down the corridor. I felt sufficiently removed from it whilst hypnotically letting the minutes tick past. It baffled me how small life could become when reduced to four walls and a ticking clock. The mundane was suddenly comforting as I was safe in the knowledge that the clock would continue to tick without any intervention and regardless of the chaos going on in the world.

After what seemed like an eternity, Dianna returned. She entered the room so swiftly that I almost fell off the couch.

"Okay. Things have been… re-ordered somewhat. No need to delve into the specifics but you're up after the next recess."

I glanced at the clock, suddenly panicked.

"Yes, I know. Some things have changed. No need to worry. Just do everything exactly as we prepared, Mhairi. You'll be great."

Dianna's confidence had been visibly knocked. It did not fill me with confidence.

"I'll come and collect you in ten minutes or so and we can get you set up in the courtroom. Ok?"

She did not wait for me to answer but instead glided out of the room. A familiar uneasiness settled in my gut. I hoped that everything would turn out for the best… but, at that moment, I did not know what the best was.

The wait before the trial had felt like an eternity. That was, until the trial itself. Although the room was much small than I imagined, the dust of Hollywood terror landed fresh on my shoulders. It was like a misty rain shower. The kind that overwhelms you slowly until you suddenly realise you're soaked. My face glistened under the fluorescent lights as I sat drenched in anxiety.

Dianna King made some passing remarks to the judge and assembled audience. Among them were a host of faces from past and present: Mary, Steph, Ian, *Tom*. In the defendant's chair sat Rab in a grey suit. He looked like a shadow of his former self. His cheeks were gaunt and his eyes sagged. Instead of being somewhere to sit, it looked like the chair was propping him up. A once buoyant man was reduced to a shrivelled heap. His thirty-nine years were more visible than they had ever been. I felt a pang of sympathy. Only once before had life seemed so vivid and tangible.

"… can you state your name for the record?" It took a moment to realise that this remark was from Dianna King and aimed at me.

I leaned forward in my seat so that my lip grazed the microphone. "Mhairi Anne Sinclair."

"Thank you." Dianna strode with purpose from one end of the room to the other as though creating space for her own testimony. It was as if she was walking in a park- she was calm and took her time to pace from one end to the other. The squat man who represented the prosecution sighed and folded his arms, clearly well-versed in her performance.

"Mhairi- what are your earliest memories of Robert Campbell?"

I took a deep breath, collecting my thoughts. "We were friends. Childhood friends."

"Do you remember what age you were when you met?"

"I was six years old."

"And how old was Robert at this time?"

"I think he was… thirteen."

"Ah, so quite an age gap."

"Yes, there was. It has never really felt like that though."

"Why is that do you think?"

"Rab always treated me like an equal. I don't remember ever noticing the age difference."

Dianna nodded, continuing her stroll. "How would you describe Robert Campbell as a child?"

"Adventurous, mischievous, rebellious… but kind. He was always very kind to me."

"Do you feel he is different now? Has he changed?"

"He is still kind. In many ways he just the Rab I remember… just with grey hair."

Amusement rippled through the courtroom.

"So how has your relationship changed as you've grown up?"

"I left Allaban a number of years ago so we lost touch. Our relationship is pretty much the same but the circumstances are different."

"Are you eluding to the fact that you are now his Boss?"

I nodded. "Yes. That's what I mean."

"How has being Robert's Boss impacted your relationship?"

"Sometimes Rab and I have differing opinions about what is good for the school so… we clash."

"Do you argue a lot?"

"We are not afraid to stand up to each other. It's important to talk things out. It's for the good of the school."

"Has that had an impact on your relationship?"

I shrugged. "Not really. We used to argue a lot when we were younger. We would fall out but we'd always fall back in again… eventually."

Dianna nodded thoughtfully, coming to a stop in-front of me. "Can you tell us about when you found out about Robert's relationship with Beth?"

My stomach churned. I inhaled, trying to push all of the voices out of my head. "A work colleague confided in me. She was concerned. I was shocked by the accusation so immediately went to Rab's house to speak to him."

"When you did eventually speak to Robert, what did he say?"

"He told me that he and Beth had been in a relationship since the summer. They had kept it a secret for obvious reasons."

"Do you truly believe that Robert loved Beth?"

I dared to look at Rab and saw the pain on his face. "Yes."

"And do you believe that Beth also loves Robert?"

"Yes I do."

Dianna took a moment to let this sink in. The prosecution was scribbling furiously. "And what did you do after meeting Robert?"

"I reported the incident."

"And what were your reasons for doing that?"

"It was a clear breech of Professional guidelines. Beth was a pupil at the school and Rab was a teacher. It was my duty as Head Teacher to pass this information on."

"So, although you believe that Robert and Beth loved each other and the relationship was a mutual decision, you still reported it?"

I nodded. "Although Rab and I are friends, work comes first."

"Thank you Mhairi." Dianna turned to the Judge. "No further questions." Dianna King returned to the Defendant's bench and whispered something to Rab. The squat man from behind the Prosecution bench stood and strode towards me. Intimidated, I sank back in my chair.

"Mhairi. Aaron Price." He gave me a warm smile that sent shivers up my spine. "May I ask what your job title is?"

"Head Teacher of Allaban High School."

"And how long have you been in your current position?"

"7 months now."

"7 months." He said, as though pondering my answer. "Have you held any other Head Teacher positions?"

"No. This is my first Head Teacher Position after completing my Standard for Headship."

"So your Headship career is actually younger than Beth's unborn baby. Is that correct?"

I stiffened, clenching my fists beneath the table. "Yes. That is correct."

"Right. So, as part of your job, you must report any 'breeches of conduct' as you put it?"

"Yes, that's correct."

"So anything that happens within the school must be reported immediately to the proper authorities?"

"Yes, that is the case."

"Right I see. So once you heard these allegations from a colleague, you reported Rab right away?"

My face felt hot. I knew where this was headed. "No. Not right away."

He looked at me with faux confusion. "No? Why not?"

"I wanted to speak to Rab first. I had to hear his side of the story."

"Yes, I completely understand that. However." He returned to his desk, plucking a piece from the top of the pile on his desk. "You didn't actually report Robert to the police until four days after your little chat. Is that correct?"

"I… I just…"

"Is that correct, Mhairi? A simple yes or no will suffice."

"Objection." Stated Dianna, eyeing up Aaron Price.

"I'll allow it." Said the Judge, pushing his spectacles back onto his nose.

I attempted to keep my voice steady. "Yes, that's correct."

Aaron smiled. "Can you tell us why you did that, Mhairi?"

"I wanted to give him a chance."

"A chance? To do what exactly?"

"To turn himself in."

Aaron paused for dramatic effect. "So let me get this straight. Someone you work with is concerned that Robert Campbell raped Beth Anderson, a pupil in your care. You speak to him, find out it's true and decide not to report such a matter until four days later? You sat on these allegations for four days?"

I swallowed but the lump in my throat stayed lodged. "Yes, that is correct."

"And what happened in the meantime, Mhairi? What happened after you *eventually* reported Robert to the police?"

"He went missing." I whispered.

"Do you mean he ran away? Disappeared?"

"Objection!" said Dianna, louder this time.

"He was reported missing." My face was growing hotter by the second.

"Do you think running away are the actions of an innocent man, Mhairi?"

"Objection!" Dianna repeated.

"Sorry, I'll rephrase. Robert Campbell confirmed the allegations, you waited four days to report him and then he ran away. Correct?"

"It wasn't like that, I-"

"As a professional with ten years of teaching experience and seven months of Headship experience, do you think your actions were timely in order to take care of Beth or allow your friend Robert to make a getaway?"

"OBJECTION!" yelled Dianna, leaping from her chair.

Aaron smirked. "No further questions, your honour."

Chapter Twenty-Three

After my spectacular grilling from the opposition, the judge decided to call a short recess. I stood up casually, vacating the chambers as quickly as possible without drawing attention to myself. I escaped through my small holding area, down the grand staircase and out into the fresh air. My eyes squinted as I adjusted to the light. The sky was a spectacular blue without a cloud to be seen. A February chill was in the air. There was a small wooden bench to the side of the building, partially disguised by the grand steps leading to the courthouse. I took refuge, sheltering from the wind. My head felt heavy with guilt and fear but my mind was surprisingly empty. The voices were quiet, if only for a moment. The tears kept coming but I felt surprisingly calm. Perhaps I was still idling in the eye of the storm. I was eighteen again, staring out of my bedroom window, not registering anything inside my head or out. Sadie had been on the phone to Mum for what felt like an eternity, the urgency of her voice echoing quietly throughout the house. The entire universe had been white noise that day. I was simply an empty vessel, locked inside my own head. That day too had been so bright and clear. Someone cleared their throat and I looked up, raising my hand to shield my eyes from the relentless glare of the sun.

"Hi." Said Tom, his hands in his pockets. "A little chilly to be outside don't you think?"

I shrugged. "Doesn't bother me."

"Well I'm bloody freezing." He pulled a packet of cigarettes from his pocket and offered me one. I declined. "Mind if I join you?"

I moved to one side of the bench, making room for him.

"Thanks for speaking today, Mhairi. I know it couldn't have been easy."

"I don't know how much good it did. That guy tore me to shreds."

"He's an arsehole. Anyone could see that."

"Arsehole or not... he's good at his job."

"Regardless of what that guy said, you really stood up for Rab today."

"I told the truth, Tom. Nothing more."

"It was a truth that needed told. Not just for the judge-for all of us." Tom took another deep drag of his cigarette. He sighed deeply. "Donna told me what happened."

My breathing became shallow. "Right."

"We had an argument."

"Ok."

"I read the letter, Mhairi."

I looked down at my hands. I could feel Tom's eyes on me.

"I hadn't realised... I didn't know..." Tom sighed, clearly frustrated. "I wish I hadn't been so adamant you tell me."

"You were just trying to look out for me, Tom."

"I wish I'd done a better job."

We sat in silence for a moment.

"It wasn't your fault. I guess I ran away to protect you. I thought it'd be easier for you to label me as the 'bad guy' rather than tell you the truth. Telling you what happened... it would have done more harm than good back then."

"What Dad-" he stopped, the word catching in his throat. "What *he* did was wrong. It wasn't your fault. I'm so sorry for all the harm it caused you. The harm it caused us." He moved closer, our knees touching.

I looked up at him. "I love you Tom. I loved you back then but didn't know it. It's only now after everything has happened that I realised... I didn't want to lose you again."

Tom took my face in both of his hands and wiped away the tears splashed across my face. "You could never lose me."

"But Donna..."

"It's you, Mhairi. It has always been you." He stared at me intently. My heart pounded. I would never stop loving this man. He pulled me close, running a hand through my hair. He edged closer and studied my expression, his breath tickling my cheek. Then, slowly and tenderly, he kissed me. I returned his kiss, my heart full to the brim. After some time, we pulled apart and I rested my head on his shoulder. He put his arm around me, pulling me close and protecting me from the cold. In spite of the February frost, I had never felt warmer.

"Tom." I whispered.

"Mmm?"

"I just have one question."

Tom turned to face me, a quizzical expression on his face. "Anything."

"The bench. The one at Feic Beach. What happened to it? Why is it gone?"

Tom sighed heavily, giving me a knowing look. "I took care of it."

"That's all I needed to know."

After the recess, Tom and I returned to the courtroom, hand in hand. I caught Rab's eye as he was being led in by Dianna King. He raised an eyebrow and then smirked. I shrugged my shoulders and then smirked back.

We all rose as the judge re-entered and sat waiting anxiously to hear the outcome.

He cleared his throat and adjusted his rounded spectacles. "When I was originally introduced to this case, I had assumed it would be merely a formality. The facts were clear and therefore I assumed the sentencing would be too. However."

My chest tightened.

"It is clear from evidence and testimony that my original assumption was incorrect. This case was not simply about misconduct or inappropriate relations. It was, in fact, about love."

I smiled at Tom and he squeezed my hand.

"Were the grounds of this improper? Absolutely. Was the defendant incorrect to act as he did? Absolutely. However, after the testimonies today, it was made clear that it was an act of love rather than an act of violence. The girl in question was of age and, by my account, consented to any relations which took place. This was made clear in her written statement to the court and also reinforced in testimony. With that in mind…" he lifted his gavel in readiness and stared at Rab. "Robert Campbell. Due to gross misconduct, your teaching licence will be revoked effective immediately. Also, for evading police enquiry and perverting the course of justice, you will be required to complete two years of community service as set by this court." The judge banged his gavel, sending a ripple through the courtroom. "Case dismissed."

***

I guess what you want me to say is that this story ended very happily and all of the strings were tied neatly with a bow. In many ways, there are lots of positive things in my life but, as life often dictates, things can be messy. Also, like the tide, the only thing constant is change. I love Tom, but it will take me a lifetime to understand what that love is. We are both happy to wait it out and walk along that winding road together. He eventually finished converting the old barn at the back of the Campbell property and we moved in. It wasn't far for me to get to school and Tom could take his place at the helm of the Campbell family business. I marvelled at his dedication to the business and tried to lend a hand whenever I could. It was clear that Tom loved the farm which made me love him even more.

Things began to settle at the High School once more and, with Iris's help and support, everything was going in the right direction. There was a new, positive energy and a sense of community in the building. There were still mixed feelings amongst the staff but many of them were starting to come around. I knew that would take time but I was willing to wait. Mutual respect did not happen overnight. We were inspected a couple of years later and they were impressed by what they saw. It was still very much a work in progress but they could see we were trying.

Oliver Stevenson, after nearly forty years of service, retired from the teaching profession in pursuit of local fishing spots. In spite of his gruff façade, we parted on good terms. He said I had a lot of guts which, although very irritating, he couldn't help but admire. He was happy to leave the school in my hands which was the biggest compliment he could bestow.

Donna left the High School to work in the local Doctor's Office. She handed in her notice not long after Rab's trial had ended. It was nice to finally walk past reception without attempting to dodge her.

As far as I knew, Steven was still working away in Inverness doing the job he loved. I was glad he hadn't married Lucy in the end- he had so much love to give and needed to find someone ready to bear that load. He messaged occasionally to check in and ask after Mum. Our communications were short. I was sorry to waste his love but our parting was definitely for the best. We had both learned a lot from each other.

Beth had her baby the week after the trial finished- a beautiful baby girl which she named Sarah. She and Rab were doting parents. I had never seen Rab so absorbed in a person that wasn't himself. Whenever he was with Beth and Sarah, his face had a warm glow. He was transformed. I often saw them around the village, walking hand in hand and pushing the pram. It had taken time for the people of Allaban to get used to the idea but the gossip mill eventually settled. Rab worked on the farm most days meaning he had plenty of time to spend with his new family.

Life was going on. However, everything was still a little messy. I had come to learn that life could not be neatly packaged and tied with a bow. Just when you thought everything was neat and tidy, you discovered you'd run out of string or paper or both. I had tried to live a life that I'd prescribed to myself and ultimately I rejected it. The call of Allaban had been too strong in the end and I was glad of it. I hoped my Grandma Sadie would be proud.

Tom and I spent every Sunday walking to Feic Beach, just as my Grandma once had. No matter how many times we visited, it always looked completely different. It could be majestically calm in the summer months and drastically violent during the winter frost. The waves would sometimes ebb and flow, barely above a whisper. Other times, they would crash against the beach, demanding the attention of any onlooker. Regardless, it would always remain Allaban's silent guardian. The beach was a place that never changed but was always changing. A place that was strongly linked to my past, present and future but remained unmoved by the sands of time. I marvelled in its presence, pulling Tom closer to me as we watched, hypnotised by the waves.

The darkness was still there. It would never leave me alone, but it sometimes gave me a brief reprieve. Most of the time, it was a little ball in the back of my mind, my silent observer. Other times, that little ball became quite large and threatened to consume me whole. Tom convinced me to see a counsellor. After a lot of arguments and resistance, I finally agreed. It was finally time for me to confront my past head on. It helped. The flashbacks would still happen but I found ways of coping when they did. I faced my past and found a little bit of myself along the way.

My story is far from over but now, maybe, I could live it instead of writing it. Maybe I would tell Tom about my baby one day. Maybe now I could finally forgive myself for everything I'd been through and everything I'd done as a result. I tried to be kinder to myself. Sometimes I succeeded and sometimes I didn't. It was a daily practice and Tom was with me through it all. I was often bewildered that we had ended up here. In many ways, moving to Allaban had been embarking on a new and mysterious journey. However, I soon realised that I was actually just returning home.

Acknowledgements

Mhairi's story was born out of a dull March day in 2020. Like the whole country I was grappling with the highs and lows of lockdown, riding the waves like an inexperienced sailor lost in the ocean. After finishing a day of work, I sat down at my laptop and inspiration struck hot and fast. I had dreamed about Mhairi the night before and suddenly the words were tumbling out to form sentences and paragraphs. I wrote three chapters in the space of a few hours and Mhairi was brought to life.

Firstly, I would like to thank my dear friends Hannah and Fiona. On a whim, I sent my first three chapters to them. Their support and encouragement spurred me on to complete this book and share Mhairi's story. They hassled me every day for new chapters which kept me writing.

Secondly, I would like to thank my other friends who took the time to read this book and offer their feedback. Their opinions and constructive comments helped my mould Mhairi's story and write the book I could never dream of producing. Thank you Jon, Kirsty, Vivien, Chantelle, Christine, Amy, Alex, Connor, Ross, Lyndsey, Sarah, Keegan and Margaret.

Thirdly, I would like to thank everyone who has been so supportive in my publication of this book. Your kind words of support and encouragement spurred me on and gave me the confidence to share Mhairi with the world.

Finally, I would like to thank my Mum. Unlike Mhairi's mother, mine has always encouraged me to follow my dreams and chase my biggest ambitions. Without her belief in me every day I could not have written this book.

In this text, Mhairi does not provide the perfect narrative. Her ambition is often detrimental to herself and others around her. She pushes people away because she is too afraid to be vulnerable. She is undeniably human. This is a story that needs to be told- an honest and open account of a woman who is not perfect.

Printed in Great Britain
by Amazon